GW00732846

THE AMAZING FARTZINI

An incredible story about an

incredible boy who found magic!

SHANE ROBINSON

ISBN: 978-1-7908-3873-8

DEDICATION

I dedicate this book to all the 'Dreamers' out there! Because, without 'Dreamers', you'd be reading this book on a stone tablet, and living in a cold and damp cave! Or possibly the human race would have become extinct a long, long time ago and then you would have definitely had no chance of reading this book!

INTRODUCTION
By The Author

In case you are wondering whether this book you now have in your possession is a 'Fictional Story Book', a 'Magic Book', or a 'Self Help Book'? Well actually, it is all three! You see I didn't just want to write yet another 'Beginners Magic Book', explaining just tricks! I hope for this book to be inspiring and enable the young reader, who this book is intended for, not only to learn some amazing magic tricks but more importantly how to become more self-confident, admired and respected by those around you through performing magic, as well as enjoying the story of course! So at its core, it is a 'Magic Book', but it is mainly about helping children gain confidence through performing magic, and I thought if I write a story this will help to get my advice across to children in perhaps a better, more effective way!

It is a fictional story about a schoolboy called Eric Fartz, who lacks self-confidence and is bullied. But, by a chance meeting at the local Christmas fair with an old magician, decides to take up performing magic, which he finds really helps him to gain confidence and eventually turn his life around for the better! However, this story could just as easily be written about many young people in the real world today, struggling with confidence issues. Maybe that is you? If it is then this book will definitely be very helpful to you as well as being an interesting and enjoyable read, plus you'll learn some really cool magic tricks too!

Throughout the story, Eric performs a number of really amazing magic tricks, and a lot of these tricks are taught in 'Eric's Magic Trick Secrets' found at the rear of the book, so you too will be able to amaze people like Eric! All the magic tricks explained in this book I have carefully chosen with the beginner to magic in mind. I wanted to choose the sort of magic tricks that are simple and easy enough for a beginner to learn, but yet effective, and that you could perform on the spur of the moment using everyday objects that you can easily find around you. Some of these tricks you will find more challenging to learn than others, but it is always good to stretch yourself so you can improve!

I have written all the magic tricks taught in the way as to how I perform them, which include a number of my own additional idea's. Some of these magic tricks date back hundreds of years, whilst some are more recent.

Amongst them is a very impressive card trick called 'Lucky Thirteen', which I created. *(I couldn't write a book teaching magic tricks and not include any of my own!)*

They are all tricks I still perform myself to this day, so I can certainly vouch for their effectiveness! Also included towards the rear of the magic book section is a 'Glossary', which you will find very useful for learning and understanding the various terms used.

I have been a professional magician for many years and my 'Stage Name' is called 'Zane'. I am also the owner of a well-established and respected magic shop business in the UK called 'Zane's Magic Shop'. So I am very qualified to write this book and the advice and motivation I give to you in these pages come from many years' experience, and trial and error. One of the things you learn from performing magic for as long as I have, is human psychology and behaviour, so you will also find in amongst the story, written in italics, advice on not only performing magic but how to become, if need be, more outgoing and confident and also how to deal with bullying.

I receive a lot of lovely comments from parents, thanking me for inspiring their children and here is an email I received recently from an acquaintance of mine I thought would be good to include as proof of the power of performing magic.

"Hi Zane,
I was performing magic for some guests in a restaurant, and they told me a nice story.

They live in Dartford and were at a nearby event, and there was a magician with a stall. Their child, around 10 years old, wasn't really interested, in fact, was not really interested in anything apart from computer games.

Anyway, they dragged the child over to the magician's stand, and within minutes he was transfixed, watching the magician perform, demonstrating tricks.

They bought quite a few tricks, and the child has spent months practising them, wanting to do them as well as the magician. He has practically given up computer games, and spends hours practising card tricks, and has even invented a few of his own.

"That magician," they told me, "changed our son's life. He was just inspirational!"

I had to ask.

"That's wonderful, what was his name?"

"Zane!"

Thought you would like to know, selling tricks is special work indeed! …"

It is always nice and rewarding for me to hear about real life stories like this! Testimony to this is how much magic has helped me in life, especially as a child growing up!

As regards my book, I recommend that you read the story first before going straight to the pages at the rear of the book to unlock the door to all the magic secrets taught, because there is advice on performing magic throughout the story; even though it is very tempting!

Well, I really hope you enjoy reading my book and that you are inspired by it, and enjoy learning the amazing magic tricks taught and have as much fun performing them as I have over the years!

CHAPTER ONE

THE BULLYING HAS STARTED!

Eric Fartz, an eleven-year-old schoolboy was being forcibly pinned up against his school locker again by two school bullies from the year above! "Give us your dinner money or else!" said David, aggressively. He was a large and overweight big mouth and the ringleader.

The other even fatter boy, whose nickname was 'Hamburger' because he was always eating them, leaned down even closer towards Eric. "You heard him, Stinky Farts!" said 'Hamburger' in his annoyingly high-pitched squeaky voice. His breath stank and Eric could feel his long black greasy hair brushing against his face. The big bully then held up his large chubby clenched fist, threatening to punch the poor boy hard if he didn't pay up!

"Okay! I have it, I have it!" squealed Eric, scared and desperately fighting back the tears. He didn't want to show them he was frightened anymore, but was a weakly boy, short in height for his years and was smart enough to realize he would come out worse, a lot worse if he tried to fight them. They were about twice his size! So like on most days he handed over his dinner money to these two horrible boys and went hungry.

It was only recently that Eric joined St. Bartholomew's C of E Comprehensive School in Ramsgate, Kent. Three weeks ago to be precise, midway through the second term of year seven. He came down with his mum Ingrid from Sheffield, an industrial city in the north of England, where he was born, to start a new life. They had to leave and relocate due to domestic abuse.

His dad Peter had a drinking problem and was sometimes violent towards Eric's mum. One time the police even had to be involved! She had all the locks to the house changed and the courts served him an injunction order to stay away from them, but that didn't seem to work, as he would often turn up at the family home drunk, shouting abuse and demanding to come in. One time smashing a window to try to gain access. Enough was enough and Ingrid knew that she and her son had to leave for their own safety!

So they did and ended up in Ramsgate. No ones heard of Ramsgate, a small, quiet and remote fishing town on the East Kent coast! Actually, his mother who was originally from Germany had heard of it; she was brought over to England on a family trip from Germany via the port of Ramsgate as a teenager. There used to be a ferry crossing from Calais in France to the port of Ramsgate back then. It was on this trip to the north of England where she had a holiday romance with her now estranged partner, and a few years later lived with him in Sheffield and fell pregnant, given birth to their only child, Eric. They were never actually married, and since she no longer wanted to use his surname - she kept her maiden name Fartz - much to the displeasure of poor little Eric.

Ingrid and her son gave up a lot to move down to Ramsgate, as although they were by no means well off, they did live comfortably in a modest but nice house and had a reasonably nice car, and always had a family summer holiday by the seaside once a year, usually to Scarborough. So they both had to make a personal sacrifice. However it was a lot better they thought, to be in living in Ramsgate without the luxuries than living in fear as they did back in Sheffield, although for poor little Eric, fear was very much still with him!

Having the surname Fartz, of course, didn't help with the bullying. Apart from being ridiculed for being short, he often had to endure children making disgusting fart noises and chanting, "Eric farts, Eric farts!" whilst holding their noses, very cruelly taunting him. How Eric wished his mum and dad had got married; then his surname would have been 'Richardson' and he wouldn't have had to put up with all the horrible name calling. He knew the old saying, "Sticks and stones may break my bones, but names will never hurt me." But it did hurt Eric's feelings. The surname name 'Fartz', spelt with a 'z', is a German name and his mum was proud of her name.

Eric hadn't told his mum about the recent bullying at school because he didn't want to worry her further, especially with everything they have been through in Sheffield. Eric an only child was a quiet lad but had a great sense of humour and a vivid imagination. He was short and rather skinny. He hadn't had a growth spurt yet like most of the other children in his class seemed to have had. He had blue eyes and must have been the fairest haired boy in Ramsgate, which no doubt he got from his mum. Although his mum had since dyed her lovely natural long blonde hair black, to be incognito. Just like his mum, Eric was kind and considerate and despite being bullied, often had a smile on his face. He had a great smile! A sort of happy, go lucky type of boy.

"Hi, Mum. I'm home, what's for tea?" Eric called out as he opened the back door into the kitchen.

"Never mind that," said his mum. "What's that mud doing on your face again?"

"It's one of your face packs Mum," quipped Eric. Eric could be very witty at times.

"Look at your face!" his mum said, slightly concerned.

"I fell over playing football," he replied convincingly. Eric liked football, although he wasn't very good at playing it, but he was a keen Sheffield United supporter. They used to live very near to Bramall Lane football ground and his dad used to take him to watch 'The Blades' play whenever the team were at home. "Sheff United!" and "Come on you Blades!" he used to enjoy chanting with his dad in the terraces. There are three things he really missed the most living in the South of England: watching his favourite team play football, walking in the beautiful Derbyshire countryside and 'Mushy Peas'!

"Okay, well go and wash yourself and your tea will be ready by the time you've finished."

Actually he told his mum a fib. He had his face pushed into some muddy grass by the two bullies on the way home from school!

"Eat grass!" said David, mockingly, laughing as he pushed Eric's face into the grass, while 'Hamburger' held him down by sitting on him.

"Hurry up David - I'm hungry," squeaked 'Hamburger', thinking of his stomach. His voice hadn't broken yet, and it sounded odd and comical to hear a high-pitched squeaky voice coming out of the mouth of such a large boy.

"Don't you dare grass on us northerner," added David, threateningly. "Grass! D'ya get it Hamburger?" then said David, just realizing what he had said. Both bullies laughed out loud in unison at this unintended pun, like a pair of hyenas. They thought it was hilarious. But it wasn't at all funny for Eric!

Both the bullies were immature for their age, especially 'Hamburger'. But at least the laughter distracted them and saved poor little Eric from further intimidation, as they then decided to leave him alone, and carried on their way home. Eric could still hear them laughing their heads off in the distance every time one of them repeated the immature remark.

Eric was becoming a good liar. He was certainly getting enough practice at it. But only because he didn't want to admit that he was being bullied!

"Here you are, love. Make sure you eat up all your tea!" said his mum as she put his meal on the table. His mum had cooked him his favourite meal. A traditional German dish, called 'Bratkartoffeln'. Basically, fried potatoes with diced fatty bacon, onions, and a fried egg on top.

Eric was starving by now and left nothing on the plate. He probably would have eaten the plate as well if it were edible. Although he was missing his lunches, his mum always made sure he went to school with a good bowl of porridge or muesli and a piece of fruit, usually a banana as he didn't like most other fruits, and always had a hearty meal at tea time. One meal he hated but got given a few times a week was beans on toast. It wasn't that he didn't like the taste of baked beans: it was because he was always worried that after eating them he would live up to the horrid names called him by his tormentors. Luckily though he didn't get baked beans for breakfast before going to school.

His mum was now bringing Eric up on her

own as a single parent, living on a council estate in a ground floor flat at number 76a, Hope Close, which the road sign now read as 'No Hope Close', no thanks to a local graffiti artist with a cynical sense of humour, and she no longer had monetary support from her ex-partner. So times were hard and it really felt like there was no hope for them at times. But she was determined not to let the current situation get the better of them and got by the best she could. Sometimes though she struggled to make ends meet and would have to miss meals herself to make sure Eric always had a good meal on the table each day. Sometimes it was the harsh decision of do we keep warm or eat. It was approaching winter now and sometimes it was very cold in their little council flat, as their electricity was one of those types on a meter, where you had to keep topping it up or it would suddenly cut off. Poor little Eric often missed out on treats that most kids in the area enjoyed and took for granted. This upset her more than anything.

Ingrid managed to get part-time work during the week at a local supermarket working at the checkout, which helped with the bills, and she also received child support allowance. Her English was very good, having lived in the UK for a number of years, but she still had an accent. A cross between a German and northern English accent, which she hated and often felt self-conscious of it. Ingrid had already made a few friends from work, and this really helped lift her spirits.

Eric, on the other hand, was struggling to make friends. He was becoming more inward than ever before and would often shut himself in his room and be self-absorbed playing one video game after another, which quietly started to worry his mum. He was a bright lad and had always done well at school, so his mum didn't worry too much about him playing video games on his old 'PlayStation', which he got as Christmas present when times were a bit better a few years ago. Besides, it kept him out of mischief she concluded.

After finishing his dinner and doing the washing up, just like clockwork, Eric went and shut himself in his room. But unlike most days, this time he didn't immediately pick up his 'PlayStation' controls; he sat quietly on the edge of his bed thinking about the ordeal he had had that day because of those two bullies, and how he could not let this carry on anymore. He knew how hard his mum had worked for that money.

The trouble was he had no idea how he was going to deal with it. He thought if he told his mum and it was reported to the school, it would only make things worse for him, and also he could see his mum seemed to be on the up and even perhaps happy once again. It had been a while! He could always tell because his mum started singing again when she cooked his food. She always did that when she was happy. She didn't make anyone else happy with her singing though. She had a dreadful voice, especially singing in English with a thick German accent. Even their cat, they used to have in Sheffield would dart through the cat flap the moment she started to sing. Eric and his dad would cringe and put their fingers in their ears just for fun, and the three of them would laugh about it together.

"If only she didn't try and attempt to sing those high notes in the Whitney Houston songs she keeps singing, and if only I had one of those buzzers like on The X Factor!" Eric thought. A grin, then a smile cracked on his face as he remembered a happier time in Sheffield before his dad started heavily drinking and the problems started.

Anyway, for now, he'd forgotten about the bullies and with an almost involuntary flick on the remote, on came the lights on his T.V monitor and he was playing a game of 'Fifa'. "Goal!" he shouted. His team was Sheffield

United of course and they were one nil up!

Later that evening his mum came to tuck him in and kiss him goodnight, but he'd fallen asleep playing his video games. She noticed a piece of paper by his bedside with just the word 'Plan' and the capital letter 'D', written on the next line. The rest of the paper was blank? Just like her facial expression, wondering what that could be about?

CHAPTER TWO

DOWN IN THE DUMPS

The next morning Eric awoke, feeling as if his eyes lids had been super-glued shut. The 'Sandman' had been again in the night. Since the bullying started Eric would often wake up in the middle of the night sobbing from having nightmares. In fact, he very rarely woke up to a dry pillow.

Eric wiped the crust from his dried tears away and quickly got ready for school, as he daren't be late again. He would have much rather stayed in bed all day! Quickly he gulped down half a slice of toast, put on his grey school blazer, followed by his grey duffle coat and went outside into the grey and dreary weather. "Tarra Mum!" he called out as he slammed the front door behind him and hurriedly dashed off to his new school in Ramsgate.

"Tarra love!" she called back. She often called him 'Love'. A term she picked up living in the north. Eric put on a brave face, but really he was dreading going to school because he knew it was likely to be another day of him being bullied.

The trouble with being repeatedly bullied is that it seems like it will never end for the victim. Eric didn't have any social media accounts like 'Facebook' or 'Instagram', as a lot of his fellow school pupils had. So at least the bullies weren't able to bully him on social media platforms as well, which no doubt they would have done. His mum didn't allow it for the time being at least, because she was worried that her ex might find out where they are now living. *(The best way to deal with 'Cyber Bullying' is to not respond to the bullies directly and to report it to your parents or guardians and the authorities immediately! Don't allow yourself to be affected by it and drawn into communicating with them. It will only cause it to escalate, which is what the bullies want!)*

To get to school Eric had to walk out of the

estate he lives on and then either walk about 200 metres along a main road, past the local shops and then cross the busy road at the zebra crossing, winding his way along a few smaller roads before he arriving at the gates of his new school. Or alternatively, once he's out of the estate, just cut across some playing fields, which is where he got his face pushed into the muddy ground the day before. But this journey is a lot shorter and could save him at least ten or so minutes and as Eric is not very good at getting up in the mornings this option was very appealing to him.

So against his better judgement, he decided to take the more precarious shortcut again, across the playing fields to school. He walked briskly across the lonely field on this cold and cloudy day thinking, "Where are they?" He had just passed the children's play area, which consisted of just broken swings, a rusty old slide and roundabout, and where the two bullies often like to hang out, usually smoking one cigarette between them and playing truant before mums with pushchairs would arrive and tell them off, but there was still no sign of them anywhere. "Strange!" Eric thought and carried on walking. All of a sudden he heard a loud scream.

"There he is, get im!" one of the two bullies

called out! They had arrived later than usual that morning, coming across the fields from a different direction and started running towards him.

Eric thought, "I wish I had one of those 'Invisibility Cloaks', like in the Harry Potter books!" Although, to some extent, Eric was invisible to most other people, because he was so quiet and unnoticeable. Except to bullies, of course, who tend to pick on the quiet ones. Thankfully for Eric, they were both very overweight and couldn't run very fast.

"Oi, come here you northerner!" one of them screeched. But Eric had already left the starting blocks, running faster than he's ever run before. Even Usain Bolt would have struggled to keep up with him. He was at least twenty metres ahead of them and could now see the school in front of him.

Eric turned his head around as he ran and retaliated from a distance, shouting back, "Catch me if you can, you southern wusses!" The other boys gave up the chase realizing it was a waste of time, panting heavily as they now walked. Eric's heart was racing so much, it felt like it was about to burst out of his chest!

"We'll get you later … Northern monkey!" David called out angrily.

"Thank God for that!" Eric thought as he

entered the school gates after his routine daily morning exercise and went straight to his classroom. "Now all I've got to do," he thought, "is to avoid them all day!"

"Your earlier than usual Fartz?" said his form tutor Mr Potter, peering over his glasses at him. "What's the matter with you, are you feeling alright?" continued Mr Potter with a dry sense of humour to lot's of giggles as Eric entered the classroom, still panting. Mr Potter, who was getting on in years and soon due for retirement, was a real character.

"Morning sir," said Eric as he headed quickly for his desk at the back of the class with his shirt hanging out and looking rather sweaty. As he sat down he just caught a glimpse through the classroom door window of the two bullies passing by. One looked menacingly into the classroom as if searching for Eric.

"Right settle down and be quiet!" yelled the teacher. "It's come to my attention that not all of you have handed in your History homework and therefore the following pupils will have detention tonight. Barker, Robinson, Williamson and oh, what a surprise ... Fartz!" Some of the kids in the class giggled again. "Silence! … Well, what have you got to say for yourselves? Fartz this is not the first time you that haven't handed homework in is it. What is your excuse this time? Don't tell me your dog ate it again!" said Mr Potter as he stroked his goatee beard trying to calm himself down.

"Well ... no sir, my dog didn't eat it ... but my neighbour's dog did!" replied Eric nervously. The class howled with laughter but quietly Eric enjoyed this newfound attention.

"Class, I said be quiet!" shouted the teacher again, throwing the formbook down onto table with a loud bang as he said the word 'quict'. "No excuses Fartz! I will see you in detention after school tonight!"

"Why did you do something wrong as well sir?" One of the naughty pupils at the back quipped to more giggles around the class.

"Right, who said that? Was it you Robinson? Right, have another detention!" The classroom went quiet, but then all of a sudden a loud rip-roaring fart sound was heard. Somebody had purposely got up from their seat and plonked themselves back down onto a 'Whoopee Cushion' making a horrendous sound followed by an uproar of laughter from the class. "Right, who did that?" demanded the teacher starting to boil over with anger. "It was Fartz, sir!" claimed the naughty prankster pointing at poor Eric. More laughter was heard as the teacher struggled to contain control of his class. "No it wasn't sir, honest!" protested Eric, embarrassed that the whole class were staring at him, laughing and giggling, some holding their noses.

"Right! There's only one thing for it," thought, Mr Potter "... To use my 'Trump Card'!" Finding it hard to keep a straight face and not burst out laughing at his unintentional word choice. So, in a last-ditch attempt to main order in his class, Mr Potter shook his forefinger in the air and yelled, "Whoever the culprit was, bring that 'Whoopee Cushion' to me now! Or ... the whole class will have detention!" not fooled for one minute as to what made the fart-like sound.

Well, it must have worked because the giggling stopped and the classroom fell silent as they all turned their gaze and pointed towards the now red-faced guilty individual, who promptly brought the soggy 'Whoopee Cushion' up to the front of the class.

"Sorry, sir!" said the boy nervously as he handed it over to the teacher.

"Consider this confiscated and you can join the other lot in detention. Go and sit down!" sternly said, Mr Potter, as he gingerly dropped the 'Whoopee Cushion' into his desk drawer. The thought of pranking the other teachers in the staff room entering his mind. Mr Potter then opened the register and began calling out pupils names.

On Eric's way out of the classroom, going to his first lesson of the day, Mr Potter remarked: "You don't seem that bothered you've got detention young man?" And he wasn't, in fact, Eric had purposely not given his home- work in even though he had finished it at home because he knew that by not doing so he would be given a detention and it would mean the bullies couldn't set upon him after school, at least for today. Given him more time to work out his plan.

Well, the day went by and Eric managed to avoid the bullies, sometimes hiding from them as they walked past. He also stopped using his locker where he knew they would sometimes wait for him and with some difficulty lugged his heavy bag of schoolbooks around with him all day. There was one close shave though. Eric was in the Boys Toilets just having a pee in one of the cubicles during one of the breaks; he would often go in the cubicles fearing the bullies might walk in. Well, luckily he locked the door behind him, as on this occasion David and his cohort 'Hamburger' did walk in. Eric could recognize their voices anywhere! He immediately froze in a state of terror, accidentally peeing down his trousers. He could overhear them just opposite him at the urinals chatting.

"We'll wait for him by the school gates again," said David. Eric knew exactly who he meant by 'him'! Eric kept as quiet as he possibly could, waiting for them to leave before he dares open the door. Eventually, they did leave and Eric quietly undid the lock and freed himself from the cubicle, relieved that the bullies had gone! He quickly washed the wet patch on his trousers, furthering his embarrassment by making it look much worse than before, and on his way to the classroom strategically covered the large damp patch with his school bag, feeling very self-conscious. Eric didn't think the bullies would wait around for him after detention, as he knew they liked their food so much and would want to get home to eat their tea. Of course, he would now have the problem of explaining to his mum why he got detention, as the school would have phoned the parents to inform them.

For a change, he came in through the flat door with a smile on his face having outwitted the bullies. That smile soon dropped though as his mum, who was now the disciplinarian told him off for not doing his homework and for telling lies about the dog they never had. As a punishment, he was banned from playing video games for one week and had his 'PlayStation' confiscated. But even worse, he had beans on toast again for tea that night. His mum tried to find out if there was anything wrong but got no answers.

"So that strategy isn't going to work anymore," Eric thought to himself. Eric made sure he got all his homework done and later that evening in his room tried to plan out his next approach to tackling the bullies. He knew they would be even more angry with him now as he had evaded giving them his dinner money and who knows what they might do to him! But nothing came to him and his mind was as blank as the paper in front of him. It was late and Eric was now feeling tired and gave up trying.

"Eric, would you like a nice cup of hot chocolate?" called out his mum from the kitchen. His mum normally made him a cup of hot chocolate before bedtime.

"Yes please Mum!" replied Eric as he was getting into his 'Marvel Comic' pyjamas, whilst at the same time trying to insert a DVD into the DVD player to watch his favourite movie 'Superman' for the umpteenth time, in bed.

"Okay, I'll put the kettle on love," then called out his mum.

Eric woke up early the next morning in a sweat; he'd been having a nightmare dreaming the two bullies were holding him by his ankles and dangling him out of an upstairs classroom window so his dinner money would fall out of his pockets, laughing their heads off. Bizarrely his teacher Mr Potter was there also, who kept shouting angrily, "Detention Fartz!" and steam would come pouring out of his ears as if he was about to blow his top like Eric had seen last night in a cartoon, whistling like a boiling kettle.

"It's only a dream, It's only a dream," he kept telling himself or at least until now as he wouldn't put anything past those two horrible boys. Suddenly he thought, "I know! I'll throw a 'Sicky', then I won't have to go to school!" but then he thought, "No that won't work with my mum, she's much too clever to believe that and then she will know something's up!" Then after some deliberation, he thought, "I know! I'll break open my piggy bank and offer the bullies what I have saved if they will leave him alone!" He was desperate now.

He discovered that he only had £22.47 in total left, most of the money he'd already spent buying second-hand video games from a video games store in Sheffield before he left. Twenty pounds of it was from his nan and grandpa in Germany, intended for his last birthday and for him to buy a present with it! "I will offer them twenty pounds, that's ten pounds each and then I won't have to hand over Mums hard earned money anymore!" he naively thought. *(This was a big mistake, and Eric would soon learn the hard way, as you should NEVER hand money over to bullies because it shows a sign of weakness and then the bullies will just keep coming back for more! You can't negotiate or reason with bullies because they often get a thrill out of it and like to be controlling. It's a power thing!)*

So off Eric went to school, taking the shortcut again with two crumpled ten-pound notes in his pocket. This time the two bullies were waiting for him, sat all cocky like on the broken swings, calling out abuse as Eric was approaching.

"What's that horrible smell? Hold your nose here comes 'Stinky Fartz'!" cruelly said 'Hamburger'.

"You're dead!" called out David sinisterly. As soon as Eric heard this, he nervously removed the cash from his pocket, holding it up in front of him, his hand visibly shaking with the look of fear and dread etched on his face!

The two boys were expecting a chase again but Eric bravely held his nerve and kept heading towards them. David flicked the cigarette away he'd been smoking just to look big, coughing a couple of times, and said, "Oh look 'Hamburger', Christmas must have come early!"

David promptly walked over to the very scared younger boy and grabbed the money out of his hand. "I'll take that," he said and pushed him against his chest, which hurt.

"You can have it, just please leave me alone from now on!" Eric pleaded with them.

David repeated what Eric had said, in a mockingly poor northern accent. "Please leave me alone. Leave you alone, leave you alone!" shouted David in an intimidating way. "I'll tell you when we'll leave you alone ... I know, let's give him a ride on the roundabout!" said David menacingly. 'Hamburger', then squeezed himself out of the swing seat to join his partner in crime, each grabbing one of poor Eric's arms, and between them, dragged the now screaming boy in the direction of the roundabout.

"No, no, leave me alone!" Eric pleaded once more, trembling with fear. Now only slightly struggling, realizing the inevitable, as sure enough, Eric's screams fell to deaf ears, and the two bullies chucked him on the roundabout and started spinning it as fast as they could. Faster and faster it went. It was too dangerous now to try to jump off, so Eric crouched down holding on for dear life, feeling dizzier and dizzier, wishing his punishment would stop.

"Enjoy the ride!" called out David. The two boys thought it was hilarious and kept laughing and spinning it and spinning it. "Get me off … pleeeease!" shrieked Eric, starting to cry.

"Why don't you learn to speak proper English, you northern cry baby?" said David.

"Yeah! Why don't you learn to speak proper English, you northern crybaby?" repeated 'Hamburger', much to David's annoyance. He would often repeat what David had said. "Oh yeah, and you wouldn't have run faster than us if it was a proper race!" then exclaimed 'Hamburger', in his usual immature way.

"Yeah, that's right you skanky northern monkey!" then called out David, in agreement. An old man walking their dog had heard the screams and spotted what was going on and called out to them, "Hey, you leave that boy alone!" shouted the passer-by in aid of the poor defenceless boy. Upon hearing this, the two bullyboys made a run for it, leaving the roundabout still spinning.

"Let's go!" said the ringleader David. Both the unruly boys now directing their abuse towards the passer-by as they ran – with a torrent of strong swear words unashamedly rolling off of their tongues with well-practised ease - being rude and disrespectful. "This isn't over Fartz!" then called out David.

Shaken up and bedraggled, Eric still managed to get to school. As he entered his classroom, with his shirt half hanging out again and slightly late, Mr Potter addressed him.

"Mr Fartz! How nice of you to drop in to see us!" The rest of the class who had by now all answered the register laughed at what Mr Potter had said. Then in a less sarcastic, more serious tone, the teacher said, "Your ten minutes late Fartz! Detention!"

Suffice to say it wasn't turning out to be a good day for poor little Eric and the rest of the week didn't get any better either. The bullying didn't stop and Eric was feeling down in the dumps. He now knew that the only way he was going to stop the bullying was if he stood up to them and put up a fight, not literally since he wasn't as big and physical as there were, but he would need to be cleverer and outsmart them, and not do something foolish like hand over his money to them. (Never let fear misguide your common sense!) But the weekend had now finally arrived so at least Eric would get a break from all that.

His mum could tell her son was feeling down and upset. She thought it was probably just because she had confiscated his 'PlayStation'.

"That's all it is," she said to herself. But she knew she couldn't go back on what she'd said already as that would undermine her authority and that could lead to all sorts of problems in the future. *(Never allow yourself to be intimidated by bullies and show weakness by letting them see that you are bothered and upset by them: otherwise they will do it all the more! Most bullies are cowards and normally only pick on those who are or appear to be weak and vulnerable, and with whom they think they can get away with it because they won't fight back.*

Eric wasn't being bullied just because of his name or that he was short: it was because he lacked confidence and showed weakness, and was an easy target!

So stand up for yourself: because by speaking up and being assertive, this will show you have confidence and that you are not frightened of them, and then they will be less likely to pick on you!

Also, by standing up for yourself and speaking up, it will alert others around you to come to your aid and draw attention to the bullying, and that's the last thing they want!

But, if you sense you are in danger - don't try to be a hero - flee to safety and seek help!)

CHAPTER THREE

CHRISTMAS MAGIC

It was now early December and people had already started to put up their Christmas decorations. Ingrid had picked up a flyer that morning, whilst out doing some shopping, promoting a 'Christmas Fair' over the weekend in the local community hall. So she thought to help cheer Eric up she would take him along to help pick out a new Christmas tree and decorations as they'd left all their old decorations in their house in Sheffield. They always bought a real tree and not one of those plastic imitation ones. It was a tradition in the Fartz family to always have a real tree and it reminded her of the wonderful and happy

Christmases she had in Germany when she was a little girl. When his mum mentioned about doing that on Saturday Eric didn't seem all that bothered though.

"There will be sweets stalls there!" she said to try an entice Eric to go. A smile suddenly appeared on his face.

"Okay then Mum, why not," Eric replied, feeling a little more spirited than before.

Eric spent most of Saturday morning still in his pyjamas bored out of his brain watching repeats of unfunny American sitcoms on T.V. His mum made him a round of sausage sandwiches to have for his lunch, German sausage of course.

"It is time you got dressed now love," said his mum as she cut the sandwiches into quarters. "We'll go to the Christmas fair straight after lunch," she added.

After lunch, Eric and his mum set off to go to the Christmas fair all wrapped up in their coats, scarves and woolly hats. It was a bitterly cold grey winters day and rather windy. She was more excited than he was!

The community centre, where the Christmas fair was being held, was very near to his school. "Let's cut through the playing fields. It will be quicker!" said his mum. The feeling of dread suddenly came over Eric at the thought of the two bullies possible hanging around there.

"Erm, but Mum, don't you want to go the other way past the shops so you can do the shopping?" Eric said panicking.

"No, I did the weekly shop already. Eric, I did tell you this already. I'm sure you never listen to a word I say," said his mum as she shook her head. "Let's step it out. It won't take long to get there," she said tightening her scarf. Eric then reasoned, as long as he was with his mum they wouldn't dare try anything on.

So they briskly walked through the playing fields. It was quiet for a Saturday with just a few people about walking their dogs and in the distance, they heard the sounds of a football game going on. Eric was constantly looking nervously over his shoulder and walking very closely next to his mum, occasionally getting under her feet and accidentally tripping her up. They walked past the children's play area where on this occasion by contrast to his ordeal earlier in the week a little girl was being gently spun around on the roundabout ride. To Eric's utter relief the two bullies were not there!

The two of them left the recreation ground through the main gates and headed towards the community centre. As they approached the building they could hear Christmas music playing. "Ah, listen to the Christmas music

Eric, int' it lovely!" said his mum now even more excited. It was certainly very busy with people cueing to get in as people were coming out. They could see the freshly cut Christmas trees propped up against the walls outside with different sizes on display.

Eric pointed to the largest tree, "Look at the size of that tree Mum!" said Eric now smiling.

"We'd never fit that in our living room," said his mum laughing. "We'll buy a smaller one on the way out," she then said.

They both entered the entrance to the main hall where there was free mulled wine for the adults and soft drinks for the children handed out. The doorway was beautifully festooned with holly all around it and as they entered their eyes lit up and glistened with excitement and delight, like the shiny tinsel they could see hanging from the Christmas trees displayed around the room! Over to their left were the Salvation Army singing Christmas carols. "How lovely," thought Eric's mum, reminding her of her childhood again.

There were so many different types of stalls to look at they didn't know where to start: stalls selling Christmas decorations, Christmas cards, Christmas gifts, Christmas wrapping paper and Christmas confectionery, all sorts! It certainly was a wondrous sight! There were lots of families there with their children; some Eric recognized from his school, but thankfully not the two bullies.

"Let's go this way, Mum," said Eric. His mum was so pleased to see her son looking happy for a change and she hadn't seen him this excited for a while. They looked at this stall and that, buying decorations for the tree as went: the distinctive smell of incense candles filled the air. "Hey Mum, this will look nice on the tree," Eric had to repeat what he said. It was very noisy in the packed hall. Eric was staring at a shiny silver star to go on top of the tree.

"Yes, that will look lovely on top of the tree. One day you'll be a star Eric," said his mum. Eric gave his mum one of those wonderful smiles of his.

Just then, Eric's mum bumped into one of her, newly found friends from work called, Carol. Quite literally as it was so crowded.

"Oh hello Ingrid, how are you. Isn't it wonderful!" said Carol, excited.

"Oh hiya, Carol. Same idea eh. Get it done early! This is my son Eric," said his mum.

"Oh I've heard a lot about you Eric," said Carol. Eric just smiled.

Both of the two women by now had got several bags of shopping in their hands and hanging off their wrists.

"Thank God for the plastic!" said Carol referring to her well-used credit card. They both laughed and got into a conversation. Eric started to get a little impatient and bored, nudging his mum slightly with his elbow.

"Mum, can we go?" asked Eric. His mum carried on chatting and Eric could see he wasn't going to be able to separate them apart for some time. "Mum ... Mum ... Mum!" he called out trying again to get his mum's attention.

"What is it?" his mum finally answered smiling with embarrassment at her son's interruption.

"Is it okay if I carry on having a look around?"

"Yes, of course, it is darling. I'll catch up with you in a minute," she replied and carried on chatting.

"Yeah right, and England will win the world cup!" he thought. Knowing that when his mum starts chatting it's never a minute. More like sixty!

So, Eric carried on along the aisle of glitter and southern accents, trying to squeeze past people and eventually he got to the end. There right at the end, he could see lot's of people, mostly children, gathered around a stall. He couldn't tell what they were selling because of all the people blocking his view. But he kept hearing, "Oohs" and "Ah's" and lots of applause with the occasional laughter. Whatever it was the audience was having a great time and Eric wanted to be a part of it. So he squeezed through the crowd on his hands and knees and suddenly popped his head up at the front of the stall. This was an advantage of him being small.

"Hello, who's this just appeared as if by magic?" said a strange looking man, wearing an outdated top hat and a fancy waistcoat decorated with stars and moons, much to the amusement of the audience. "Pick a card young man, any card you like," said the strange man behind the even stranger stall counter as he offered little Eric the choice of a card from the pack.

As Eric glanced around wide-eyed, bewildered at first by the odd-looking objects he saw displayed on the counter; shiny silver cups and balls, red sponge balls, packs of playing cards, various books, large fancy-looking boxes piled up one on top of the other and a black stick with white tips. He then quickly realized he was at a magic shop stall. His face lit up and he smiled from ear to ear!

He'd always liked watching magicians on the

telly but had never seen a magician performing in person before.

All excited Eric removed a card from the pack of cards presented before him and the magician asked him to remember the card, which was the nine of hearts and then instructed Eric not to show him the card. The card was returned and the pack thoroughly shuffled. The magician held his fingertips to his forehead in a mystical fashion and said, "Think of your card," and after a dramatic pause the magician declared … "Your card is a red one correct, then another pause, "The suit is a heart I believe," Eric nodded in amazement. Then after an even longer pause, the magician raised his voice and announced, "The card you are merely thinking of is the nine of hearts."

"Yes!" said Eric totally mesmerized and wondering how on earth this strange and captivating man, wearing a top hat and a mystical waistcoat could have read his mind. Eric was speechless, which was not unusual for the usually quiet little Eric anyway. It filled him with a sense of wonderment! And the whole crowd immediately burst into spontaneous applause.

The magician took a bow and then started his sales pitch, explaining that this is a 'Trick Pack of Cards' called the 'Svengali Pack', and with this amazing pack of cards, you can perform lot's of amazing easy to do card trick miracles. He then went on to demonstrate even more amazing feats of magic you can perform with it, and caused Eric's chosen card the nine of hearts to continually rise to the top of the pack after being placed into the middle but it was the finale that really blew everybody's mind, when he turned every single card into the nine of hearts!

The crowd erupted into even louder applause this time shaking their heads in disbelief. To Eric, this was real magic!

"I'll buy one!" called out one of the onlookers.

Then somebody else said, "Yes I'll buy one also please," followed by somebody else wishing to buy one and another and another. In fact, everyone there bought a 'Svengali Pack'. Except for Eric, he couldn't afford one. He only had two pounds odd in his pocket, which is what he had left in his piggy bank after giving most of his savings to those two bullies. If only he hadn't of done that he thought to himself, then he could have bought one of these amazing packs of cards. He wanted one so badly. Maybe he could persuade his mum to buy him one, he thought. Even if it meant not having any sweets he was promised. Even though he loved sweets as most kids do, Eric thought that he would much rather perform amazing card tricks as he'd just witnessed. It was no competition!

The crowd started to disperse, but not Eric, he wanted to see more. A spark went off in his brain and Eric was hooked.

"Show me more, show me more!" said a thrilled and excitable Eric.

The magician showed Eric and other people who had just arrived more incredible and amazing magic tricks he sold at his shop, including a classic of magic called 'The Ball Vase', much to the delight of the audience, where with the wave of the magicians wand and some magic words, a little ball appeared and disappeared to and from an odd shaped little plastic cup. A number of the adults among the crowd remembered this trick from when they were children, having received it in a box set of magic tricks. "A little miracle that anyone can do!" he declared. The magician then took a little red coloured silk handkerchief out of his waistcoat pocket and waved it in the air saying, "Watch the hankie!"

The magician then proceeded to poke the hankie slowly, bit by bit, into the top of his fist, using each fingertip in turn, finally pushing it all the way in with his thumb. He made a magic gesture and then to everyone's surprise, when he opened his hand the hankie had disappeared! The audience once again applauded.

"What's that stuck on your thumb?" suddenly called out an unruly older child at the front, pointing at the magicians slightly swollen looking thumb. The magician quickly and slightly suspiciously, dived his hand into his trouser pocket, ignoring the remark and swiftly carried on with the next demonstration.

Next, to everyone's amazement, including the unruly boy, he turned a large die into lots of tiny dice! This one was called the 'Dice Smash', Eric noted. But still out of his price range.

The magician then demonstrated an astonishing magic trick called 'The Dynamic Coins'. Nobody had a clue how that trick was done. It completely baffled everyone! Eric really wanted to buy this trick too, in fact, he wanted to buy all the tricks, but alas he couldn't afford any of them. He would have to put them on his Christmas list he thought.

"What's that?" Eric asked the magician curiously, pointing towards a gruesome looking miniature guillotine on the magicians stand, about 10cm tall with a shiny metal blade.

"Ah, that is what is known as a 'Finger

Chopper'," replied the magician, chuckling to himself.

"A finger chopper!" exclaimed Eric, looking a little frightened.

The magician laughed. "Don't worry it doesn't really chop your finger off," then explained the magician. "Watch, I'll show you." He raised the miniature guillotine's shiny metal blade and then asked for a volunteer to place their finger through the hole in the apparatus. No one wanted to volunteer at first, "… Don't be frightened!" said the magician. And then a brave man cautiously extended his right forefinger and inserted it into the strange contraption.

Some people around the stand closed their eyes, but not Eric, as he wanted to watch. "On the count of three!" announced the magician. The volunteer quickly withdrew his finger and then to the sound of nervous laughter reluctantly reinserted it. You could feel the tension building! Everybody there joined in the counting and upon the count of 'three' the magician sharply pushed down the blade and to everyone's astonishment, the blade appeared to go right through the volunteer's finger! To lots of applause and much relief, the man removed his finger showing that no harm had come to it, not even a scratch. Eric really liked that trick.

Then the magician picked up a red velvet cloth bag with a wooden handle attached and turned it inside out showing there was nothing inside. "Prepare to be amazed!" he said in his mystical, slightly gravelly voice. He then gave Eric the magic wand to wave over the bag and say the magic words, 'Abracadabra', but as Eric went to take the wand, it collapsed in his hand as if he'd broken it. "Oh dear!" said the magician. "What have you done to my magic wand?" Everybody laughed including Eric, who thought it was hilarious. Then to everyone's amazement, the magician reached into the bag and pulled out lots of different coloured silk handkerchiefs one by one followed by what seemed to be a never-ending beautiful multi coloured silk streamer. The audience loved it and applauded loudly again.

The magician then thanked Eric for being a good sport and helping him. Some of the children who come to his magic stall were sometimes less helpful though and were naughty and rude, interrupting his performance by calling out how they thought the trick was done. The magician could see that Eric, however, was a polite boy and very enthusiastic about magic and so he gave him some sound advice about performing magic, and as he'd helped him during some of his tricks, gave Eric a free pack of 'Svengali cards'. "Thank you very much!" replied Eric, very, very pleased.

As the magician handed over the pack of cards, he then leant down and quietly whispered something in Eric's ear so only Eric could hear. What was it that was said? Was it a magic secret? Maybe the magician recognised in this boy something in himself when he was a child - something rare, that's inside all the best magicians perhaps? "Don't forget what I told you will you young man!" said the wise old magician as he left Eric to serve a customer down by the far end of the counter. Eric was so glad he'd decided to come to the Christmas fair after all. Any fears he had disappeared like magic on this day!

For the whole time, he was there, which must have been at least half an hour, Eric had been completely transfixed and had forgotten all about his mum who was by now searching for him. Being small it was hard to spot him amongst the crowds. Then as she came past the magic stall again for the second time she spotted her son through a slight gap in the crowd watching the magician perform.

"Excuse me please!" she said as she moved past people up to the front, struggling with even more bags of shopping. "Eric I've been looking for you. I was worried because I didn't know where you were!" said his slightly flustered mum.

Still excited Eric replied, "I've been here all the time Mum, watching lots of amazing magic tricks and I want to be a magician!" He held up the pack of cards the magician had given him and said, "Look, Mum, the magician gave me a free pack of magic cards for helping him." Well, when she saw how much fun he'd had and how happy he was she decided to leave it at that. Besides her feet were now killing her after all that traipsing around Christmas shopping.

"I've bought you a bag of those sweets that you like love. I didn't forget! Let's go now and choose a nice Christmas tree to buy!" said his mum with a big smile. Eric thanked his mum and off they went together to buy a Christmas tree, calling out goodbye to the kind magician as they left. Eric helped his mum carry the shopping bags; it was less busy now and easier to move along the aisle.

When they got back outside his mum had a look inside her purse to see what money she had left as the man selling the Christmas trees would only accept cash. When she counted up the money she had only just enough left to buy the smallest tree there, which was about 4 foot high. Most of the other trees had already sold and you could now see parts of the walls of the community centre again, which you couldn't see when they first arrived. So his mum bought it and they were both happy to have a real Christmas tree!

So off they went back home. Eric had the job of carrying the tree and his mum carried the bags. On their way home, Eric did not stop talking about all the wonderful and amazing magic tricks that he had seen.

"You should have seen what he did with the playing cards!" he said to his mum, clearly inspired and eager to learn the tricks with his very own 'Svengali Pack'. "I can't wait to get home and practice," he said excitedly.

"I bet I can guess what you want for Christmas this year," said his mum smiling. Eric smiled back and nodded. His mum thought taking up magic as a hobby was a great idea for her son, as it would give him something positive to do and it would also help her son gain the confidence he lacked and be good for his social skills by getting him out meeting other children more. So she was all for it.

As they headed across the playing fields battling against the cutting wind with all that shopping they were carrying, Eric could see two large boys in the distance kicking a football around. His immediate reaction was to instinctively cover his face with the Christmas tree, so they wouldn't see him. But then he bravely lowered the tree from his face, remembering what the magician had told him and walked the rest of the way home, believing he was a superhero!

CHAPTER FOUR

A NEW FOUND PASSION

For the rest of the day, Eric spent most of the time in his room with his door closed learning the secret to the 'Svengali pack' and how to perform the amazing card tricks taught in the instructions, while his mum made a start with putting up the new Christmas decorations. Eric helped every now and then, between learning his magic tricks, hanging up the baubles and fairy lights and he putting the star he had chosen on top of the tree, which he could only just about reach. His mum put some Christmassy music on and started singing along in her native tongue, "Stille Nacht! Heil'ge Nacht! Alles schlaft, einsam wacht. Nur das traute hock …"

Eric remembered fondly, the most magical and enchanting story his mum used to tell, which her mother in Germany used to tell to her as a young child about the fairies, thousands of them in fact, that lived in the Christmas tree and how it was the warmth from all their bodies when they flapped their tiny wings that would generate enough heat and electricity to light up the tree! And would then explain, "That's why they are called 'Fairy Lights'!" As he reminisced, a big gleaming smile lit up his face! Both of them were very happy for a change.

"Eric, Britain's got talent, is starting!" called out his mum as she hung another bauble on the tree.   Eric normally never liked to miss this T.V programme, but even this would not stop the protégé magician from learning his new found passion. He practised and practised, over and over again, determined to get it right, sometimes getting frustrated as cards would fall to the floor and he would have to pick them up and start again. Eric had read, quoted in the instructions and what he'd often heard his mum say, 'Practice makes perfect!' and 'If at first, you don't succeed try, try again!' *(Two old proverbs worth remembering! You should always practice and rehearse your magic tricks before you show them to anyone so that you don't make mistakes and ruin the trick by revealing the secret!)*

It was getting late in the evening by now and even though he desperately wanted to show his mum the card tricks he had learned, it had been an exhausting day and he was feeling rather tired, so he called out, "Goodnight" to his mum and fell straight to sleep still holding the pack of cards in his hand.

Sunday morning Eric woke up around 8:00 am to find just about all the cards were now scattered in a mess on the floor by his bedside, some cards were face up and some face down. Having relaxed his fingers as he drifted off, the cards cascaded from his grip flowing off his bed like a dry waterfall. No nightmare this time but instead he had a very pleasant dream of him standing on stage in front of lots of people performing an amazing magic act with everybody cheering and applauding him. He had just one 'Britain's got talent' and that's when he woke up! He jumped out of bed with a big happy smile and reassembled his pack of cherished magic cards, carefully putting them back in their case.

Now armed with his special deck of cards in his hand again, he went in search of his first ever volunteer, his mum, who didn't take long to find in their small flat.

"Guten Morgen! I'm in here!" called out his mum in her native German tongue. Eric found his mum sat at the dining table finishing her breakfast cereal.

"Mum, pick a card, any card you like -" said the very eager protégé magician as he offered her the choice of a card.

"Have your breakfast first love," she said chuckling and admiring her son's enthusiasm at that early time of Sunday morning. To Eric that was like someone firing a starting pistol at the start of a race and Eric had left the blocks! He gulped his cereal down as fast as he could, some missing his mouth completely. He even declined the offer of toast with peanut butter, which he normally loves. "Wow! You made that disappear quickly!" laughed his mum, thinking she was being very witty with her reference to magic. With food still in his mouth, Eric offered his mum the choice of a playing card again.

"Pick a card, any card you like Mum ..." Eric repeated. He had remembered virtually all the patter the magician had said during his demonstration yesterday and went on to perform a couple of the tricks he had learnt from the instructions. There are so many tricks one can perform with 'The Svengali Pack' and

Eric performed the same trick he had seen the magician perform at the Christmas fair called, 'The Ambitious Card', where the chosen card despite being placed in the centre of the pack, repeatedly rises to the top! His mum was well impressed!

Eric really liked that trick and it was the first trick he learnt. He then performed another incredible trick where the chosen card is seemingly lost in the pack and as the magician deals the cards face down onto the table one card at a time, the spectator is asked to call out "Stop" at any time they like and when the card stopped at is turned over, it is the chosen card! Both these tricks are classics of magic and normally performed with a regular pack using skilful sleight of hand, but by using the 'Svengali' pack it makes it easy to perform these amazing tricks.

"Can I show you one more trick please Mum?" asked Eric still buzzing with excitement.

"Yes alright darling," his mum replied pleased to see her son so enthusiastic.

"You see all the cards are differ -"

"What's that burning smell?" suddenly said his mum interrupting Eric. "Oh eck! It's the toast!" She quickly went and switched the grill pan off and threw the blackened toast in the waste bin, having completely forgotten about it because she was so transfixed by her sons amazing magic tricks. "Nevermind, carry on Son -" Suddenly the smoke alarm went off, startling both of them and his mum watched Eric perform his finale, miraculously causing all of the playing cards to turn into her chosen card, whilst at the same time standing on tiptoes and waving the tea-towel frantically around in the air trying to perform her own magic trick and make the smoke disappear!

Finally, the smoke dispersed and the beeping stopped and his mum gave him a big round of applause, pleasantly surprised at how good he was! What an eventful morning it was turning out to be!

"How did you do that?" she said amazed and impressed that he had learnt these magic tricks so quickly!

"A good magician never reveals his secrets!" he replied, which is one of the rules of magic he had read in the instructions. *(Yes, that's right because if you reveal the secret, it will no longer be special and it would spoil it for your spectators, plus you will get less credit as a magician!)*

"Actually, I don't want to know how you did it because then it would spoil it! Well done love!" said his mum still in amazement.

He did make a few minor mistakes whilst performing the tricks, but his mum pretended not to see those and just gave him encouragement and praise. She thought he'd done brilliantly especially as it was the first time he'd ever performed magic.

Eric couldn't wait now to get out and show more people his magic. He liked the response you get from performing magic and found it very rewarding and empowering.

"I have arranged to go and see my friends from work for afternoon tea at one of their houses. Why don't you come along and perform your magic for everyone!" said his Mum thinking what a good idea that would be.

"Yes, alright," said Eric in an enthusiastic albeit slightly nervous way.

"Their children will be there also," his mum added thinking it would be good for her son also to mix with other children.

"I'm going to my room to practice Mum," said Eric.

Eric started to head for his bedroom when his mum suddenly said, "Wait a moment Eric, I have something for you?" His mum reached into her large bag searching for something.

"What is it Mum?" enquired Eric inquisitively, wondering what it could be? His mum then handed him a book, but not just any book it was a magic book for beginners. "A magic book!" shrieked Eric delighted, "Oh thank you, Mum!" Ingrid had secretly gone back to the magic shop stall, leaving Eric waiting at the entrance, telling him a little white lie that she had forgotten to buy something. She had intended to wrap the book and give it to him as a Christmas present but she could see how interested he was in magic and so decided to give it to him that morning.

Eric went off to his room and promptly closed the door behind him, while his mum got on with some household chores singing merrily along to herself as she did. His appetite had been wetted and he wanted to learn more magic tricks performed with different objects other than just cards, like the magician he was so inspired by, performed the day before. He was so excited and immediately sat down on the edge of his unmade bed and started reading his new magic book.

He had never had a magic book before. He turned one of the pages and came across the heading 'The French Drop', "Oh that looks interesting!" he thought. It was a technique on how to make a coin disappear. It reminded him of when the magic shop owner would go to give a customer their change and just for fun he would suddenly make it disappear! Of course moments later he did give the change back. Eric thought this would be a fun trick to perform and began learning how to make a coin disappear! *(Learn the secret to this very useful coin sleight called 'The French Drop', and many more amazing magic tricks in 'Eric's Magic Trick Secrets' found at the rear of the book!)*

He must have read through the explanation at least half a dozen times just to make sure he got it. Eric practised the coin vanish in front of the mirror to start with, as was advised in the book. He kept dropping the coin at first but would pick it up and kept practising. He even amazed himself when he looked at the reflection in the mirror and laughed at himself. He was now the proud owner of his very first magic book and he was delighted! *(It is recommended to read 'Magic Books' as well as watching magic taught on video, because although it is good to watch other magicians teaching you on video to see how others perform the tricks and perhaps a quicker way to learn the tricks taught, by reading books you will find that you will use your imagination more and will, therefore, be more creative and your presentation will be more original. After all, you don't want to be a carbon copy of another magician!)*

CHAPTER FIVE

A SURPRISING AFTRENOON TEA

"Eric it's time to go love!" his mum called out. Eric picked up his magic cards and both of them headed off to her friend Carol's house. It was cold outside but the wind had dropped and the sun was out. Much nicer than it was the day before. The house they were visiting wasn't very far away. In fact, it was just a few streets away. Ingrid had not been to there before and was really looking forward to having a nice chat with her friends from work. "I think this is the one," she said. It was a nice looking three-bedroom house on one of those modern housing estates. All the lawns were perfectly manicured with gleaming and sparklingly clean family cars on the driveways.

"Eric do you want to ring the bell?" asked his mum. Eric reached up; he could only just about reach it and rang the bell. They could hear a lot of noise coming from inside so they thought this is probably the correct address. Suddenly they heard a loud barking and clawing sound on the other side of the door. As the front door opened, a hairy leg suddenly popped into view.

"Hello!" said Carol desperately trying to hold back the dog and stop it keep jumping up. It was the families pit bull terrier. "Do come in," said Carol trying to sound calm. Both Eric and his mum looked a bit frightened and surprised.

"Hiya Carol!" said Ingrid slightly nervously.

"Oh don't worry about Bruiser. We've just had him castrated and he's a bit grumpy today," said Carol as she bent down and gave the dog a quick cuddle and kissed him on the head. "You are a grumpy dog today aren't you bruiser. Yes, you are, yes you are," repeated Carol as if she was talking to a small child and not a dog. Carol pulled the dog away by its collar, struggling to control it, so the visitors could come in. "I'll put him in the front room for now until he settles down."

Ingrid was thinking, "I hope she keeps him there!" She didn't like dogs, especially dogs that barked a lot. As they entered the hallway they could also hear a loud noise of gunfire and explosions coming from upstairs.

"We're all in the conservatory come on through," said Carol in a bit of a fluster, her hair, less tidy than before she went to answer the door. Eric followed his mum into the conservatory eager to show more people the magic tricks he'd learnt.

"I like all your Christmas decorations!" Ingrid commented to Carol. "Aren't they lovely Eric ... Eric, aren't they lovely?" Ingrid repeated, giving him a slight nudge. Eric was miles away.

"Yeah," Eric then just replied.

"Thank you dears," replied Ingrid, pleased to hear that for the third time that afternoon. Carol certainly went to town when it came to Christmas decorations, not wanting to be out down by the neighbours. There were decorations everywhere!

"Hello!" everyone said in unison.

In the room, there were Ingrid's other newly found friends Julie and Fiona with their children. The men were all still down the local pub. It was a bit of a tight squeeze in there but they managed. All the mums introduced their children in turn and then Carol said, "And these are my two, Abby and Mary and my oldest boy is Gary, who's upstairs in his room playing video games."

On the table were a variety of freshly cut sandwiches and a choice of 'Victoria Sponge Cake' or 'Chocolate Cake', which all the children kept eyeing up. All the adults immediately started chatting to one another and the children, who already knew each another, started playing a board game in a corner of the room. Except Eric, who was sat staring against a wall, analysing when would be the best time to perform his magic show? He thought it probably best to perform it after people had eaten. Also he didn't feel quite up to it yet.

His mum saw Eric was by himself and looking slightly uneasy and said, "Why don't you join in with the other children Eric?"

"Why does my Mum always say embarrassing stuff like that?" he thought to himself, much to his annoyance, but the other children were two or three years younger than him and he didn't think that would look cool. "I'm fine Mum," he replied rather abruptly. Besides, Eric was still thinking about performing his magic and what trick he ought to perform first and the nerves were starting to kick in a bit.

"Isn't your boy shy?" Carol said to Ingrid to no reply, just a polite smile, not realizing that she had hit a nerve by making that comment to Ingrid. "Right, is everyone ready for a cup of tea?" asked Carol trying to get up from her seat. Carol was a rather large lady who clearly liked her splodgy cream cakes. "I'll go and put the kettle on then."

Before going into her plush new fitted kitchen to make a pot of tea she called up to her son Gary from the hallway. "Gary darling! Would you like to come and join us for tea and cakes. I bought your favourite chocolate cake you like!" She had to ask him again because the noise from the video game was so loud and then the dog started barking again.

"No, I told you I don't want to. Are you deaf?" Gary eventually replied, very rudely. "I'm playing video games, leave me be!"

"Would you like me to save you some cake?" his mum called up.

"YES! NOW STOP DISTURBING ME! OH - NOW YOU'VE MADE ME GET SHOT!" The rude boy screamed down to his mum even louder in his high-pitched voice. His mum thought it best to leave him to it so he wouldn't have one of his temper tantrums. Her son had anger issues.

Meanwhile, in the conservatory, the adults were still busy talking and discussing a whole manner of topics and the children were getting into their game, laughing with excitement every so often and everyone was having a jolly time. Well except Eric that is, who was now staring at a framed photograph on the wall he had just spotted, of someone he immediately recognized dressed in his school uniform. It was one of the bullies - 'Hamburger'! Whose real name was Gary!

"OH NO! GET ME OUT OF HERE!" was the immediate reaction he screamed in his head as that overwhelming feeling of dread once again started to envelop him. The poor little fellow started to panic and sweat for a moment not knowing what to do, but for a change, he didn't show any obvious signs of fear. Eric kept calm by repeating to himself what the magician at the magic stall had confided in him. Before the weekend if he'd been faced with this situation he would probably have run for the door. So he was definitely gaining more confidence.

Anyway, he had a job to do, put on a magic show and amaze everyone! At that point, Carol came in carrying a tray with a large pot of tea, cups and saucers and a pile of plates.

"Here we are," she said as she put the tray onto the coffee table. "Now, who's ready to eat?" she said.

All the younger kids screamed "Yeah!"

"Please help yourselves to sandwiches and cake… I better just cut off a slice of Gary's favourite chocolate cake for him," she added. Well, Carol must have cut off a third of the cake for him. Everyone looked at each other in surprise.

Carol carried on being her usual chirpy self as if the episode with her son just now hadn't happened as if she was used to it. But Eric was not the only person to be bullied by Gary, she was too! Carol was always pampering Gary and was too soft with her son, letting him get away with how he treated her much too often. Her husband was not any better either and he often worked away from home as a long distance lorry driver or was out with his mates drinking, leaving poor Carol to mostly deal with his poor behaviour.

"I like your pink furry slippers," said Ingrid to Carol, noticing them on the floor.

Carol laughed saying, "Oh they're not mine, they're Gary's! He got a thing for pink and just loves the soft feel of them for some reason?" Eric's ears pricked upon hearing this and his eyebrows raised involuntarily. "He's a big softy really," Carol added smiling.

"He's big alright, but a softy?" thought Eric.

"Is Gary not coming down to join us?" said Julie.

"No," said Carol, "He's happy where he is, bless him," she added. "More tea anyone?" Carol said smiling with a tinge of embarrassment, quickly changing the subject. Everyone had heard the screaming from upstairs. Eric overheard this conversation and gave a big sigh of relief that 'Hamburger' wasn't going to be joining them.

By now all the guests were tucking into their plate of sandwiches and cakes and enjoying them.

"Did you make these yourself? Their lovely!" said Ingrid. Everyone one else who had their mouth's full nodded in agreement.

"Yes," replied Carol. Actually, that wasn't true, she bought them from ASDA up the road. She always liked to make a good impression even if it meant telling a little white lie occasionally.

Carol could see that Eric didn't want to join in with the other younger children and was bored so she said to Eric, "Eric, after you've finished eating why don't you go upstairs to Gary's room and play video games together?" Eric went quiet, even more so than he normally is, not replying.

Eric's mum could see that her son was keen to start his magic show so spoke for him in a proud 'Dance Mom' or in his case 'Magic

Mom' kind of voice and said, "Eric would like to put on a magic show for you all!" On hearing that, everyone, especially the younger children got excited and moved to get a better position, the draft caused from the sudden rush of bodies nearly blowing over some of the carefully placed Christmas cards situated around the room. They all sat crowded around together on the fake suede, tan coloured furniture, with some of the kids spilling off onto the floor by the feet of their mums ready to watch Eric perform his tricks.

Eric was naturally a little nervous to start with performing in front of a room full of people and as he pulled the pack of cards out of his pocket he accidentally dropped them on the floor and a few slid out of the box. Some of the younger children giggled followed by the sound of, "Ssh!" from their mums. But Eric smiled and carried on as he removed the rest of the cards from the box.

"I'd like to show you some card tricks," quietly announced Eric. He then showed the cards to be all different and proceeded to have one selected. "Remember your card and place it back in the middle of the pack please ..." he said as he offered the pack forwards for the card to be re-inserted.

Eric then performed a few of the amazing

tricks he had learnt with the 'Svengali pack' that he showed his mum earlier, only this time he didn't make any mistakes. Everyone there cheered and applauded as he finished performing each trick, which kept waking the dog up, who would then bark loud each time. The mums all looked at each with raised eyebrows clearly impressed and surprised at how a normally quiet boy was now confidently standing up in front of them performing these amazing tricks!

Eric's confidence grew and grew and like everyone else in the room he too was really enjoying himself now and had completely forgotten about 'Hamburger' being upstairs. Feeling a lot more confident he decided to perform another magic trick he had learnt from his new magic book and picked up a teaspoon from one of the saucers.

"Carol did you know that your spoons are made of rubber!" Suiting the actions to the words he held the spoon handle between both of his hands and pressed the bowl of the spoon against the table bending it almost in half."

"Oh dear, what have you done to my nice spoon!" said Carol genuinely worried for a moment. Everybody else began to laugh.

"Don't worry! I am a magician!" Eric said as he covered the damaged spoon with his hands and wiggled his fingers, "... Abracadabra!" Eric lifted his hands away to reveal the spoon was now completely restored and back to normal! *(Learn the secret to the amazing 'The Rubber Spoon' trick at the end of the book)* Everyone burst into loud and spontaneous applause drowning out the sounds of gunfire coming from upstairs and the barking dog. Eric said, "Thank you very much," and took a bow but the children all chanted, "Do one more trick! Do one more trick!"

Eric wanted to perform the 'Vanishing coin trick', but didn't feel he was quite ready for that one just yet. It still needed a bit more practice he thought. He could only remember one other trick he had learnt, which was a mind reading trick. So, he performed that trick.

Eric gave Julie a small square of paper and asked her to secretly write the name of a famous person in the circle he had drawn on the paper, "Now so as to get a strong mental picture in your head, please write down the name of a famous person, dead or alive in the circle I have drawn, but don't tell me or let me see what you are writing," asked Eric politely.

So after giving it some thought, she wrote down the name of her favourite singer 'Elvis Presley', being careful not to let Eric she what she had put. Turning his head away Eric then requested her to, "Fold the paper into quarters so I can't see what you've written ..." All said in a very serious and dramatic manner just like how he remembered seeing 'Mind Readers' on the telly.

Still with his head turned away he took the folded paper back from Julie and tore it up into tiny pieces. "... We won't need this anymore," he said and threw the bits of paper away. Holding one of his hands to his forehead he looked at Julie mysterious like and said, "Now look into my eyes and concentrate on the name of this famous person in your head."

Except for the distant noise coming from 'Hamburger's' room upstairs, the room went completely silent, even the dog had stopped barking.

"Try to visualize this person ..." he added as Julie concentrated, trying to keep a straight face, unsure whether she should take it seriously or not. Then after a dramatic pause, he announced "The name of the person you are thinking of is ..." Another dramatic pause. "Elvis!" The audience was stunned, especially Julie and everyone burst into spontaneous applause once again! How could Eric have known that? *(Find out how to read peoples minds at the rear of the book! The trick is called 'The Centre Tear')*

Eric took his final bow to even louder applause and cheers, which woke the dog up again and as the show came to an end so did this wonderful afternoon tea party. As people were leaving they were all praising and complimenting Eric on his performance. The children were still pestering him to perform more! Eric's mum gave him a big hug and said she was very proud of him. They said goodbye to everyone and Ingrid thanked Carol for inviting them and they left as they entered to the sounds of the dog barking and gunfire and explosions in the background.

Eric's confidence had really grown and as they walked back home together he felt about ten feet tall!

"Everyone was surprised at how good you were Eric!" said his mum.

"It had been an afternoon full of surprises alright!" thought Eric.

CHAPTER SIX

ERIC FORMS A NEW FRIENDSHIP

They both arrived back home from Carol's house. Eric's mum put the dinner on and Eric, a little tired but still elated by the great response he got from performing his magic show, went straight to his room to learn more magic tricks. He couldn't believe though that his mums best friends son was one of the bullies! Eric tried not to focus on it but every now and then kept getting flashing images in his head of the grossly overweight 'Hamburger' wearing pink fury slippers. He would shake his head each time to try and get the image out of his head and every now and then would burst into laughter.

"What were you laughing about?" asked his mum inquisitively.

"Oh nothing!" replied Eric smiling. During dinner they both talked about what a wonderful day it had been and Eric's mum said, "You can have your PlayStation back and play video games tonight if you like Son," But Eric wasn't interested in that anymore and only wanted to learn and practice more tricks.

Eric quickly finished his desert, which he hadn't lost interest in and said, "Thanks Mum," as he jumped up from his seat and went straight back to his magic den. His mum was pleased that he had now found another pastime rather than playing video games all the time, like a lot of children she thought.

The next morning Eric went off to school and his mum went off to work. On the way there, Eric bumped into his classmate Jack Robinson. By now the two of them had got to know each other better by spending a few detentions together. Jack had never really noticed Eric before that.

As they made their way to school, Eric would jump every now and again to avoid stepping on the cracks in the pavement. The superstitious behaviour he picked up from his mum. Superstitions and fears and self-doubts are often passed on from generation to generation. "It's unlucky to walk under a ladder!" and "Thirteen is an unlucky number!" he would also sometimes hear his mum say. *(Don't allow other people's irrational and unfounded fears and anxieties or doubts, superstitious or otherwise, to be passed onto you. As fear can stop you from doing the things you want to do in life, which could also prevent you from achieving your goals and succeeding!*

If you believed all the superstitions and fears you heard you wouldn't do anything - You'd be too frightened to even leave the house!

If you think about it rationally and logically: walking under a ladder, for instance, is not unlucky in the sense that something bad might happen to you in the future, as it is largely perceived to mean - It's because the ladder might accidentally fall on top your head! (Ouch!)

As with most superstitions: it is told with the intention of protecting you and to merely prevent you from the risk of danger and harm by striking fear into you, which is really only sensible and sage advice and nothing more! But also, fear-mongering, which plays on people's fears and anxieties, has been used through history, and still to this day, as a means to control people!)

Eric and Jack got on very well and had a similar sense of humour. Jack, however, by contrast, was a confident and very popular boy, deemed as one of the cool kids and part of the 'In crowd', who loved sports and was tall and well built, unlike Eric. Jack was in all the school sports teams and especially liked rugby.

Eric had noticed that Jack had a couple of elastic bands around his pencil case because the zip had broken.

"Jack, can I borrow those elastic bands you keep around your pencil case for a minute? I'll show you a magic trick," asked Eric. Jack gave Eric the two elastic bands and he performed an amazing trick, causing the two elastic bands to link and unlink in a most magical and mystifying way.

"How did you do that?" Jack said amazed. "That was sick!" he added.

"It's a secret!" replied Eric smiling. Jack thought Eric was cool and was pleased to call him his friend. The magic trick he had shown him was a simple trick with just two elastic bands called 'The Penetrating Bands'. *(Find out the secret to this amazing trick at the rear of the book)*.

On the way to school, they passed by the community centre where Eric had been to the

Christmas fair over the weekend.

"I went to a Christmas fair there on Saturday and there was a sick magic shop stall there," said Eric. Eric had often heard Jack use the word 'sick', so decided he would adopt that word too when describing something he thought was cool. "Did you go Jack?" asked Eric.

"No," said Jack. "I wish, but I had to do some chores," he added sounding disappointed.

The community centre looked very different now though. The entrance door was shut. No more Christmas trees outside or festive music playing. A completely different atmosphere compared to the fun and exciting atmosphere experienced over the weekend, just the drab looking grey walled building it normally is for most of the year.

During the school mid-morning break that day, Eric was in the playground and after some hesitation plucked up the courage to perform his amazing magic to other children in his year. Before he knew it, pupils prized their eyes away from their mobile phone screens and looked on in wonder as he performed his amazing magic tricks, as if transfixed and under his spell, completely forgetting about their mobiles phones!

He got quite a crowd around him in the playground watching and applauding him, even some of the children who had called him names in the past joined in the applause. He got, the occasional, "I know how you did that!" Mainly from kids that just wanted to sound clever in front of their friends but didn't really know how it was done.

It caused quite a commotion and one of the teachers on break duty came over to see what was happening and to make sure that there wasn't a fight going on. At the unusual sight of all the pupils refraining from staring at their mobile phone screens for a change, the teacher thought, "Now that is what I call magic!" as they also watched on in delight and amazement.

The bell was heard, which meant that the mid-morning break was now over and Eric, Jack and a few other classmates who now also wanted to be Jacks friend went off to their lessons together.

"Oh, I've just remembered. I've got to get a textbook from my locker. See you later!" said Eric as he rushed off.

"Yeah see you later!" replied his new friend Jack. Eric hadn't seen the two bullies at school and thought that they were probably playing truant again. But just as Eric began to close his locker door, to his surprise there they were stood there, like as if they had suddenly appeared by magic. It startled Eric.

"Watcha Fartz! Ahh, did we make you jump?" said the menace David, as cocky as usual.

"Ahh, did we make you jump?" chimed in 'Hamburger', repeating what David had just said. His bad breath made Eric wince.

"Will you stop keep repeating everything I say!" David quickly said to 'Hamburger', finding it annoying. He then continued addressing Eric. "If you don't hand over your dinner money now, you'll get much worse happen to ya than us making you jump!" said David, as he pulled a menacing face and punched the locker right next to Eric's head, creating a loud bang and making Eric jump again.

"Okay, okay I'll get it for you," said a now frightened and distressed Eric. To David, Eric was just a 'Cash Machine' that he could draw money out of whenever he wanted to.

David let him go and backed off a little bit as Eric reached it his pocket and pulled out all the money he had, which he was supposed to pay for his dinner with.

As he was removing the coins from his trouser pocket, his inner voice kept telling him,

"DO THE FRENCH DROP! DO THE FRENCH DROP! DON'T LET THEM HAVE IT!" It was like the magician at the Christmas fair was speaking to him?

Eric by now had practised the 'Coin Vanish Move' a lot more and bravely as he went to hand over his dinner money to David, he did the 'French Drop', and upon opening his hand all the coins had vanished!

The two bullies both stepped back in stunned silence completely surprised at what just happened and were lost for words for a change! 'Hamburger' even sort of smiled, like he forgot for a moment to be 'The Bully' and enjoyed that moment of amazement. The smile soon dropped though as he caught David's glance towards him.

Then David, clearly irritated and annoyed at the thought of being fooled by his 'victim', said in a frustrated and condescending tone, "It's obvious, it's in your other hand!"

The two bullies were now staring intently at Eric's other hand thinking that they had caught Eric out, but then Eric slowly opened his hand to show that there were no coins there either? David looked was completely dumbfounded and looked crestfallen.

'Hamburger' started to smile again in wonder, and then laughed at David, saying in his irritating voice, "He's just mugged you off!"

"Shut it!" snapped back David angrily, giving 'Hamburger' a 'dead arm' with his tightly clenched fist.

"Ouch!" replied 'Hamburger', feeling the pain and no longer laughing as he rubbed his sore arm.

While the two bullies were still bickering and stunned by what just happened, Eric sharply turned on his heels and deftly slipped away and headed off to his Geography class, which Eric hated but on this occasion had never got there as quick!

Eric had fooled his enemy and was very pleased with himself as he sat down and began to take notes on irrigation systems in West Africa. He was especially pleased as he had pulled off the 'French Drop' technique so well, seemingly vanishing the coins, but hadn't really of course. But he also realized that he'd only just escaped by the skin of his teeth and knew this probably wasn't the end of it.

After his geography lesson the school lunch bell rang out and off he went to the school dining hall and for a change had a school dinner that day. Eric was sat around a table with Jack and a couple of his rugby teammates. Jack said, "Show us a trick, Eric!" So Eric performed a few tricks for them including the

'Bending Spoon' trick with their spoons, causing much hilarity and amazement.

And then, Eric picked up a napkin, holding it by the top two corners and draped it over a bowl of bread rolls in front of him, "What's he going to do now?" thought the bedazzled onlookers. Suddenly one of the bread rolls rose up from out of the bowl under the handkerchief, it's form clearly seen. Eric struggled to keep control of it at one point, as the roll seemed to want to fly away dragging Eric up from his seat. Everyone looked on in amazement and by now even pupils on other tables started to take notice.

Eric noticed a pretty girl with long dark brown hair on the adjacent table constantly smiling at him and enjoying his antics with the bread roll. It was a girl called Emily, who was in Eric's class but he had never spoken to her before. Eric smiled back at her still struggling with the bread roll as it darted here and there above the table. The roll then suddenly popped halfway into view momentarily above the top of the napkin causing a sudden gasp from around the dining room. The roll then went back under the napkin and floated back down and nestled back in the bowl. Eric whipped the napkin away to the joyful sound of cheers and applause. One of the pupils at the table immediately grabbed the roll, out of the bowl, cautiously examined it and took a big bite out of it causing everyone at the table to laugh out loud. *(Learn the secret to 'The Floating Bread Roll' at the rear of the book.)*

"Quieten down!" shouted out one of the dinner monitors. Eric then thanked his audience of fellow diners, thinking he'd now get to eat his meal, but now pupils from the adjacent tables wanted to watch him too.

"Show us another trick!" someone at the table called out, ignoring the dinner monitor's pleas to be quiet.

"Okay, okay, sure," Eric replied, taking a quick bite out of a boiled potato before carrying on. Eric asked to borrow a coin and covered it with an empty glass, which was nearby. "To shroud the secret in mystery I shall cover the glass with this napkin," Eric then announced. "I shall cause the coin to penetrate and pass through the solid table!" He said the magic words 'Abracadabra' and lifted the glass but the coin was still there. "Oh!" he said and quickly covered the coin once again. His friends laughed thinking the trick had done wrong, but after a bit of friendly banter, Eric suddenly smashed the palm of his hand against the top of the glass, squashing the paper napkin flat on the table. The glass was gone! Sounds of amazement were heard. Eric was getting used to hearing that wonderful sound and liked it a lot!

"Oh … My … Gosh!" someone screamed.

Eric then coolly reached under the table and brought the glass up into view. The glass, it would seem had passed right through the solid table instead! *(Learn how to cause a glass to pass through a solid table at the rear of the book. The trick is called 'The Glass Through the Table'.)*

The school bell did its job indicating it was the end of the lunch break and all the children went off to their respective classes. Those that watched Eric perform were still talking about how amazed they were. "He's like that magician on the T.V!" someone said!

As Eric and his new friends were leaving, Eric heard a voice from behind him say, "I really liked your magic tricks!" It was Emily, the girl who had been admiring his magic. Eric turned around.

"Thank you," said Eric. He then realized who it was and went a bit quiet and shy. He had noticed her before in his classroom and thought how nice and pretty she was but had been too shy to go over and speak to her.

"My name is Emily. Emily Ryan. What's your name?" Eric already knew her name and just stared into her beautiful brown eyes, speechless for a moment. The girl laughed, "Have you forgotten your name?" she enquired.

"Eric. I'm Eric," he said, bottling up enough courage to just about be able to get his name out.

"Are you coming?" called out Jack who was now way ahead of him.

"Yeah, hold on!" replied Eric.

"Bye then, nice to meet you," said Emily smiling.

"Tarra. See ya in class," said Eric slightly more confidently. Emily nodded and Eric quickly turned and run after his friend, smiling broadly as he did.

Jack teased Eric giving him a nudge, "I think she fancies you mate,"

"No she doesn't, get out of here," said Eric still beaming.

"You fancy her too don't cha," said Jack grinning, sure that he was right.

"Do I 'eckers like. Shurup up Jack!" replied Eric in his northern dialect, still smiling away, but slightly red-faced and embarrassed as both the boys headed off to the classroom.

The school day had come to a close and Eric met up with his friend Jack, who he had invited to come back to his flat after school. As Eric and Jack were leaving, Eric noticed that the two bullies, David and 'Hamburger' were standing by the gates, probably waiting for him. The two cowardly bullies did not dare try anything on though while Jack was with Eric because they knew Jack was a popular boy at school and they wouldn't stand a chance against him in a fight. So, both the two bullies carried on talking to each other pretending not to notice Eric and Jack as they walked past them. Both unconsciously bursting the pus from their spots; both wondering how come Jack is now a friend with that loser Eric?

"What's Jack doing with that Northern Muppet?" said 'Hamburger', trying to act hard in front of David.

"The expression is Northern Monkey, not Muppet! You Muppet!" replied David, still peeved he hadn't managed to collect Eric's dinner money earlier that day.

"Oh!" just grunted 'Hamburger' in reply.

David was suddenly aware of a horrible smell. "Oh! Have you farted again Hamburger?" said David to his grinning friend. " ... Oh, it stinks!" added David, holding his nose. 'Hamburger' just laughed, seeming to relish the smell of his own farts.

It was Monday and his mum always cooked 'Bratkartoffeln' on a Monday. Both boys could smell the pleasant aroma from her cooking as they walked up the shared garden path to the flat.

As they entered at the side kitchen door Eric called out, "Um smells good!" He had got used to that smell and knew exactly what it was.

"Hiya love!" called out his mum. She then noticed the other boy as he entered the kitchen as well. "Oh hiya, who's this then, Eric?" his mum asked.

"This is my friend Jack. Is it alright if he stays for tea?" Eric asked, knowing that his mum always cooked more than enough food.

"Course it is! Nice to meet you, Jack," said Eric's mum.

"Nice to meet you too Mrs Fartz ..." replied Jack in a confident and polite manner, assuming she was married. Ingrid didn't bother to correct him on her marital status, as was often the case: so as to avoid people asking too many questions. "... I like your Christmas decorations. We haven't put ours up yet," then said Jack admiringly.

"Thank you, love. Oh I love Christmas!" replied Eric's mum thinking what a nice polite lad he is. She was very pleased that her son had found a friend in their new town of Ramsgate. "Have you shown Jack any of your magic tricks yet Eric?" she then asked. Eric nodded and smiled.

"Yes his magic tricks are amazing!" said Jack, smiling enthusiastically. "I haven't got a clue how he does them!" Jack added.

"Me neither, and he won't even tell me the secrets, and I'm his mum!" she agreed.

"A good magician never reveals his secrets!" Eric reminded his mum.

His mum carried on with the cooking and Eric and his new friend Jack took a football outside for a kick about until tea time. She could hear them laughing together and having a great time. Jack had been ribbing Eric again about how he and Emily fancied each other.

It was now Jack's turn to show Eric his skills at 'Keepy Uppies' with the football. Eric was equally impressed at Jack's skills with a ball as Jack was with his magic skills. He kept the ball in the air for ages and if it weren't for Eric's mum shouting "Dinners ready!" he would have probably kept the ball up for even longer!

"On my head!" Eric called out to Jack, who kicked the ball up in the air and as Eric went to head it, he missed the ball completely and both boys burst into fits of laughter. They then went back inside the house to enjoy Eric's mum's skill at cooking. A new friendship had formed! *(Eric soon realized that the more confident and popular you were, the less chance there was of* being bullied and performing magic certainly helped with that, and was a great way to be noticed and make friends! Bullies normally target individuals rather than those who have friends around them, and those who show a lack of confidence or are seen as being weak or different! So making friends will not only make life more enjoyable for you but could also prevent bullying!

Making eye contact when you are talking to people, smiling and holding your head up and not slouching is very important as well, and it will make you look confident! Also if someone doesn't articulate or pronounce their words very well, it makes it hard to communicate with others and then it's easy to become isolated like Eric and be picked upon. Eric found that by performing magic his speech really improved, he spoke up and pronounced his words a lot better and as a result was more easily understood, and by being able to communicate better, more people were interested in what he had to say, he got more respect and he didn't get ignored like he used to anymore.

Speaking correctly and communication is very important! That doesn't mean you have to speak with a plum in your mouth as they say. It doesn't matter what type of accent you have, but you should speak loud enough to easily be heard, pronounce your words clearly and not speak too quickly! This will also help to give you a look of confidence even if you don't feel it at the time.

People will judge you on how you come across to them. You see it's all about perception, the same as a magic trick, which is really only an illusion. In other words, if you act like you are confident, then that's how people will perceive or judge you to be. Simple really but it's true!

Also, the more you show you are confident, the more you will get used to being that way, and before you know it will become the norm! But also remember that you don't have to be loud to be confident. You can have an inner confidence and that is fine! Anyway back to the story.)

CHAPTER SEVEN

THE MYSTERIOUS LETTER

Eric and Jack often met up and walked to school together, having a bit of banter with each other on the way.

"Where's your girlfriend?" said Jack, grinning.

"She's not my girlfriend Jack. How many more times do I have to tell you that?" replied Eric grinning too as he shook his head. Jack changed the subject.

"So where is Sheffield then?" Jack asked, knowing full well where Sheffield was all along.

"It's up in the north of course!" replied Eric, surprised he didn't know.

"Oh yeah. I remember now … Sheffield

United nil!" said Jack trying to hold his laughter in, but couldn't any longer and burst out laughing. Eric got the joke and also joined in the laughter.

There were no sign of the bullies on the way to or from school for most of the week and during school time Eric only saw them occasionally. The bullies were keeping away now that Eric had made some new friends.

On Thursday morning all the children were sat at their school desks ready for their form teacher Mr Potter to call out the register. "So what do you aspire to be when you grow up Jenkins?" asked the teacher.

"A computer software developer sir," answered the boy.

"A computer software developer eh! Very good! ... And what about you Patterson?"

"I want to be a teacher like you sir," replied a girl sat at the front. "Good for you Charlotte ... Patel - what about you?"

"A nuclear physicist sir! - or a doctor - or maybe a lawyer?" confidently answered one of the brainy students. "Wow! ... And what about you Fartz?"

"A magician sir!" immediately replied Eric without hesitation. There were a few pockets of laughter and sniggers heard around the classroom.

"Right, everybody, sit still and shut up or you'll get detention … Atkinson?" yelled Mr Potter as he started to call out the register.

"Here sir!" a boy at the back called out loudly.

"Brown?"

"Here sir," a girl at the front answered in a quietly spoken voice.

"Clarke?"

"Here sir!" called out another girl, eagerly raising her hand.

After calling out several other pupils names, Mr Potter's finger moved down a line to the next name on the register. "Fartz?" Mr Potter called out to no reply. "… Fartz?" He repeated slightly irritated. "Wake up Fartz! Are you daydreaming again?" Eric was a dreamer. Slightly startled Eric's gaze immediately shifted from the window to Mr Potter's glaring eyes.

"Sorry! Here sir!" promptly replied Eric, now back into the land of reality, clearly feeling and looking tired after staying up late reading his magic book.

"Ah, you are alive!" said Mr Potter with his dry sense of humour to the sound of more laughter around the room. "Maybe I should have announced you as the wizard, or the magician, or perhaps the conjurer? … I like wizard best! Have you got a stage name boy?"

asked the eccentric Mr potter inquisitively.

"No sir, I haven't," replied Eric slightly puzzled, not quite sure where the questioning was going?

"Well if you are going to perform magic Mr Fartz, then you are going to need a stage name. All the great magicians had one. Like Harry Houdini!" Mr Potter told Eric as he paused from reading out the register.

"Who's Harry Houdini?" asked Eric very interested to hear the answer.

"Who's Harry Houdini! Who's Harry Houdini!" Mr Potter repeated twice. "Call yourself a wizard and you don't know who Harry Houdini was!" Mr Potter then said in a raised theatrical voice. "Houdini was only the greatest magician of all time, that's who!

"But sir, I thought Merlin was the greatest magician of all time?" responded Eric - Eric had read the story of the Arthurian legend 'Merlin the Wizard' many times.

"Ah, yes! But Merlin is a mythological magician ..." answered the teacher.

"Oh!" just said Eric.

Mr Potter then went on to say, "One can even find the name Houdin in the dictionary, symbolizing somebody who escapes from perilous danger! He performed all over the world at the turn of the twentieth century!"

added Mr Potter starting to calm down now. Mr Potter liked magic and even dabbled with it himself in the past, and he had the goatee beard to prove it!

"Did you go and see him perform live Mr Potter?" said a cheeky boy at the back to lots of laughter from the class.

"Watch it boy. I'm old but I'm not that old!" Mr Potter replied indignantly, trying desperately to keep a straight face, secretly thinking the remark was actually rather witty. "Right, everybody be quiet and let's continue or you'll all get detention!" he demanded as he glanced at his watch, realizing the time. "… Johnson!" called out the teacher, raising his voice once again. And he then carried on calling out the rest of the thirty or more names, which made up the overcrowded class.

"Robinson?" called out the teacher, relieved to now be on names beginning with the letter 'R', thinking, "Almost done, and then I can get rid of this lot!"

"Here!" confidently replied Eric's friend, Jack Robinson from his slumped out position.

"Here - sir!" Mr Potter bellowed shaking his head.

"Sorry, here sir!" replied Jack, quickly sitting upright.

"Ryan … Emily Ryan that is?" emphasized

Mr Potter, as there were two pupils with the surname Ryan in the class.

"Yes, here sir!" called out Emily confidently. Eric couldn't help but stare at her admiringly from across the classroom.

As all the children were leaving the classroom, Mr Potter handed each of them a letter to take home to their parents. "Here you are ... So, you fancy yourself as a bit of a wizard, do you Mr Fartz? - This might be of interest to you then?" said Mr Potter as he handed Eric the letter from the school.

"Okay thanks, sir," replied Eric wondering what the letter was about?

"Shame you can't always conjure up your homework in time," dryly added Mr Potter almost cracking a smile.

On the way to their lesson Jack said to Eric, "Old Mr Potter was really going off on one wasn't he about that famous magician, what's his name? Larry Hou, Houd, Houdi," Jack couldn't remember his name.

"Harry Houdini," laughed Eric as he reminded Jack. "I'll have to borrow my mum's laptop and check him out on 'Wikipedia'," thought Eric, keen to find out all about this famous magician.

"Mr Potters right though. You should have a stage name," said Jack as they both headed off to their first lesson of the day. Eric hadn't thought about that before.

All day long Eric wondered what the letter he was given could be about, but didn't open it as it was addressed to his mum. What did Mr Potter mean by, "This might be of interest to you?" he pondered and then he thought, "Oh I hope I'm not in trouble again," and started to feel a mixture of worry and excitement all at the same time. He didn't remember getting another detention. "What could it be about?" he kept thinking. Eric couldn't wait to get home and learn all about 'Harry Houdini' and discover what this letter, which was driving him nuts was about!

The bell sounded for home time and as Eric walked alone along one of the corridors on his way out of the building he could hear loud music being played, coming from the music room up ahead on his left. Out of curiosity he peered through the music room door window and could see that it was a band rehearsing in there and then quickly moved his head out of the way and crouched down on the floor by the door as he realized playing the drums was the bully David!!

"What on earth are you doing down there?" said Miss Hopkins, one of the music teachers, as she happened to be passing by.

"Oh I'm just tying up my shoelaces miss," replied Eric spontaneously, pretending to be tying them up.

"Off you go home now then unless you are here to rehearse?" said the teacher.

"Rehearse, rehearse for what?" Eric repeated in his head as he dashed through the reception area, knocking a bauble off the Christmas tree on his way out of the school building.

He walked home by himself because his friend Jack had rugby practice after school. "At least if David's in there then he's not out here bullying me," thought Eric as he slowed his pace down and started to relax more. "But where was 'Hamburger'?" he then suddenly thought. He hadn't seen him in the room. He told himself not to worry and carried on passed the row of shops on his way home. On the corner was the local 'Chippy' and just as he passed the entrance by a stroke of bad luck, 'Hamburger' was walking out the door stuffing his face with a double hamburger with cheese! They both looked at each in wide-eyed surprise!

"Oh eck!" yelped Eric as he made a run for it, his heart now beating fast with his school bag swinging back and forth across his back to the same beat.

'Hamburger' nearly choked on his

hamburger as he tried to speak! "Oi come here you!" he spluttered incoherently. His heart was beating even faster as he chased after Eric with his school bag doing the same motion on his back and with half a cheeseburger still in his mouth, some of it spilling out onto the pavement as he ran, with the other half still in his chubby right hand.

"You'll never catch me!" boasted Eric, feeling confident as he ran up one of the quieter side streets as fast as he could home, with 'Hamburger' several metres behind him in hot pursuit, the gap getting even greater with each stride! 'Hamburger' finished eating the bulk of what was left in his mouth but was struggling to catch up.

"Wait I just wanna talk to ya mate. Wait!" he yelled out to Eric in a less harsh voice now, panting and spitting the remains of his food as he spoke. Eric was having none of it and kept running as fast as his little legs could carry him, as he knew 'Hamburger' was just trying to trick him because he couldn't catch up with him. "You wait till I get you Fartz!" then angrily called out a red-faced 'Hamburger', realizing that Eric was not going to stop and now showing his true colours.

All of a sudden though Eric lost his balance, hurtling forwards and hit the ground with a loud thud! "Ouch!" murmured Eric, shaken and slightly injured. Luckily for him, he held his arms out in front of him instinctively, which protected his face from the fall. But now there was no getting away. Just as Eric tried to get up, a sweaty, panting 'Hamburger' was now standing straddled over him, shirt un-tucked with his flabby belly flopped out, and with now just a tiny bit of the burger bun still left in his grip. 'Hamburger' gave Eric a pathetic kick to the ribs. Then stopped and crouched over with both hands resting on his knees and waited to catch his breath before continuing.

"Get on with it then. What are you waiting for?" muttered a sore and bewildered Eric, turning his neck around to look at him as he said it.

"Gimme me a chance!" replied a now even redder faced 'Hamburger' still panting heavily with his sweat dripping onto Eric's face. Eric could smell his B.O even from where he lay!

"Call yourself a bully!" exclaimed Eric. It was a really weird conversation they were having.

"Bully? I've never called myself 'A bully'. I'm not a bully!" snapped back 'Hamburger', not liked being called 'A bully'. *(Bullies or abusers never do and often they are in self-denial and won't admit to their problem. Eric's father never admitted to it either.)*

"Well what do you call this then?" argued Eric, hurting. 'Hamburger' couldn't give a reason or an answer to that. "If you punch me I'll bleed all over you!" then said, Eric. Eric almost accepted his fate, but then heard the magicians voice in his head again. He managed to painfully turn over onto his back and just as 'Hamburger' was about to throw a punch at him. Eric held his palms out towards the bully in an attempt to stop him and quickly said, "I know all about you Gary!"

"What?" snapped 'Hamburger' in an aggressive tone, pausing with his fist tightly clenched and poised just in front of Eric's defiant face, distracted by what Eric had just said. "No you don't!" he added; sweat still pouring off of him.

"I am psychic and if you don't leave me alone I will tell everyone about the pink furry slippers you like to wear!" threatened Eric.

"How on earth could he know that?" thought 'Hamburger'. He knew he could perform magic tricks but this was a closely kept secret, or so he thought. "What pink furry slippers?" said 'Hamburger' acting in denial.

Eric sat up and put his fingers to his temples and went into a sort of a trance swaying his head as he did so. "Your mother's name is … Carol!" said Eric in a mysterious manner.

"What the ..." 'Hamburger' said under his breath. He was actually starting to freak out and get scared. "You are just guessing!" then said 'Hamburger'. "Okay, go on then, how many sisters have I got?" challenged 'Hamburger'. Eric knew all this information of course from the time he went round to his house unbeknownst to 'Hamburger', who never knew he was there!

"Two ... You have two sisters. One's named Abby and the others name is ... Mary!" answered Eric in an even more mystifying voice, releasing one of his hands to support his aching ribs.

"Stop!" said a slightly scared 'Hamburger'. He didn't like it! Ever since a young child, he got easily frightened over weird and spooky things like that.

"You also have a dog named ... Let me think ... 'Bruiser'. Don't you?" continued Eric really playing it up now, almost forgetting he was injured and started to weirdly enjoy it. This was Eric's way of getting his own back.

"Stop I said. That's enough!" said 'Hamburger' with a slight quiver in his voice as he took a step backwards now visibly scared! "You're weird. Just stay away from me!" 'Hamburger' shouted as he ran away from the horizontal psychic.

Well, Eric had never seen 'Hamburger' run as fast and started laughing and then quickly stopped as this action hurt his ribs even more. And as Eric lay on his back staring at the dark clouds above, he suddenly heard a sweet caring voice calling out, "Are you alright Eric?" A dark shadow then suddenly came over him. At first, he thought it might be an angel and that maybe he was dead, but then quickly realised he wasn't dead after all as his vision of dark clouds changed to a vision of beauty. Crouched over him was Emily Ryan trying to help him up, "Let me help you up," said Emily concerned he was all right.

"Oh, hi Emily, thank you but I'm okay. I just tripped over that's all, I'll be all right," said Eric trying to act tough. "I saw that big horrible boy chasing after you from across the street," said Emily as she helped Eric up to his feet. Emily was the athletic type and about two inches taller than Eric.

"Oh, we were just having a race that's all," responded Eric, lying, not wanting Emily to know that he was being bullied.

"Well, it didn't look like that to me? You should tell your parents and report him to the school!" then said Emily in a forthright manner as she put her arm around his body to help support him as they slowly made their way down to the end of the road together.

Eric just listened and then said, "Actually my parents split up and I now live with just my mum,"

"Oh! I didn't realise, sorry to hear that!" said Emily thinking she'd said the wrong thing.

"That's alright, anyway tell me about you, Emily, where do you live?" said Eric quickly changing the subject.

"I live on the other side of Ramsgate in the Pegwell Bay area," said Emily.

"Oh, the posh side!" quipped Eric. Emily just smiled.

"You mean you came out of your way to help me!" then said Eric very pleased that she had.

"I was just about to get the bus when I saw you looked like you were in trouble."

"That was really sweet of you Emily," said Eric thinking what a lovely and sweet girl she is, as well as being drop-dead gorgeous.

Emily and Eric had enjoyed chatting and getting to know each other a little better and reached the end of the road.

"Well, I'm very near home now, I just live over there. I can manage from here," said Eric; pointing towards the housing estate he lived on.

"Are you sure you're going to be all right?" asked Emily as she removed her arm from around him.

"Yes I'm fine, honest!" answered Eric with a big smile despite the pain he was feeling.

Emily leaned over and gave Eric a peck on the cheek. "See you tomorrow then, bye!" said Emily as she turned and walked back up the road she just came down.

"Tarra Emily!" called out Eric as he turned and headed in the other direction home.

Eric slowly managed to get back home, limping and crossing his arms to support his ribs as he did. His big winter coat had protected him somewhat and he was lucky to escape with just some bruised ribs and grazed knees!

Eric staggered into the flat with a huge grin on his face still thinking about the kiss Emily gave him and dropped his schoolbag down on the floor by the dining table in the living room, which he normally does when he comes home from school ready to do his homework. Only this time it was more of a drop rather than a toss.

"What are you grinning about?" asked his mum.

"Was I?" replied Eric shrugging it off as if it was nothing.

"You are later than usual today love?" said his mum enquiringly.

"Yeah I stopped and played football with

Jack for a bit," lied Eric again, still in pain but not wanting to tell her what really happened, although he was tempted to tell her about him pretending to be psychic and how 'Hamburger' run away from him scared!

"Did ya now?" "Yeah, honestly - Mum, I've decided that now I want to be a magician when I grow up." "I thought the last time you said you wanted to be a policeman?" replied his mum, thinking he's forever changing his mind and whatever next.

"Well - I do - but I also want to be a magician."

"Take ya coat off and sit down love," she then said, noticing he was in some pain and found it hard to stand up and then fired a number of questions at him. "Are you sure you're okay? You look a bit winded. You are not hurt are you? You're not being bullied at school I hope?" his mum said concerned.

"No, I'm fine Mum, honest. I went in goal and just got hit with the ball a few times," said Eric reassuringly, still hurting but trying not to show it. "I'm glad she can't see all the bruises and nasty grazes under my clothes!" he thought.

"Have you got any homework to do today?" asked his mum, checking to make sure. Eric was getting a bit neglectful about his homework lately.

"No," Eric replied with a one-word answer, which was not unusual for him.

"Well, you just relax. Put the T.V on and I will go and make you a nice tea love." His mum said to Eric affectionately as she cupped both her hands around his cheeks and kissed him on his head of bright blonde hair. Eric then slouched further down on the settee and watched some T.V. He was that tired he forgot to tell his mum about the letter he was given and was supposed to have given to her!

"After tea, why don't you have a nice hot shower and then have an early night for a change, Son," said his mum seeing how tired he was.

"Yes Mum," answered Eric thinking, "I must find out about that bloke 'Houdini'!" And soon after tea, Eric went to his room and got into his pyjamas, climbed into bed and went onto the 'Wikipedia' site but fell fast asleep before he even had a chance to learn about the magician 'Harry Houdini'.

Eric went to school the next day still very sore and having only washed half his face because he didn't want to wash the side of his cheek where Emily had kissed him. And, totally oblivious to the fact that the crumpled up mysterious letter was still in his school bag! He didn't have any problems from the bullies that day, David was preoccupied with something else and 'Hamburger' was clearly trying to stay well away from him! *(If you recognise in yourself that you are a bully, then don't be, because you do have a choice: it's a matter of self-control!*

Maybe you have anger issues? Or maybe you are being pressurised into being like this by your so-called friends because that's how they act? Or maybe you too are a victim of bullying? It is recognised that bullying is often the result of the bullies having been bullied and abused themselves and they then take their own frustrations and anger out on other people.

Try to put yourself in the shoes of the victim; it is horrible and you wouldn't want to be treated in this way yourself! Behaving like this will only lead you down a very negative and dark road and make your life miserable and unhappy as well! Nobody likes a bully and although you may think you have friends, the truth is probably the opposite, not real friends anyway. So try to think about other peoples' feelings and be kind and turn your negative energy into positive energy.

Taking up 'magic' as a hobby, for instance, will definitely help you to focus on being positive. You will find that you can achieve great things by being positive and nice to people and live a much happier and more rewarding life!

If you are suffering from physical or mental abuse yourself and have anger issues, for whatever reason, and are struggling to deal with it; for your sake and those around you, seek help as soon as possible!)

CHAPTER EIGHT

NO TIME TO WASTE!

It was now the weekend and on Saturday morning while Eric was playing outside with Jack, his mum was hovering his room. As she went to move his school bag, which he'd left open untidily in the middle floor, some of his books spewed halfway out and she noticed there was an envelope sticking out between two of the books. Eric often forgot to give letters from the school to her and he'd had quite a few recently regarding detention. "What's this letter about now?" she thought worryingly as she began to open it, thinking it was probably to inform her that Eric has another detention. As soon as she unfolded the

A4 size letter, the title immediately put her mind at ease. It read 'ST. BARTHOLOMEWS GOT TALENT!" Then Ingrid saw the date the competition was to be held on, which was Friday the Thirteenth of December, and for a moment made her feel uneasy, sending a cold shiver running down her spine. 'Friday The Thirteenth' is supposed to be an unlucky day and the superstition apparently dates back many centuries! Ingrid thought it best not to worry Eric by telling him about this superstition.

As Eric came back into the flat for his lunch his mum said to him, "Who forgot to hand in a letter to me again young man?" Holding the letter in question aloft as she said it. Eric suddenly remembered covering his hand over his mouth as it dawned on him.

"Oh sorry Mum!" said Eric curious again to know what the letter was about.

"I'll give you sorry, this letter should have been given back into the school with an answer by the weekend!" said his mum in a jocular telling off sort of way.

"Given my answer in for what?" asked Eric, now even more curious.

"Your school is holding an end of term talent show on Friday The Thirteenth of December!" announced his mum, which immediately got

Eric's full attention.

"So that's why I kept hearing musicians rehearsing for the last few days!" thought Eric.

Eric wasn't even aware it was supposed to be an unlucky day anyway! *(The funny thing is because Eric had never heard about this date being a superstition and supposedly unlucky it never occurred to him to fear it, so he didn't!)*

Eric did have a few other reservations though about entering the competition that troubled him.

"Are you going to do it Eric?" asked his mum positively. Eric shrugged his shoulders unsure. "You should do it, you are really amazing!" she added.

Eric quickly read through the letter. "I don't know?" then replied Eric, contemplating it. "This isn't going to just be performing in front of a few people like before, it means performing in front of the whole of the lower school and the participant's families will be there as well!" he stated to his mum sounding apprehensive.

"Oh don't be silly darling, of course, you must!" exclaimed his mum, all excited, "This is a great opportunity for you and you might win a cash prize!" she added trying to encourage her son.

"I don't know if I'm ready for it Mum," said

Eric still unsure?

"Of course you are ready! Don't you worry, and I'll find you a nice magicians costume," she replied.

"Yes but it is now only one week to go before the competition and the tricks that I have learnt are too small to perform for a large audience. I need bigger tricks like the ones you see on the telly, and besides I never win anything!" said Eric making excuses and starting to panic. Eric really wanted to enter but was anxious and full of self-doubt. He was a worrier like his mum.

Eric's mum then remembered, "When we were at the Christmas fair I picked up a business card from the magic stall. I think it's still in my purse." Upon saying that, she removed her purse from her handbag, opened it and there amongst lots of folded receipts was the business card. "… Here you are love," she said as handed Eric the now slightly crumpled business card. Eric now started to get excited again. "Why don't we have a look at his website and you can then choose a few tricks to perform in the talent show. I'll buy you them as an early Christmas present!" announced his mum. A big smile instantly appeared on Eric's face.

"Oh thank you very much, Mum!" said a delighted Eric and gave his mum a big hug. His mum was pleased to do that as she knew how good it would be for her son to take part in the competition and what valuable experience it would be for him.

"I hope you are not too late to enter though now Eric," said his mum in a slightly concerned voice.

"Me too!" said Eric enthusiastically having now made up his mind he would go for it after all!

So after Lunch with no time to waste Eric and his mum sat together at the dining room table with the laptop in front of them and Eric typed the domain name into the browser and as if by magic the online magic shop website appeared!

"There's the magician we saw at the Christmas fair!" said Eric pointing to a photograph of him on the website header.

"My gosh! Look at all the magic tricks they sell!" his mum said surprised. There certainly were lots of magic tricks, from classic magic tricks to some of the very latest and you could see photo's and descriptions of the tricks, and even video demonstrations so you could watch the trick performed before deciding whether to buy.

All the various categories of magic were listed in the menu bar. Eric was looking for

'Stage Magic Tricks'. "Ah here they are," he said and clicked on the button. Eric then scrolled down the page as he started to look for magic trick products he thought would be the best ones to perform in the talent show.

"I'll leave you to choose then love, so I can get on with the washing and the ironing. Call me when you have decided and I will pay for it on my credit card. Remember I'm not made of money! Love you, Son!" she said, blowing her son a kiss as she left him alone so she could get on with some of the weekly chores.

"I love you too Mum!" said Eric with his eyes still fixed to the laptop screen.

Eric continued the serious task of finding the tricks for his show. As per the letter the contestants only had five minutes max to perform so he wouldn't need too many tricks. He remembered some of the performance advice the magician gave him at the magic stall. He had told him when putting together an act for a show, you need a beginning, middle and an end. You should start with a quick flashy trick to get the peoples attention and create interest and then during the middle of the act the tricks can be longer and more drawn out, but still, be engaging to keep the audience attention and your finale should be spectacular and be your most impressive trick that people will remember!

Eric watched several magic trick video demonstrations and realized it was going to be hard to pick them, as there were so many good ones he'd seen! The magician advised him to vary the type of tricks he performed so they weren't too samey. "Oh, what's this?" Eric thought. He watched as a magician poured himself a glass of 'Seven-up' soda. He then let go of the glass and while the liquid was still pouring the glass remained suspended in mid-air! "That's amazing!" thought Eric and read the description and noticed one of the bullet point's, claim that it was 'Easy to do'! "That would be a really good opening trick!" decided Eric thinking out loud and promptly clicked on the buy button adding it to his shopping basket, "Oh these tricks are really going to impress Emily!" he thought.

Eric spotted the 'Change Bag' that he saw the magician at the magic stall demonstrate. He liked that trick as it was very entertaining and thought that would be a good one for him to perform. Eric, having a fun sense of humour also liked to make people laugh as well as amaze them when he performed magic. He remembered the magician telling him to always make the magic tricks entertaining! Also, you can do a lot of different tricks with it and it's nice and showy. So Eric clicked on the buy button again and added the 'Change Bag' to his ethereal shopping basket. "Oh I better have some 'Magicians Silk Handkerchiefs' as well!" he thought, so he added those as well.

Eric kept scrolling and then saw the same type of magician's wand for sale that the magician at the magic stall also had, which collapses when given to someone to hold. Eric thought, "I've got to have one of them!" and added it to his basket. Eric thought that was one of the funniest things he'd ever seen!

He found another trick called the 'Six Card Repeat', which he thought might be a good one to include and that was also added. He then saw another trick he liked, where a handkerchief changed colour as you pulled it through your hand, so promptly added that too. But he still hadn't found his closing trick!

"Haven't you finished looking yet?" asked his mum as she came back into the room.

"No, not yet. I'm still looking, there are loads of tricks on this site Mum!" said Eric excited with his eyes still glued to the screen. Then he saw a trick, titled, 'The Nest of Boxes'. "Um, this looks interesting," he thought and started to read the description closely. The trick had all the ingredients for a good finale. It was showy and spectacular and seemed like an astonishing trick, but most importantly it would be very entertaining. The description said it was a classic of magic, where a borrowed finger ring wrapped in a handkerchief, vanishes and then after some comedy byplay, re-appears inside the smallest innermost padlocked box of four wooden nesting boxes, which are all tied shut with ribbons! "Oh, I'd really like to perform that trick but it's a bit more expensive!" said Eric to his mum.

His mum looked at the cost at the checkout and said, "That's alright Eric. I will buy those tricks for you, but are you sure those are the ones you want?" She thought that she could do some extra overtime to help pay the bill.

"I'm sure!" said Eric confidently. So his kind mum paid for the goods and now all Eric had to do was wait for the parcel of wonder to arrive next week. Oh and of course learn the tricks in time for the competition now less than one week away!

Eric was so excited! He couldn't wait to start learning his new tricks. He thanked his mum once again and went to his room to plan his show. He also decided to go onto the 'Wikipedia' website and read and learn about 'Harry Houdini'.

Eric discovered that they shared the same first name, as his real name was Erik Weisz and that 'Houdini' was actually a 'Stage Name'. Eric also learned that 'Houdini' was born in Budapest, Hungary in 1874 and moved to the U.S as a young child. And as well as being a famous magician, 'Houdini' was even more famous as an escapologist, or escape artist and escaped from a whole manner of restraints including chains and handcuffs, straitjackets suspended high up from tall buildings and even police cells! He was a superstar of his day and became a legend, still talked about to this day! "Wow and he was a magician!" thought Eric totally engrossed in what he was reading.

But sadly 'Houdini' died an untimely death on Halloween 1926 when a stunt he performed went horribly wrong and despite the doctors advice, refused to go to hospital as he was booked to perform at a sell-out theatre in Detroit in the U.S.A, and being the true showman he was, believing in the old adage that 'The show must go on', he ignored the advice and collapsed backstage at the end of the show. He was taken to hospital but sadly died a few days later from a ruptured appendix. A tragedy!

When Eric found out that 'Houdini' was a 'Stage Name', it reminded him that he needed a 'Stage Name' as well. Over the weekend Eric also started to learn about other well-known magicians from the past like 'Slydini' and discovered that a number of them also added the letters "INI' like 'Houdini' to the end of their names too. So Eric thought, "That's it! I will call myself 'Fartzini'!"

He told his mum with great excitement and enthusiasm everything he'd learnt over the weekend about 'Houdini' and other famous magicians whenever he saw her and his mum really liked his 'Stage Name' and thought, what a good choice!

On Monday Morning Eric met Jack as usual and they went to school together.

"I am entering 'Bartholomew's Got Talent' competition," said Eric enthusiastically.

"You're brave! I wouldn't have the confidence to do that! I'd be too nervous," replied Jack admiring Eric for having the guts to stand up and perform in front of lots of people. As although Jack was a very confident boy in normal everyday life, like a lot of people he wasn't when it came to something like that! "Good for you," Jack added patting Eric on the back. Eric was quite surprised to hear Jack saying that and it made him think. *(Quite often, people who are 'shy' or on the quiet side like Eric, like performing! Whether it's performing magic or something else, as a way to come out of their shell and connect with people, and also because of a desire to be liked and accepted! And if you are normally 'shy' and inward, then performing magic can be used as a bridge to connect with people and a vehicle to put over your personality.*

Lots of well-known stars of film and Television, theatre and in the music industry are actually quite shy! The confidence comes from being well versed at whatever it is you do and have gained enough experience to the point where you are self-assured at what you do! Now back to the story.)

As soon as Eric got to school he ran up towards the school reception desk. "No running!" called out one of the teachers on their way to their classroom. Still, slightly out of breath he handed over the even more crumpled up, completed 'St Bartholomew's Got Talent' entrants form confirming he would like to take part desperately hoping it wasn't too late!

"You're a bit late handing this in aren't you. This should have really been handed in by last Friday!" explained the receptionist, as she looked down at this little figure at her desk. Eric was tempted to tell a porky again about his make-believe dog eating the original one but resisted.

"I'm sorry about that miss," said Eric with

his fingers, and his toes crossed.

"We've had a lot of interest in the competition this year and not everyone will be able to enter it otherwise the show will go on until Midnight!" stated the receptionist "What is your talent then?" she asked inquisitively.

"I am a magician!" Eric replied proudly.

"Oh, I don't think we've ever had a magician in our talent show before?" she announced trying to remember.

"May I borrow your pen," he asked the receptionist. She handed Eric the pen she was holding wondering what he needed it for? Eric removed the pen cap and displayed the cap on the palm of his left hand and announced, "Watch. When I count to three the pen cap will disappear!" Before she could protest Eric started to count to three and upon each count, he would tap the pen against the cap in his hand, but as he went to tap it for the third time the receptionist's pen had disappeared!

The receptionist stood there speechless with her mouth open for a couple of seconds, then said, "Where's it gone?" Eric grinned and after a moment turned his head and pointed towards his ear. The pen had reappeared behind his ear! "How on earth did it get there?" she thought, completely astonished.

"Let me try again," Eric said still grinning,

knowing full well that the trick was supposed to happen like that. So Eric once again counted to three and this time the pen cap, to the receptionist's surprise and amazement did disappear! *(To learn this amazing trick called 'The Vanishing Pen Cap', go to the rear of the book!)*

"How did you do that?" asked the very befuddled receptionist, completely forgetting for a moment that she was there at work, not noticing that by now there was a queue of people behind Eric.

"It's magic!" said Eric as he returned the pen.

"That was amazing! What's your name?" she asked. "'Fartzini'!" Eric replied.

"No, your real name 'Silly Billy'," said the receptionist, chuckling.

"No it's not Billy, miss!" innocently replied Eric. "It's Eric, Eric Fartz!" then answered Eric, a little confused having not heard that expression before.

"Are you having me on, young man. You should be a comedian!" then said the receptionist, her chuckle morphing into laughter. "Well Eric, I hope that we will see you in the talent competition. All the entrant's names should be displayed on the notice board by school home time today." Eric quickly thanked the receptionist, gave her one of his big smiles and briskly walked away. "… Hey young man, what about my pen cap?" called out the receptionist, but Eric had already left making his way to his classroom for another week of monotonous page turning. He would much rather be studying magic all day at 'Hogwarts' if a place such as this existed!

"Ah, good morning young wand wielder," said an upbeat, slightly wired Mr Potter as Eric entered the classroom. Having drunk copious amounts of strong black coffee in the staff room before going to his classroom.

"Oh, good morning sir, sorry," eventually answered Eric, who as per usual was in a bit of a daze.

"Well?" said the teacher inquisitively.

"Well what?" replied Eric, clearly somewhere else!

"Are you going to be entering the talent competition?" asked his teacher, as if to say what else!

"Yes I hope so sir, but I don't know yet? I have to wait to see if my names on the notice board," answered Eric as he sat down at his desk.

"Well, I do hope so too. I like to watch a bit of magic and try to figure out the 'Modus Operandi'!" said Mr Potter buoyantly, even cracking a smile. Eric and the rest of the class looked at him bewildered? Once upon a time Mr Potter used to teach Latin and would suddenly come out with the odd Latin words every now and again. "It's Latin, meaning the methods for how the tricks are accomplished!" explained Mr Potter.

"Oh!" said the rest of the class all at once, even more, convinced their teacher was from a different planet.

"Have you come up with a 'Stage Name' yet?" then asked a curious Mr Potter.

"Yes, sir…'Fartzini'!" answered Eric fairly quietly. There were a few giggles around near where Eric was sat.

"I think that's a really cool name Eric!" said Emily standing up for him.

"I took your advice sir and looked 'Houdini' up on the Internet and that's how I came up with the name," said Eric more confidently and pleased to be talking about it.

"Well I also think that's a very good magicians name!" said Mr Potter.

"Thank you, sir," replied Eric, pleased.

"Is that The Amazing Fartzini or just plain Fartzini?" enquired his teacher smiling.

"The Amazing Fartzini sir!" answered Eric proudly and confidently, smiling.

"Well good luck to you boy or 'break a leg'

as they say in the theatre!" said Mr Potter engrossed in the conversation and forgetting for a moment that he should have been calling out the register. "Okay, quieten down class ... Who threw that eraser?" Then howled Mr Potter as he took back control of his noisy classroom.

A lot of the topic of conversation amongst the class had been about the upcoming talent show. All day long Eric wondered anxiously whether his name would be on the list of entrants and he popped by the notice board during every break and even made an excuse during class to go to the toilet just to take a look to see if the list of names were now pinned up yet. But alas it wasn't and Eric would have to wait now until school home time to check. The anticipation was almost unbearable!

He never had any bother from the bullies that day either. 'Hamburger' was still too scared to go anywhere near Eric and David was now too pre-occupied with rehearsing his band desperately wanting to win the Talent show!

There was still about three-quarters of an hour to go before school home time and in the school office were the organisers of the talent show. The Deputy Head, the School Governor and a couple of the teachers were still trying to decide whom they should select to be in it.

"What about Eric Fartz?" asked one of the teachers.

"Well, he is very late in entering! I don't think we will be able to fit him in now. What does he perform?" replied the Deputy Head.

"He's down as a magic act?" answered the teacher looking at his form.

"Oh, a conjurer eh! Well we don't have a conjurer in the show do we?" said the Deputy Head, mulling it over.

This year they had an unprecedented number of hopefuls enter, and so as not to make the show too long, limited the number to a maximum of sixteen with each participant having a five-minute slot with an interval in between. It may have had something to do with the fact they have raised the prize money to £100.00 for the winner this year. For the organisers, it was important to present a well-balanced show and obviously try to pick the most talented and entertaining individuals because they would be representing the school, plus the public had paid money to see a good show.

The organisers finally made their decision and with only about ten minutes to spare before the home bell was due to be rung, one of the staff members quickly ran round to pin up the list of entrants on the school notice board.

The bell sounded and loads of excited school children quickly rushed out of their classrooms, all heading in the one direction, to the school notice board! It was almost like a stampede along the corridor with teachers and other staff members clinging to the walls lest they get crushed!

"Good luck Eric!" Emily called out as Eric darted for the classroom door.

"Thanks!" Eric called back.

As Eric entered the packed reception area - he was immediately confronted with a lot of screaming and shouting with excited pupils barging and shoving one another in their quest to reach the notice board. It was very noisy - a mixed sound of joy and disappointment..

"Calm down, calm down!" yelled the Deputy Head in a commanding, authoritative voice from behind the safety of the reception desk.

As Eric got closer to the notice board, amidst the chaos, he could see the bully David bulldozing his way back through the crowd with a big smile and a re-assured look upon his face. "His band must be on the list?" he thought, still not knowing if his name was on there too - there were still too many people in front of him to be able to see?

Eric finally got to the notice board where his

eyes immediately started moving downwards from the top of the list, searching desperately for his name. And there it was, third from the bottom, 'Eric Fartz'! Eric was so delighted he jumped into the air with his arms above his head and screamed, "Yes!" Anyone would have thought he'd won the competition already! Eric then quickly turned and ran out of the reception to the sounds of pupils rehearsing nearby, smiling joyfully at the receptionist as he did and ran all the way home with the smile never leaving his face. He couldn't wait to tell his mum the good news!

CHAPTER NINE

A DASTARDLY PLOT, A FALLING OUT, AND A SPECIAL PARCEL

"**M**um, Mum, I'm in the Talent show!" yelled Eric filled with joy and excitement as he came bounding into the house. His mum came through to greet him.

"Oh, I'm so glad to hear that love," said his mum thrilled that her son made it into the school talent show. "I must buy a ticket!" she said in a slightly panicked way. "How many acts are there going to be in it?" then asked his mum.

"I think about fifty or so," replied Eric.

"Wow! That's a lot!" exclaimed his Mum

surprised.

"Well it's a big school," said Eric as he removed his coat, hat and gloves, shivering slightly. It had been a particularly cold December's day. His mum had put some more money in the electric meter though, so at least the flat was nice and warm.

"Feels like it could snow," said his mum, as she took his coat from him. "Wouldn't it be lovely if it snowed over Christmas Eric!" she added, reminiscing about white Christmases when she was about Eric's age in Germany. You could tell Christmas was coming because Christmas cards had started to fall through the letterbox. "Oh yeah! A Christmas card arrived from your nan and grandpa in Germany," then said his mum, suddenly remembering. The postmark read: 'Munich' Eric noted, and smiling happily, ripped open the envelope.

After doing his homework and finishing his tea, Eric went off to his magic den to continue planning his show, ready for the coming Friday. Eric was very excited at the thought of his parcel of magic tricks arriving the next day and tried to picture himself performing the tricks in the order he had already planned out.

Inspired by reading about 'Houdini's' many incredible 'Escapes', Eric thought it would be a really good idea if he learnt an 'Escape' stunt himself. "This looks like a good 'escape' to learn for my show," thought Eric as he found someone on YouTube, teaching an 'Escape' called, 'The Siberian Chain Escape'. *(Learn how to escape from a chain or a rope yourself! Find out the secret at the rear of the book!)* Eric watched the tutorial a few times and then went and fetched his old bicycle chain and padlock. He no longer had the bike just the chain and padlock. The bike got nicked in Sheffield a while back!

He soon realized that he couldn't tie himself up by the wrists himself, so he had to call his mum into his room to do it. So with his sleeves rolled up like his idol 'Houdini' as seen in the old magic posters, he practised escapology.

For the rest of the evening, his mum was in and out of his room tying him up by the wrists with the chain and padlock as instructed by her son and every time he escaped he would call her back in to tie him up again. Eric would roll around on the bedroom floor trying to make his escape. Sometimes embarrassingly he couldn't get out and she'd have to come and unlock the padlock to release him.

"You getting much quicker!" said his mum who by now was desperate to have a cup of tea and relax on the sofa watching T.V.

"Yes I've got it down to about three minutes

I think?" said Eric rubbing his now sore wrists.

"I think it's time you went to bed now Eric," then said his mum as she could see her son was tired and his wrists were a bit red. Plus he had school the next day.

"Can I just do it one more time please Mum!" said Eric, clearly tired and aching.

"No, it's time for your bed now Son," she replied more assertively. Eric would have gone on all night practising if he'd have been allowed!

"Okay, then Mum. Thank you for helping me. Goodnight!" said an exhausted Eric.

"Goodnight, sleep tight!" his mum replied kissing her son on the head.

"Oh, Mum! Don't forget to watch out for the postman will you!" called out Eric as she started to leave the room.

"No, don't you worry I won't forget! Night, night now," his mum replied as she pocked her head around the door.

"Night, night!" said Eric yawning.

The next morning arrived and the weather was much the same as the day before although it looked like it had tried to snow during the night. Just before leaving to go to school Eric once again reminded his mum to keep an eye out for the postman so she didn't miss his precious parcel of wonderment being delivered. They were expecting a large parcel and it certainly wasn't going to fit through the letterbox!

"Bye Mum!" Eric said all excited.

"Bye! Mind how you go love. Don't worry I won't forget!" called out his mum reassuringly.

He met up with his friend Jack again on their usual route to school along the main road, passed the shops.

"Hiya Jack!" said Eric smiling

"Watcha Eric! What's up?" replied Jack, wrapping his coat tighter around him. "It's freezing isn't it mate!" said Jack, really feeling the cold and blowing into gloveless cupped hands.

"No, it's lovely and warm! What are you talking about? You southerners just aren't cut out for the cold," joked Eric teasing his friend for a change. They both laughed, stepping it out to get to school quicker for a change. Actually, Eric was cold too but didn't tell Jack. He was a proud northerner and hand a reputation to uphold. "I'm in the talent show Jack!" said Eric in an upbeat way.

"Oh, well down mate! You're gonna smash it!" said Jack positively helping to boost his friend's confidence ahead of the competition on Friday night.

"D'ya think so?" said Eric being the modest

boy he was.

"Yeah!" Jack replied straight away.

"Ta, Jack," said Eric appreciating Jacks encouragement. Just then Eric heard Emily's voice from across the road, "Eric, Jack!" she called out. Emily crossed the busy main road,

"Hi, do you mind if I tag along with you to school," asked Emily.

"If you want," said Jack feeling slightly awkward.

"Of course you can Emily!" replied Eric very pleased to see her.

"It's freezing today isn't it," said a very rosy-cheeked Emily. Both boys nodded in agreement.

"Well look, guys, I'm going to dash on ahead," announced Jack feeling that three is a crowd.

"Yeah, alright, see you later pal!" called out Eric as Jack jogged on ahead of them.

"How are you now after your fall Eric?" asked Emily caringly.

"Still a bit sore but I'm doing good. I'm going to be entering the talent competition!" announced Eric all in one breath, still excited by the thought.

"Oh, that is good news. I'm pleased for you. I am sure you'll do well, you are a really good magician!"

"Oh cheers Emily," replied Eric moving closer to her as they walked.

"Call me Em, all my friends call me Em," said Emily smiling at Eric. "I never really liked magic until I saw you perform Eric. It's much better when you see it live rather than on the telly!" added Emily. Just then Emily was about to walk under a ladder propped up against the wall of a shop building. Eric, acting instinctively quickly grabbed Emily's arm and pulled her away.

"It's unlucky to walk under a ladder!" Eric told Emily. But just as he said it, he accidentally tripped on a crack in the pavement. Both laughed.

"You're not superstitious are you?" replied Emily, curious.

"No! Of course not!" said Eric denying it. Both continued to laugh at Eric's funny mishap.

"Hey! I know a magic trick too." Suddenly said Emily, keen to show Eric the one trick she knew.

"Yeah? I'd love to see it!" replied Eric. Both of them stopped and Emily took a five-pound note out of her coat pocket and then removed a couple of paper clips from her pencil case. Eric looked on curious.

"My grandfather taught me it!" said Emily as

she folded the banknote into thirds and clipped the note together with the paper clips, clearly showing that the clips were well separated. She held the banknote between both hands and suddenly to Eric's surprise, snapped it open and somehow the two paper clips flew off and linked together in midair!

"Wow! That was really clever! I've never come across that trick before?" said Eric genuinely impressed.

"Did you like it?" asked Emily pleased the trick had worked.

"Yeah! Will you teach me it?" asked Eric Excited.

"Yes it's easy!" announced Emily and quickly showed Eric how to do the trick.

Meanwhile, while Eric and Emily were still walking and chatting on their way to school, David and 'Hamburger' were at their usual haunt in the children's play area, sitting on the roundabout plotting!

"No way, I'm not going to do it! Look I don't want to be a part of it," 'Hamburger' told David feeling uncomfortable. 'Hamburger' wasn't the brightest of students but he knew what David was planning was going a step too far! The conversation was by now starting to get heated and ugly.

"Don't be a chicken! Bruck, bruck, bruck,"

David responded, making a noise like a chicken as he moved his arms up and down like a pair of wings.

"You could get expelled for that. No, forget it!" said a defiant slightly nervous 'Hamburger'.

"Don't be a scaredy cat, it will be a laugh Hamburger, go on," said David still trying to coax 'Hamburger' into something he clearly didn't want to do.

"No, not this time mate," 'Hamburger' said shaking his head.

"What's gotten into you? You've changed!" David questioned 'Hamburger'.

"I just don't want to do it anymore, and besides if you're so confident that your band will easily win the competition and bank the £100.00, you don't need to worry about Fartz being in it, do ya!" said a wiser than usual 'Hamburger' trying to evade being involved with David's dastardly plot.

David laughed, "What? I'm not worried about him being in it. Don't be silly! What makes you say that? He's got no chance against my band, we're much better than he is!" snapped back David in an arrogant and cocky manner. Actually they had both noticed the amazing reactions that Eric was getting performing his magic at school and it made David jealous and even angrier towards Eric.

"… Actually, come to think of it, I've noticed you seem to have been avoiding Fartz lately!"

"He knows things! He's one of those um … psychics or whatever ya call em!" exclaimed 'Hamburger'

"What things?"

"Nothing," said 'Hamburger' as he got off the roundabout and started to walk away, not wanting to talk about it.

"What, are you scared of him or something?" David called out to 'Hamburger', laughing. "You are scared of him aren't you - and that's why you won't do it!" David made a noise like a chicken again. "Bruck, bruck, bruck. I'm gonna call you Chicken Burger from now on!" called out David, laughing again.

"No, of course not!" replied 'Hamburger', turning his head around to say it as he continued to walk, and now starting to feel a little bit of what's it's like to be on the receiving end for a change.

"Get lost then! I'll do it on my own, I don't need you, loser!" David angrily shouted to 'Hamburger', who was now walking with his back to him some distance ahead. "Fatso!" David then added.

'Hamburger' had his private reasons to keep out of Eric's way, but he thought that what David was planning to do to Eric was going a step too far!

David was used to getting his own way you see. He came from a well-off family and was a spoilt brat, always getting what he wanted whenever he wanted it. His father David Snr was a successful businessman who owned several businesses in the area and his mum Penelope was a lady of leisure. They lived in a wealthy part of Ramsgate in a four-bedroom executive home and had flashy cars and so on and liked to show off their wealth. His father also happened to be a Governor at the school and had some influence over how it was run. It was he that suggested the school should have a talent show this year.

All day at school Eric kept thinking about his parcel arriving and couldn't wait to get home and open the box and start learning all the new tricks. During class, he would daydream - thinking about performing his magic show in the talent competition and imagine himself winning it. There was a real buzz in the air with lots of groups of pupils discussing it and who they thought might win.

Eric was sat at his desk in a history lesson with five agonising minutes still left to go until home time - his eyes flitting back and forth between the clock on the wall and his open textbook showing a picture of Henry VIII seemingly smirking at him - eagerly waiting for the home bell to ring out its joyous sound.

Time was really dragging on. At one point it seemed to Eric that the hands on the clock were moving backwards!

"The time won't go any quicker by you staring at the clock young man," said Mr Potter to Eric, looking over his spectacles and raising his bushy eyebrows.

"10 – 9 – 8 - 7 – 6 – 5 – 4 – 3 – 2 - 1!" Eric counted down the seconds in his head, but the bell didn't ring? Eric's face dropped, then a minute or so later the home bell did ring and all the children jumped straight up out of their seats, bags swinging over their shoulders as they scrambled for the door. "Why is the bell always late rather than early?" thought Eric as he picked up his bag and joined the rush.

"Hold up! Hold Up!" yelled the teacher. The children froze in the positions they were in. "Who said you lot could go? I didn't say you could go. The bell is not there to tell you that you can go, the bell is there to tell me to tell you that you can go! Okay, off you go!" said Mr Potter, showing who ruled in his class.

Eric sprinted home again for another day on the trot, buzzing with excitement and anticipation at the thought of discovering the secrets that would behold him once he opened the parcel.

"Mum I'm Home! Has it arrived?" Eric called out excitedly as he opened the front door.

"Hiya love, yes it's on the dining table!" replied his mum, knowing exactly what he was referring to. Eric immediately rushed through to the lounge diner, and there it was, sitting in the centre of the table still wrapped up in brown parcel paper. Eric didn't waste a second, he threw his coat off on the floor beside him and started ripping off the paper. It really did feel like Christmas was here, he was so excited!

He finally opened the well-packed box and there they were inside, all the tricks that he had ordered from the magic shop. Eric's face lit up! His mum watched on enjoying seeing her son being so happy and enjoying himself. Eric reached into the box and picked up one of the magic trick products called 'The change Bag', which he immediately recognised and put that down on the table for a moment wondering how that works, and then he removed the 'Breakaway Wand' smiling as he did, thinking back to how funny it was when he watched the magician perform it at the Christmas fair.

He had to use two hands to remove the next magic trick, as it was such a big box. He read the title on the package, "Oh yes, that's the

'Nest of Boxes'," he thought, remembering what he'd ordered. He was planning on performing this trick or maybe the 'Siberian chain escape' he had learnt, for his finale. He then had a quick look inside the box to make sure the other tricks he ordered were there, still buzzing with excitement. "Thank you so much, Mum!" Eric said to his mum delighted.

"You are welcome Son," she replied, smiling.

"I had better start learning all this magic now!" said Eric, realising the urgency.

"Yes, love…Oh by the way I went to one of the local charity shops and bought you a nice black jacket and bow tie and I even managed to find you a top hat, although it may be a little on the large size," commented his mum as she picked up his coat from the floor and started clearing away the ripped up pieces of paper discarded all over the table and floor. "You can try your costume on later love. I can always adjust things if need be?" She added.

"Great! Ta Mum," said Eric feeling slightly overwhelmed by it all. Eric didn't know what to start learning first. He opened up one of the products and removed the written instructions and started reading it as he carried all his new magic props to his bedroom to start learning and practising them in time for the talent show, which was now only in a few days time!

CHAPTER TEN

THE RUGBY GAME

The next morning Eric struggled to get out of bed, still feeling tired after staying up late practising his magic act. His mum had to call him about six times before he finally got out of bed and got ready for school. On his way out of the door, he suddenly remembered it was the 'Lower School Inter-House Rugby Tournament' that afternoon and quickly dashed back inside and grabbed his rugby gear with a feeling of dread. Eric hated rugby, as apart from the fact he wasn't the physical type, he knew that David and 'Hamburger' would be playing on the opposing team. So, with his heavy bag of schoolbooks over one shoulder, his P.E kit over the other shoulder and his dirty rugby boots tied together by the laces around his neck, which he neglected to clean from a week ago, off he finally went to school.

Jack was already waiting for him on the corner; also with his schoolbag and P.E kit over his shoulders but his rugby boots were spotlessly clean! Jack took his rugby very seriously and played for the school team, usually in 'Fly half' position and couldn't wait to get out onto the sports field and play his favourite sport.

"Look at the state of your boots!" laughed Jack. "Mr Jones is going to give you a right telling off if he sees them like that!" stated Jack shaking his head in bewilderment. Eric wasn't really listening and just grinned, as he had other things on his mind; namely Magic and Emily.

Mr Jones was their P.E teacher from The Valleys in Wales who spoke with a thick Welsh accent and was passionate about rugby. He was a big tall strapping fellow who once played at a professional level as a 'Lock'. Eric didn't like him because he was always shouting and telling him off and would always make the boys have showers even if the water was cold. Mr Jones was very 'O.C.D' with the rules when it came to rugby.

"The weather has improved a bit today. The grounds still a bit hard but we should still be able to play!" commented Jack enthusiastically.

"We?" laughed Eric. "I never get to play a game! I'm rubbish anyway and can never remember the rules!" piped up Eric self mockingly, his mind now focusing on the conversation Jack was trying to start about the rugby tournament today.

"Well I am the team captain and I get to pick the team! I'll see if I can get you a game today Eric," said Jack reassuringly as they now both headed for school.

"The house will only lose if you pick me Jack!" replied Eric half-jokingly. So far Eric had always been a substitute, which he didn't mind at all and would rather Jack didn't pick him.

Jack noticed Eric kept looking across the road, probably looking for Emily, "Hey, have you asked Emily out yet?" asked Jack being nosy and now changing the subject. Eric ignored the question, "Go on tell me -"

"Mind your own business! We're just friends!" replied Eric wishing Emily and him were more than just friends.

"Yeah, sure you are. Don't be a melt! Why don't you just ask her out, you know you want to?" said Jack with a huge grin. Eric didn't answer, just smiled and shook his head at his friend's persistence to find out the truth, "Look do you want me to ask her out for you?" said Jack genuinely trying to help his friend out.

"No, I don't! I can do it myself," responded Eric realizing he had just spilt the beans.

"Oh, so you do admit you fancy her then!" said Jack with an even bigger grin.

"Is it that obvious?" said Eric.

"Err, yeah!" replied Jack nodding as if to say you can't-fool me this time.

"She kissed me the other day!" Eric suddenly announced.

"What! She actually kissed you? Shut up!" said Jack surprised and slightly jealous as Emily was probably the prettiest girl in the class.

"Yes! she did!" said Eric with a big smile.

"Yeah, sure she did?" questioned Jack not believing it.

"Don't believe me then," said Eric still smiling.

"Straight up?" asked Jack.

"Straight up!" replied Eric.

"You lucky thing!" said Jack now starting to believe Eric.

"I suppose I am," thought Eric as they both walked through the school entrance grinning at one another.

In the afternoon, all of the year seven pupils

headed towards the sports field for the house rugby tournament. The usual racket was heard much to the annoyance of teachers in nearby classrooms trying to teach. The house rugby teams made their way to the changing rooms to get changed whilst the pupils not taking part lined the pitch ready to support their house teams. The changing rooms were in the sports block in the old part of the school, which was well due for a refurbishment, adjacent to the sports field.

The groundsman had done his job and the all the lines had been freshly painted on the rugby pitch ready for the tournament. Mr Jones the sports teacher was inspecting the pitch already and keen to start, kitted out in his shorts and wearing his Welsh national rugby shirt with pride, spotlessly clean rugby boots and with his whistle on a string around his neck. "What on earth is taking them so long?" he thought, getting impatient.

In the boys changing room Eric was showing Jack and some of the other boys some magic tricks. "Lend me your tie Jack," asked Eric. So Jack picked up his crumpled up tie, which he had just removed and tossed onto the bench.

"There ya go," said Jack as he handed his tie to Eric. Eric took the tie and proceeded to tie a knot in the centre. Pupils looked on wondering what Eric was going to do?

"Now watch!" said Eric, raising his voice so as to be heard above the din of noise in the testosterone and bravado-filled room. He blew on the knot and to everyone's amazement, the knot dissolved away! *(Learn this quick and amazing trick called 'The Magic Knot' at the rear of the book!)*

"Wait! What? Do that again!" said Jack and turned to one of his mates saying, "Did you see that?" Pupils shook their heads in disbelief.

There was one boy sat on the bench nearby listening to music through his earphones.

"Can I borrow your earphones a minute pal?" asked Eric loudly to him. The boy didn't hear him very well at first and took one of the earpieces out and said "What?" Eric repeated his request as Jack and the others encouraged the boy to do so. What for? The boy said, unsure about what was going to happen to his precious earphones.

"He's gonna do another trick!" said Jack still trying to work out the last trick. The boy then cautiously handed them over to Eric.

"You better not ruin them," the boy said as he watched Eric produce a pair of scissors from his school bag.

David and 'Hamburger' were at the other end of the changing rooms with the rest of their house team but sat on different benches to each other. David could be heard from the other end of the room, bragging as usual about how good he was at rugby to his bandmates and anyone else who cared to listen, and how they were going to thrash all the other teams! The normal rivalry you get between schoolhouses. He wasn't the captain of his house rugby team but liked to think he was.

The three other house teams were doing the same, taunting each other as they were getting changed and putting on their rugby boots. Not the majority of Eric's house team though. They were watching him about to cut a pair of expensive earphone wires in half!

"Look, you can clearly see the wires have been cut in half!" exclaimed Eric after he cut them to everyone's surprise and shock, especially the boy who lent them. "Now Watch!" He tucked the ends of cut wire into his fist and then rubbed the two ends together with the fingers of both hands." The tension built and then Eric quickly moved his hands out of the way to show the earphone wires had now been completely restored! *(Discover the secret to this amazing trick called 'The Cut and Restored Earphones' at the rear of the book!)*

Jack and Eric bumped fists together and all those that could see what just happened applauded and praised Eric. Eric then handed back the earphones to the much-relieved boy who checked that they were indeed working again. "That was well cool!" he said and carried on listening to his music.

David noticed it was Eric getting the applause, which he hated and was now even more determined to follow through with his dastardly plot on the night of the Talent competition!

"What's all this commotion I hear going on in hear then!" shouted Mr Jones as he came bounding into the changing room carrying his clipboard. "Quieten down! Come on you lot - you should have been on the pitch by now - Come on hurry up, hurry up!" he yelled in his strong Welsh accent as he stood by the doorway studying the boy's rugby boots closely as they passed him on their way outside. He was a real stickler for having clean boots and having the studs securely tightened.

Eric had still not cleaned his filthy boots and tried to hide behind some of the bigger boys as they went out. He thought he'd got away with it as he walked past the stern looking teacher. But then he heard, "Fartz! Come here Boyo!" Eric knew then that he was in for it!

"Sorry sir," said Eric before the teacher had even told him why he had stopped him.

"They make those boots in black as well you know," said a displeased and annoyed Mr Jones sarcastically as he looked down at Eric's muddy brown boots shaking his head. Eric kept his head lowered and didn't dare argue. He'd seen boys do that before and regretted it because they then had their punishment doubled. "Right, once around the field, off you go Fartz!" demanded the stern P.E teacher.

Before long there were other boys who also hadn't learnt their lessons joining him running around the large sports field. Some boys would be very disappointed at missing out on the rugby games but to Eric, it was the lesser of the two evils. Eric also saw it as a good opportunity to go over his magic act in his head and was purposely running slowly. The other boys had already caught up with him and were now well in front of him.

The rest of the year seven boys' rugby teams were now on the pitch doing warm-ups and throwing the practice balls back and forth to each other. Jack was one of the first on there, keen as ever. Mr Jones blew his whistle loudly and shouted out to everyone in his booming voice to gather round.

"Right, listen up! The first two teams drawn to play each other are St. Georges versus St David's. After that game, the other two houses will play. Then it will be the losers of both games to play each other to determine 3rd and 4th place, followed by the winners who will play each other in the final. Have you got that?

"Yes, sir!" replied the players: some less enthusiastically than others.

"Well you better had because I'm not going to repeat it!" demanded the teacher, showing his authority. "So get yourselves into your house teams and put your house bibs on and if you're playing in the first game; into your positions please as quick as possible and let's see some good rugby played today lads ... I shall be refereeing so I don't want to see any silly business going on, do you hear me?"

"Yes, sir!" yelled back the players this time.

"Good luck to each of your houses!" Mr Jones announced and then went to help his assistant pick up the practice balls from the pitch. Eric and Jack's house was 'St. Georges'. So Jack and his team got into their positions ready to play against 'St. David's'. Eric was still running as the whistle blew for the first game.

A 'St. David's' player dropkicked the ball, having won the toss, into the oppositions half. The backs charged forward after the ball and the first game had commenced! Eric by now had joined the rest if his house as a sub.

After a well fought game Eric's team 'St.

Georges' won the first game 12 to 7 with two tries and one conversion and all the house cheered them from the touchline as they came off the pitch.

"Well done pal!" said Eric to Jack as he came off the pitch smiling. Jack scored the first try. "Well down lads!" said Eric congratulating the team as they grabbed their water bottles and plonked themselves down on the grass. Eric had got to know quite a few of them by now by showing his magic tricks to them.

The next game up was David's team 'St Patrick's' versus 'St. Andrew's'. "We've got this!" shouted David as both teams ran onto the pitch as the other teams were coming off. David and 'Hamburger' didn't play for the school team but being so big when they played rugby at school they were always picked to play as 'Forwards'; David usually played in 'Prop' position and 'Hamburger' played in 'Lock' position at the rear of the scrum. Anyhow they went on to easily beat 'St. Andrews' and secure a place in the final.

During the playoffs for the 3rd or 4th position, Jack gathered his team around him, having made a few substitutions, to talk tactics. Jack knew the next game against 'St. Patrick's' was going to be even harder as they were up against some very good school rugby team players as well as the biggest two boys in the year, David and Hamburger. Eric was very relieved that he still remained a sub.

The game just finished with 'St. David's' house team coming out the victor. Trying not to show he was biased Mr Jones mildly smiled thinking at least his patron saints team didn't come last!

After a short interval, Eric watched on from the touchline as his friend Jack and his team swapped places with the losing team ready to play in the final against St. Patrick's'. Even before all the players got into position there was some unpleasant taunting going on between the two teams, started by big mouth David of course.

"Hurry up into your positions lads. We haven't got all day!" said Mr Jones impatiently as he ran with the ball towards the halfway line. The weather had warmed up a bit and the sun even appeared out from behind a cloud occasionally. It was ideal weather for a rugby game as the ground had by now softened somewhat, which lessened the chances of players becoming injured and breaking bones as they fall.

All the houses made a wall of sound around the pitch as they chanted for their house teams. This was a chance for the winning team to gain some valuable house points and both teams were determined to win!

"Come on St. Georges!" shouted Eric along with the rest of his house. Emily was with her girlfriends in a group further along the line. Occasionally Eric and Emily would catch each other's eye smiling at one another.

The ref blew his whistle for the start of the last game of the day, the final, and Jack kicked the ball high well into the opponents half. Both teams were rested by now and were abound with energy as they darted for the ball hoping it would be their team who put the first number on the scoreboard. The ball landed with a bounce and was caught by one of the opposition players, who ran forwards with it several metres before passing it behind him to his team-mate and then he made some more ground as he passed it to 'Hamburger', the ball spinning through the air as it travelled.

But 'Hamburger' decided not to pass it as he'd been taught, but instead selfishly run forwards with it looking for glory, bulldozing his way through his opponents. He managed to barge his way through a couple of players and reach the opponents 20-metre line still dragging a player who was holding him by the legs with him, but 'Hamburger' was then tackled to the ground with a loud thud.

Eric gave a big cheer upon seeing him fall over, thinking back to about a week ago when he was the one doing the falling over. As 'Hamburger' landed, the ball fell out of his grip and he lost possession as the scrum half from the 'St Georges' team quickly picked up the ball to cheers from his house and ran forwards passing it, backwards along the newly formed line, continually moving forwards unchallenged and making ground as they did.

As they reached the 5-metre line the ball was past to the winger who found open space and sprinted to the try line running right round behind their opponent's posts before touching the ball down to the ground.

"Come on what are you playing at. Get it together!" shouted an angry David at the other forwards assuming the unauthorized role as captain.

'St. Georges' had made a good start. Now it was up to the fly half, Jack to put the ball between the posts. The ball was placed into position on the ground carefully on its end and Jack stepped back several paces ready for his run-up. There was silence in the air, apart from a few taunts for him to miss, from the other house. Jack paused holding his nerve and then ran and kicked the ball. The ball did what it was supposed to, going over the crossbar right between the two freshly painted white goal posts to loud cheers again from his house.

"Get in … Get over there!" Eric screamed loudly quickly remembering it wasn't football and changed what he was saying mid flow not to look stupid, but even still it didn't come out right. He looked around slightly embarrassed to see if anyone, especially Emily had noticed and carried on cheering as the players got back into their starting positions.

"That boy down there keeps looking at you!" said Georgina, one of Emily's friends pointing towards Eric.

"What boy? replied Emily knowing full well whom she meant.

"The blonde haired boy who does magic tricks," described Georgina.

"Really!" she replied, not letting onto her friend that she secretly had a crush on him.

"He's actually very cute," remarked her friend.

Mr Jones blew his whistle and the game continued. After about five more minutes of head colliding and bone-crunching scrums, rucks, nasty high tackles and furtive foul play, mostly committed by David, and lot's of whistleblowing, it was now 'St. Patrick's' turn to score a try and they too converted it making the score now 7 – 7. What an exciting game this was turning out to be. The halftime whistle blew and the players left the pitch to get refreshments. The game could go either way as both teams were well matched.

Jack didn't make any substitutions and Eric sat quite happily on the grass watching the teams go back onto the pitch at the opposite ends to start the second half. Jack needed to keep his best players on the pitch to stand a chance of winning the game against this tough opposition. So, therefore, understandable Jack was not likely to make a substitution and bring Eric on after all.

The second half started and the opposition was in possession. Only the opposition knew what was said to them during the pep talk they had, but whatever it was it seemed to be working, as three minutes into the second half despite 'St. George's' best efforts, they managed to score another try and make another successful conversion. The score was now 14 – 7 with 'St. Patrick's' now in the lead!

"Don't get downhearted lads, come on now, we can do it!" yelled Jack clapping his hands as he and the rest of his team made their way quickly to their starting positions, waiting to hear the ref's whistle play its monotone tune. The rest of the house made as much noise as they could to cheer them on.

The whistle blew and Jack once again kicked the ball into the oppositions half. It was a caught by one of the less brave backs who ran with it a metre or so and then panicked and quickly kicked the ball into touch rather than pass it before being pounced on, for a 'St. Georges' team line-out just beyond the halfway line in their half.

Mr Jones blew his well-used whistle again not impressed by what he just saw and the ball was thrown. Up jumped the forwards but it was one of the 'St. Patrick's' team who managed to win the ball and throw it straight over to one of his team-mates, and the ball was then passed in succession along the forty-five-degree angle line of players albeit rather jagged. 'St Patrick's' were now well into the oppositions half, but then as the ball was thrown one more time - it was deftly intercepted by one of the forwards who kicked the ball forwards high up into the air. Everyone's eyes following it as it made an arch and started it's decent. Jack acted quickly and made a dash for it catching it in his arms and cradling it like a precious newborn baby.

He crossed the twenty-metre line with it and just before he was grappled by the ankles and brought crashing down to the unforgiving ground, he threw the ball back to one of his players, who in turn threw it to the winger. The winger then sprinted with lightning speed down the wing as everyone in the 'St. George's' house came closer to the touchline and loudly cheered him on as he ran past them. No one was going to be able to catch this boy. He was the fastest runner in the year! Was this going to be their opportunity to equalize?

The winger who had played in both the games suddenly developed a cramp in his legs and collapsed to the ground in agony accidentally dropping the ball forwards. The whistle blew for a scrum awarded in favour of 'St. Patrick's' team, but as the ref and linesman got nearer they soon realized that the boy was not going to be able to carry on and needed assistance. The boy was helped off the pitch by the P.E teaching assistant and applauded as he left. "What a shame!" thought the 'St. Georges' house team and supporters. They may not get this chance again?

So now Jack had a dilemma. His fastest player was now off the pitch and he needed to make a substitution. Did he bring on one of the larger boys who weren't very fast but have played before or did he risk bringing Eric on who had never played an actual game before and by his own admission was 'Rubbish'. "Eric was very fast at running though," thought Jack. He'd certainly had plenty of experience and practice at that recently: being chased by the bullies! So Jack called Eric over, much to his surprise and slight horror, and Eric was no longer a sub but now a player.

"You're up Eric!" called out Jack to his friend as a matter of urgency. There were only another three minutes left to play! Eric came running on overshadowed by all the other larger boys around him. "If you get the ball just run as fast as you can along the wing and touch the ball down over the try line!" said Jack secretly to Eric, covering his hand over his mouth as he said it, so the opponents wouldn't know what he'd said. Eric nodded and adopted his position as winger. "Come on lads we can do it!" shouted the very determined Jack. The tension was really high!

"Form a scrum!" The ref shouted to the forwards. "Quick as you can now boys!" Mr Jones added.

As David passed Eric to join the scrum he nudged him on purpose and quietly but menacingly threatened him, "I'll get you now Fartz!"

"Crouch, bind, set!" called out the ref and on hearing this both teams of forwards interlocked with one another forming the scrum. The scrum was just beyond the twenty-metre line at the 'St. Patrick's' team end and the

'St. Patrick's' scrum half had the ball in his hand poised and ready to throw it into the darkened cave of bodies. The ball was tossed into the scrum, the scrum half quickly ran round to collect the ball from the rear as the hooker did his job and extracted it out with his boot, as did the other forwards. The ball was picked up and thrown and the game was underway again.

'St. Patrick's' were now in possession and quickly took advantage making ground as the ball was tossed along their line. One of their players then fumbled the ball, which was swiftly grabbed by Jack he could see Eric was in a good position to make a run.

"Run Eric!" roared Jack as he booted the ball over towards him on the wing. Eric ran courageously towards where the ball was headed with his arms out ready to try and catch it. The ball descended and much to everyone's surprise, especially Eric's, he caught the ball and with only a slight hesitation sprinted along the wing. His first touch and he caught the ball! All the supporters cheered and screamed as Eric whizzed past them. No one was really marking him so he had space in front of him. The rest of the team ran into the opposition half in support of him. He almost reached the 5-metre line before a tackle was made by one of the backs bringing him to the ground.

Eric rolled on his side holding the ball on the ground behind him like he'd been shown to do in previous rugby lessons. The ref called out, "Ruck over!" which was the cue for the forwards there, which included David and 'Hamburger' to move in. "Ruck formed! Rules of ruck apply!" then called out Mr Jones.

David who was right by Eric then purposely stamped on the back of poor Eric's right hand as he lay on the cold ground with his metal studs. Eric screamed in pain but it went unnoticed by the ref in the noisy confusion. At the same time, the 'St. Georges' scrum half quickly grabbed the ball shouting, "Balls out!" and threw it backwards, towards his teammate, who caught it and passed to the next player in line and so on. Every time the opposition went to make a tackle the ball was securely passed evading them. The atmosphere was electric and the crowd cheered their team on as they got nearer and nearer to the try line.

Poor little Eric got up but realized his hand was injured. He could still see the boot studs impression on the back of his hand. "Oh no! The talent competition!" he immediately thought trying to open and close his hand with difficulty. You can't perform magic with a badly injured hand!

Over at the other side of the pitch, the ball was finally passed to Jack, who zig-zagged his way past his opponents and spectacularly dived over the try line near the corner flag, touching the ball down and successfully scoring a try!

The tatty abused ball was placed on its end ready to be kicked yet again for the umpteenth time, but being at this extreme angle, the conversion, and those crucial two extra points would be difficult to make! Jack kicked the ball but it was way off this time and so, unfortunately, the team did not get any extra points!

The score was now 14 – 12 with only one minute left before the full-time whistle! The 'St. Georges' team had put everything into the game but were now exhausted and feeling despondent, even Jack! Eric carried on despite an injured hand not wishing to make a fuss about it at this desperate time in the game.

The 'St. Patrick's' supporters were already celebrating. The whistle blew and the game, what was left of it, commenced. The ball exchanged sides a few times but it didn't look like either team would add any more points to the scoreboard. With now only about ten seconds remaining the ball landed into Jack's arms - it was a pivotal moment in the game –

glory or defeat. So, with nothing to lose, Jack made one last-ditch attempt at scoring from a position just off centre, near the 20-metre line: he kicked the ball with great force up towards the target and in what seemed like slow motion, the ball hit the post and bounced over the crossbar between the two posts scoring three points! The whistle blew for the last time and the final score was 14 – 15. 'St. George's' house had won!

The whole house jumped up into the air with joy and all the teams that took part were congratulated! What a fantastic game it had been!

All the boys were in the changing room taking a compulsory shower, getting changed, flicking wet towels and throwing smelly socks at each other and making lots of noise! None more so than the winning house team, 'St. Georges!

"Well done boys!" said Mr Jones very pleased with the standard of rugby he had seen today.

"You played really well today Eric!" said Jack to his friend congratulating him on his first game. "Hey what's the matter with your hand?" said Jack seeing Eric holding his slightly swollen hand in some pain.

"Oh, someone trod on it during the ruck," replied Eric trying to play it down and act big and tough in front of Jack and his friends. Eric's view was shielded at the time and so didn't know who did it, even though he had his suspicions.

David left the changing rooms feeling angry - cursing and swearing - having lost. David hated losing.

On the way out of school, David caught up with 'Hamburger'.

"Fartz won't be entering the talent show now!" he exclaimed all smug.

"Yeah, I saw what you did," replied Hamburger, unusually not impressed as David passed him and carried on walking at a quicker pace. But this wasn't what David had originally plotted against Eric!

Eric and Emily had arranged to meet at the school gates and walk part of the way home together.

"Alright lass!" said Eric as they met.

"Good thanks, well apart from all the homework I've been given! How are you?" asked Emily smiling.

"Fine thanks," said Eric smiling back at Emily and wondering if she had noticed him today on the rugby pitch. Both felt a little awkward to start with not saying much to each other but then on the way home the conversation soon picked up.

"You played really well today!" said Emily as they walked, pleased that their house had won.

"Did you see me? Thanks, Emily!" replied Eric, chuffed that she had noticed him on the rugby pitch.

"Yes and stop calling me Emily. I told you I prefer *Em!*" said Emily in a jokingly telling off sort of way.

"Sorry Emily, I mean *Em!*" replied Eric realizing he'd done it again. Both just laughed.

"Your hand looks sore. Did you injure it playing rugby?" asked Emily holding his hand whilst they stopped for a moment.

"Yeah," Eric just replied.

"Does it hurt?" asked Emily concerned as they carried on walking.

"No!" replied Eric trying to act big and tough in front of her too, but it did hurt really. Eric explained again what had happened!

"You poor thing you!" said Emily. Eric was loving all the attention! I am looking forward to watching you in the talent competition tomorrow," then said Emily.

"Oh are you going then?" asked Eric excitedly.

"Duh! *Yeah!* I wouldn't have said I was looking forward to it if I wasn't going *would I, silly?*" replied Emily sarcastically, smiling and giving Eric a bit of a shove. Eric realized it was a silly question and both laughed again.

"That's grand!" said Eric, pleased that she was going to be there, but at the same time now feeling the pressure even more.

"My older sister is in one of the dance troupes. I'm going with my mum and dad and nan and granddad to support her – and *you,* of course, Eric," said Emily as they were approaching her bus stop.

"Cool!"

"Let's have a Selfie together!" announced Emily, moving very close to Eric, not waiting for an answer as she quickly took a photo of the two of them on his mobile phone. "We should exchange phone numbers …" suggested Emily, being the more forward out of the two of them, hoping he would. "… But only if you want to that is Eric?" added Emily.

"Yeah, sure!" said Eric coolly; really glad she had suggested it. So, both of them exchanged phone numbers and then went their separate ways home.

When Eric got home his mum saw he'd injured his hand. The swelling had got worse.

"Oh dear, how did that happen?" she said examining his swollen hand. "You need some ice on your hand to help take the swelling down!" She then went off into the kitchen to get a bag of frozen peas from the freezer to place on his hand. "I suppose you're going to tell me it was playing football again?"

"No, it was rugby Mum and our house won! I even got to play!" said Eric very excitedly as he looked up to her with his innocent butter wouldn't melt in your mouth expression, forgetting for a moment about his injured hand and the possibility of him now not being able to enter the talent show. His mum was used to his little stories, so wasn't sure if this was another one of them. "I caught the ball Mum and you should have seen how fast I ran with it!" Eric added.

"Oh that's wonderful Eric!" she exclaimed as she put her arm tenderly around him. Concerned though, Eric's mum quickly turned the conversation back to how he got his injury. "You will tell me if your being bullied won't you," she said trying to get the truth out of him.

"No! I mean yes! Stop asking me that, I've already told you I'm not … Don't worry Mum," said Eric as he leaned away from her slightly irritated. His mum was all too aware of a period of bullying her son went through at his previous school. She stepped in then and made the school aware straight away, and they dealt with it. *(If you are being bullied: it is always best to tell your family and people in authority straight away - nip the bullying in the bud as they say, so it doesn't continue! Don't suffer in silence like Eric!)*

Eric got a bit gloomy and upset. "I'm not going to be able to enter the talent competition now!"

Ingrid tried to reassure her son by saying, "Luckily for you, you haven't broken any bones! The swelling will come down by tomorrow. You'll have a big bruise and it will be sore still for a few days but your hand should be okay for Friday my darling." Eric's mum used to work as a nurse back in Sheffield. She chose not to work locally as a nurse because she didn't want her ex to find out where they were now living and she thought hospitals would be the first place he would search. "'Houdini' wouldn't have let something like this stop him performing would he now!" said his mum encouraging her son to not get despondent and give up.

"Your right Mum!" replied Eric thinking about his hero. Eric felt much happier after hearing his mum say all that. Still buzzing he then told his mum all about the rugby game and once again how fast he ran with the ball and that Jack his friend scored a try and won the game with a dropkick!

"I have got your favourite dessert for you after tea Eric!" said his mum with a big smile on her face.

"Apple Strudel and ice cream!" Eric called out very pleased.

"Yes!" replied his mum pleased that Eric was happy again and would still be entering the talent competition.

After his tea and a second helping of dessert, Eric decided to go to his room to practice and rehearse his act ready for Friday. He had learnt the tricks and what to say but he just needed to polish up his act. By this time the swelling had already come down a lot and he was able to move his hand quite freely, although it was still sore.

Ingrid could hear her son rehearsing in his room. "The magician counted one, two, three, four, five, six cards, then threw away one, two, three cards. But to everyone's amazement when he counted the cards again he still had one, two, three, four, five six cards left!" said Eric reciting his patter as he performed the trick throwing the cards all over his bed.

"Don't overdo it love will you? Your hand needs to rest!" called out his mum.

"I won't, I'll just practice for a bit longer that's all!" replied Eric from the other side of the door, keen to get it right.

CHAPTER ELEVEN

A SURPRISE VISITOR

Thursday morning at around 10:45 am, Eric was at school and Ingrid was at work serving at the checkout.

"Good morning madam," said Ingrid to a customer.

"That accents not from around here?" said an elderly lady placing her shopping onto the conveyor belt. "Where are you from? No don't tell me, let me guess…somewhere in Yorkshire am I right?"

"Yes, top marks! I'm from Sheffield," said Ingrid as she scanned a tin of cat food.

"I have a small bed and breakfast in

Addington Street, near the harbour. We use to get a lot of tourists from all over, not so much now mind you but you get to recognize the various accents after a while.

"I'm sure you do," said Ingrid suddenly distracted by a commotion going on nearby on the frozen foods aisle. "Somebody, call an ambulance!" screamed one woman. A crowd was gathering and as Ingrid stood up she could just about see someone lying on the floor not moving. Ingrid immediately asked a colleague to take over and ran round to help. "Move out of the way please, move out of the way. I'm a trained nurse! Give me some space!" announced Ingrid. Ingrid acted without thinking and did what she was trained to do.

It was a large man probably in his sixties. He had collapsed possibly with a heart attack still holding a frozen pizza in his hand! She removed his scarf and unzipped his winter coat. He was wearing a smart suit and tie so she undone his top shirt button and loosened his tie to make sure he hadn't just fainted or slipped and hit his head. She took his pulse and said, "Can ya hear me, love?" But she was unable to make the poor fellow come round, so without hesitation, she tilted his head back and performed CPR on him as the crowd looked on.

After a few attempts, it worked! The man soon opened his eyes, totally bewildered to what had just happened. Soon after that, the ambulance arrived and the medics took over. Luckily he was okay and was wheeled out to the ambulance. The medics said if it hadn't have been for Ingrid's quick response it could have been a different story! Everyone was full of praise for her and the man's wife couldn't thank her enough.

"I didn't know you were a nurse?" said her friend Carol who was on the checkout next to her. "Aren't you a 'dark horse' then!" added Carol surprised and impressed by her friend.

"You were amazing!" called out another checkout girl.

"Okay girls the drama is over, less of the chatting and back to work please, we have a store to run. Somebody pick that pizza up for Pete's shake in case somebody falls over on that!" said the business-minded duty manager not wanting any more incidents that day.

In the afternoon, Ingrid, as usual, walked home from her shift at the supermarket, sidestepping the cracks in the pavement as she did, feeling very pleased that she had been able to help potentially save somebody's life.

She arrived home to be greeted outside her flat by a photographer snapping pictures of her and a zealous young local newspaper reporter keen to get her story.

"Hello! Mrs Fartz?" Questioned the reporter as Ingrid was trying to open the front door.

"Who's asking?" asked Ingrid inquisitively: always suspicious of any strangers!

"My name is Sally and I work for the local 'Gazette' newspaper and we would like to feature your story of how you saved The Mayor of Ramsgate's life today!"

"The Mayor!" thought Ingrid, surprised. "… Oh, I don't think so love. I don't want a fuss made of me. I just did what anybody else would do in those circumstances," said Ingrid humbly.

"Lot's of people have been contacting the paper and saying what a heroine you are and the local community would love to hear all about it Mrs Fartz.

"Well …"

"It is Mrs Fartz isn't it and not Mss? Where is your husband, is he at work?

"Erm," just muttered Ingrid.

"You're not from around here, are you. Have you just arrived in the area?" asked the reporter continuingly firing lots of questions at Ingrid, which she didn't want to answer.

Ingrid then quickly stepped inside the flat and shut the door on them, leaning her back against the door suddenly starting to panic. The letterbox then opened and the reporter's slightly annoying voice could be heard again. "If there are any questions you don't want to answer that's fine Mrs Fartz you don't have to answer them. We just want about five or ten minutes of your time. That's all! I shan't ask too many questions …"

"Well, if they are going to print this story anyway, I had better make sure they have all the correct facts. Besides it's only for a local newspaper," Ingrid thought to herself. So, she reluctantly opened the door and let them in to do the interview. She also secretly quite liked the attention. "Okay, please come in. I have never done this sort of thing before," said Ingrid feeling butterflies in her stomach.

"Don't you worry Mrs Fartz, we'll be in and out of here before you know it!" stated the reporter as she stepped over the threshold.

"Would you like a cup of tea?" asked Ingrid politely.

"Yes, milk with no sugar please," said the reporter as she got her notepad out.

"Milk and two sugars please," then said the photographer.

Ingrid brought the drinks into the lounge. "I hope I have got these the right way round?" said Ingrid slightly overwhelmed by the whole thing.

"Just smile for the camera!" said the photographer in a blasé done this a million times sort of way.

"I haven't done my hair!" said Ingrid feeling self-conscious as she ruffled her long black hair with blonde roots.

"I understand you are a nurse?" asked the reporter smiling and poised ready to write down every word.

"Used to be. I *used* to be a nurse," replied Ingrid giving only brief answers.

"That's a northern accent, isn't it? Where are you from originally?" inquired the reporter after taking a sip of tea.

"Sheffield," answered Ingrid reluctantly, not wanting to give too many details away.

"Oh, Sheffield! That's a long way away!" then commented the reporter. "What brings you down here then?" The reporter added trying to appear friendly. Ingrid didn't answer that question. The reporter then noticed a photo framed picture of Eric on the mantelpiece and after a slightly awkward pause asked Ingrid, "Oh, who's that? Is that your son?" asked a determined reporter trying to get as much information as possible out of her.

"I thought you said you weren't going to ask too many questions," said Ingrid abruptly and sounding very guarded.

"Sorry! Sure no problem. Now, Mrs Fartz. In your own words please go ahead and tell us what happened!" The reporter wrote down everything Ingrid told her and another pot of tea and one hour and fifteen minutes later they finally left. "Oh, look at the time! Doesn't time fly! There should be still time for your story to go to print today before the deadline and make it into the 'Gazette' tomorrow! Thank you very much Mrs Fartz, goodbye!" said the very pleased looking reporter having got her story.

"Thanks for the tea!" called out the photographer as they left.

"Tarra," replied Ingrid as she shut the door behind them, relieved that it was over. Ingrid felt very tired and weary after all the questioning.

Ingrid had said more than she would have liked to about herself and her family but thought, "What is done is done now," and shrugged it off thinking no more of it. Ingrid then set to work making some alterations to her son's stage costume, adding a shiny silver ribbon trim around the lapels of the jacket ready for tomorrow night.

At the school that day the main topics of conversation were the rugby tournament and the upcoming talent competition. The tickets for the show had completely sold out and the school organisers were very busy still preparing for it. There was certainly a lot of excitement in the air at St. Bartholomew's and especially because the school was breaking up for the Christmas holidays the following week. The pupils were finding it very hard to concentrate on their school subjects, which was normally the case for Eric anyway but even more so this week. All he could think about was the talent show!

Eric's mum was right, the swelling had gone down completely by the next day and apart from the obvious sign of a bruise and some slight pain still, his hand was functioning as normal, much to their relief. Eric even managed to perform a few card tricks during the breaks, he had learnt from his book with a normal pack of cards, and once again amazed pupils and staff with his spellbinding magic! *(Go to the rear of the book to learn some of Eric's favourite card tricks with a normal pack of cards!)*

And so after a day of thinking of nothing much else but magic, Eric made his way home from school pleased at the thought that he'd been able to perform magic and would be able to enter the talent competition after all.

Meanwhile, in a small B&B guesthouse in

Ramsgate, a tired, slightly unkempt looking man, wearing dark sunglasses was checking in at the reception desk.

"Please fill in your details on this form if you would sir," said the old landlady to her guest, feeling slightly uneasy in the stranger's presence, not being able to make eye contact with him.

"Tah love," said the stranger as he picked up the pen. Finally sliding his glasses up onto his forehead, revealing his piecing steely blue eyes.

"Long Journey?" she then asked, shooing away her meowing, over-familiar tubby black cat as it brushed itself against the slightly irritated stranger's leg one last time.

"Aye!" he just replied not wishing to get into a conversation.

"Will you only be wanting to stay the one night? Only we do have availability if you wish to extend your stay?" inquired the landlady smiling, hoping to get more business.

"Aye, just the one night will do for now, maybe more if need be?" he replied invasively, keen to get to his room and rest. He quickly filled in the form and handed it over.

"Okay, here is your room key Mr Smith. Breakfast is from 8:00 am till 9:00 am. I hope you have an enjoyable stay with us!" said the landlady handing over the keys. The stranger took the keys and carrying just a sports type bag went upstairs to his room.

"I'm home Mum!" called out Eric as he slung his school bag done in their tiny hallway and removed his coat and hat before entering the living room.

"I'm on the phone love!" said his mum in a quiet voice as she covered the mouthpiece with her hand. "… Sorry Julie, please carry on," said Ingrid smiling at her son and indicating she won't be, long.

"I was just saying, typical of me to have a day off when on the rare occasion there's some drama at work," said Julie finishing what she started saying.

"I couldn't believe it, Julie, when I heard it was the Mayor of Ramsgate!" said Ingrid to her friend.

"What you didn't know who he was? asked Julie, slightly surprised.

"No! I didn't have a clue!" replied Ingrid.

"Didn't that big gold chain around his neck give you a clue then?" quipped Julie making light of the situation.

"No, he didn't have a chain around his neck!" replied Ingrid chuckling as she said it. "You are terrible you are Julie -" remarked Ingrid at Julie's wicked sense of humour.

"What's that about the Mayor, Mum?"

interrupted Eric overhearing the conversation.

"Julie, I've got to now, Eric's home!"

"Okay, thanks for calling me and letting me know. I will look out for the 'Gazette' tomorrow. Wish Eric good luck from me for tomorrow night, bye!" said her friend.

"Will do, see you tomorrow at work. Bye!" said Ingrid as she put the phone down. "Hello, Love! How are you, how's your hand?" asked his mum, still not come down to earth quite from everything that had happened earlier.

"My hand's fine, but what was that about the mayor?" asked Eric keen to find out.

"Tell you what love, I'll make us a nice cuppa tea and I will tell you all about it!" said his mum as she got up to go to the kitchen and then started singing.

Eric promptly shoved the headphones to his mp3 player into his ears, turned up the volume and then got out his cards and started practising a 'Riffle Shuffle', 'Card Fanning', and even attempting a 'One Handed Cut', while he was waiting, curious to know what had happened.

"Here we are love, a nice cup of tea for ya," said his mum as she sat down to tell her son all about what happened. Eric listened to his mum telling him all about saving the Mayor of Ramsgate's life and about the interview she had with the local 'Gazette' newspaper who wanted to tell her story. "Wow!" thought Eric feeling very proud of her.

Later on, his mum helped him move the dining room table over to one side, and wearing the stage costume his mum had put together for him, Eric performed the complete act from beginning to end in front of her, adding the final touches to it. Eric's mum was very impressed by how his magic act had come on, giving him lots of applause with high hopes for her son doing well in the talent show the next day!

"I wish Dad could see me perform my magic act," said Eric.

"Yes but you know that's not going to be possible darling," replied his Mum being realistic.

"I suppose not," then said Eric looking a little disappointed.

At the guesthouse, the next morning at 8:00 am on the dot the stranger was sat down at the only setup breakfast table, alone in the slightly musty smelling room waiting for his breakfast.

"Your early for breakfast, guests aren't normally this early?" said the old landlady as she came in. "I trust you slept well?" The stranger didn't reply. "Would you like beans or tomatoes with your breakfast?" she asked.

"Beans, ta love," replied the stranger of few words looking out the window towards the sea, occasionally hearing the muffled sounds of seagulls squawking.

"Tea or coffee?" she then asked.

"Oh, tea, please - Hey, I don't suppose you've seen this woman and this boy before, have ya?" enquired the stranger showing her a small photo of what looked like him several years younger together with a woman and a young boy both with blonde hair with his arms around them.

The landlady took the photo from him and looked more closely. "No, sorry I can't say I have," she said shaking her head, although, she thought the woman's face did look familiar. "Why?" then asked the landlady, curious.

"Don't worry," said the stranger curtly, seeming slightly on edge as he took back the photo and placed it back in his wallet. The landlady went to fetch his breakfast.

"Here you are dear," said the landlady as she put his plate of food down in front of him. "You're from up north aren't you?" she then asked. The stranger confirmed he was with just a nod and half a smile. "Whereabouts?" continued to ask the lady, trying to be friendly.

"Sheffield," he then replied to be polite.

"Sheffield … Come to think of it I did meet

a lovely young lady who said she was from Sheffield yesterday. What a coincidence!"

"Oh yeah!" he replied, ears now pricked, stabbing his fork into a sausage and swirling it around in the blood red tomato sauce before taking a bite. "Whereabouts was that then love?" eagerly inquired the northern guest, mouth full of food.

"Erm … Oh yes, I remember now, how could I forget. It was at the supermarket and she saved a man's life! Apparently, she used to be a nurse? I was buying some tins of cat food for my cat 'Tiddles'. He must be around here somewhere? 'Tiddles'!" she suddenly called out. "He's very sociable normally around strangers! That's strange I wonder where he's got to? Usually, he's sat on the windowsill by the -"

The stranger then interrupted her rather impatiently. "D'ya remember which supermarket?" quizzed the northern guest, raising his voice and seeming desperate to know the answer.

"I think it was 'Tesco's'? It's a job trying to remember things these days!" replied the slightly confused old landlady a bit taken aback by his brusque tone. She then suddenly realized she'd forgotten to bring him his tea! "Oh let me go and get you your pot of tea!" So off she went to get it while he ate his breakfast.

"Scatty old woman," he thought. "She probably doesn't know what the heck she's blithering on about. It will probably be just another wasted search!"

Back she came with the pot of tea and a newspaper folded under her arm. "The local newspaper has just arrived if you'd like to take a look at it?" asked the increasingly more warily old landlady.

"Ta!" he said as she handed it to him. And just when he was contemplating giving up the ghost and heading straight back to Sheffield after breakfast, he casually opened the folded newspaper, dated Friday 13th of December, and there featured on the front cover starring him right in the face was his ex-girlfriend's face, now with black hair! The headline read, "Checkout Girl Saves Mayor's Life!" He immediately got up leaving the rest breakfast and quickly left without saying another word!

"Mr Smith! Where are you going you haven't finished your breakfast?" called out the bewildered landlady. Not believing for a minute that was his real name, as 'Smith' was a name often used as an alias in hotels and guesthouses so as not to reveal someone's true identity!

Mr Smith, AKA, Peter Richardson, put on

his 'Ray-Ban' copy sunglasses despite the dull and dreary winter weather in a vain attempt to look cool whilst incognito, and sped off in his souped-up Ford Fiesta with empty crushed beer cans and a couple of empty whisky bottles rattling around together on the back seat, in search of his ex-girlfriend and son.

He had finally tracked them down to Ramsgate! He had been searching high and low for them, contacting hospitals and so on to no avail. Although he did have a hunch it could be Ramsgate, as in the past his ex, had often talked with fondness about Ramsgate, with its beautiful harbour and beaches and quirky Victorian buildings. And he now knew for sure that Ingrid worked at the local 'Tesco's' as a checkout girl. But that's as far as he knew.

Peter parked up in the 'Tesco' car park at around 8:30 am with his car purposely facing the entrance, waiting in hope to catch a glimpse of her. He had no idea what shifts she worked or even if she was working that day. There were just a few other parked cars there at this time, belonging to members of staff who he could just about see through the shop window rushing about getting ready to open the store at 9:00 am. He couldn't see Ingrid among them and it had now started to rain and the visibility through the windscreen was poor. As he waited and listened to the monotonous sound of his windscreen wipers and the amplified raindrops hitting his car roof, his thoughts turned to the grim reason why he was there!

It was the day of the talent show and Ingrid kissed her son goodbye as he went off to school and she hurried off to work slightly late with her umbrella over her head dodging the puddles.

After about fifteen minutes or so had passed Peter suddenly noticed a group of women come round the corner of the building but because they all had umbrella's open obscuring his view he could not see if his ex, was among them. The three women entered the store to be greeted by the duty manager not looking very pleased.

"And what time do you call this then ladies?" sarcastically said the manager to them. It was Ingrid, Carol and Julie arriving slightly late for work.

"Sorry!" they all said as they quickly headed for the staff changing room chatting away as they did.

"Hurry up then! These are not self-service tills!" called out the manager hurrying them along as he looked at his watch.

"I saw you in the paper," said Carol walking behind Ingrid and Julie.

"Yeah me too, you're now a celebrity in this area!" added Julie, both thrilled their friend got recognition for what she did.

Ingrid smiled saying, "Celebrity? I'm hardly a celebrity!" thinking as she said it, "I'm just glad the newspaper only has a small circulation and my ex won't read it up in Sheffield!" Little did she know he was parked outside waiting for her?

It was now two minutes to nine and the three checkout girls sat at their checkouts adorned in their uniforms ready for a busy Friday shift. The car park by this time had started to fill with customers poised in their cars ready for the store doors to open, waiting until the last minute so as not to get wet.

Peter leaned his head forward to get a better view as he now noticed more women had sat down at the tills and scanned his head along the row of tills looking for a dark haired woman that resembled his ex-girlfriend. Then he saw someone that he thought might be her on the end till. So, at 9:00 am when the store doors opened he walked into the store still wearing his 'Ray-Bans' and blended in with all the others, pretending to be a shopper.

He got to the aisle on the far side that led down to where Ingrid was sat. He needed to get closer to her though to be sure it was her but didn't want to get too close in case she saw him. So he walked down the aisle trying his best to be inconspicuous, slightly distracted by all the bottles of spirits and booze he could see lined up along the way tempting him to buy. He then stopped, pretended to look at what was on the shelves and then leaned back and made a quick glance over towards her. He then quickly leaned forward again so he was out of her sight, turned and walked away and out of the store. Peter had found who he came looking for!

He went and sat back in his car waiting for her to finish work, as he wanted to confront her somewhere private and alone like a predator waits for the right time to strike its prey! So he waited and waited, sat put in his car starring at the store's entrance not wanting to miss her leave.

At 2:00 pm Ingrid and her friend, Carol finally finished their part-time shifts and left the supermarket together. It was still pouring with rain as they started to make their way home together, umbrellas aloft, merrily chatting to one another. Peter's body suddenly jerked forwards, his eyes widening as he spotted them leave. He then stealthily got out of his car and started to follow them. Walking some twenty metres behind them, soaking wet and concealing something in his hand hidden behind his back. After a while, he suddenly stopped as they stopped!

"Bye Ingrid!" said Carol.

"Bye Carol … Oh! Are you coming tonight?" asked Ingrid referring to the talent show.

"Yes and Gary's coming too! Surprisingly I didn't even have to coax him into it? It will make a nice change for him, rather than being stuck in his bedroom playing video games all night shooting at zombies!" replied Carol raising her eyebrows. Ingrid agreed, nodding her head. "Anyway must go, wish Eric good luck from me. Bye!" Carol called out a final time as she started to walk in another direction.

"Tarra Love! Mind how you go! Remember its Friday The Thirteenth today!" replied Ingrid. Both chuckled and Ingrid walked the rest of the way home alone, or at least so she thought!

Peter continued to follow her all the way to where she now lived. Ingrid opened the door, shaking her umbrella before closing the door really feeling the cold. She put the kettle on and went to get changed. She'd just got changed and there was a knock, knock at the door. "Who could that be? It was a bit late for the postman?" Ingrid thought as she made her way out of her bedroom and into the hall. "Oh, it's probably another newspaper reporter again or maybe a T.V reporter!" she convinced herself as she flung open the door unusually unguardedly. But it wasn't a reporter; it was Ingrid's ex and father of her son standing there dripping wet! Fear immediately spread all over her body as she suddenly realized, who it was!

"Hiya love!" he said as he started to remove his suspiciously shielded hand from behind his back. Ingrid screamed loudly fearing the worst and immediately slammed the door shut on him! He always told her jokingly that he would kill her if she left him, but was he really joking? "I'm not gonna harm ya lass! I just want to talk that's all!" Peter called out from the other side of the door, his voice now slightly muffled.

"Go away or I'll call the police!" Ingrid shouted back frightened, her heart pounding.

"I miss you both and I had to find you. Can't we just talk things through? Ingrid, please, we need to talk!" he pleaded, the rain still pouring down. Ingrid didn't answer and kept silent. She then pulled the net curtains aside a little and peeped through the window to see the surprise visitor. There he was, holding only a now sorry looking bunch of somewhat wilted flowers, her favourite, Carnations. Ingrid couldn't help but laugh and let out a big sigh of relief, feeling slightly silly that she had screamed like she had over some flowers.

Peter continued talking to the door, "I've changed Ingrid! Honest, I have! I've stopped the drinking and I'm getting help. I haven't touched a drop for about a month…any road I'm really sorry for all the heartache I've caused you and Eric. I love you!" He had apologized, which she knew never came easy for him and Ingrid could see he was genuinely upset and remorseful.

He then stopped talking and with his head dropped down, he turned and started to walk away. Then the door opened.

"Aren't those for me?" said Ingrid feeling somewhat emotional, more reassured now for her safety as she invited her wet and bedraggled but still handsome ex-boyfriend into her new home and back into her life, albeit temporarily. "You can't stay long Peter as Eric will be home from school in about an hour or so and seeing you here out of the blue like this would be very unsettling for him!" said Ingrid assertively, still feeling slightly shocked and unsettled to see him herself. This was her new home now though and she wanted to make it clear that she was only allowing him in under her terms. "Your right we do need to talk Peter, come in, and take those ridiculous sunglasses off!" she said to him shaking her head grinning and full of mixed emotions.

He walked into the tiny flat, compared to where they once lived together, his shoes making a squelching sound as he did and handed her the flowers, both smiling, both hurting inside.

"You look beautiful Ingrid … even with dyed black hair!" said her ex, jokingly, referring to her new incognito look. Peter preferred her hair blonde.

"Do I, are you sure?" replied Ingrid, flattered but unconvinced as she caught a glimpse of herself passing by the mirror on the wall as she hung up his wet coat.

"What were thee screaming for ya daft thing, anyone would think I was trying to kill ya!" said her ex, chuckling and trying to make light of the situation, pleased to be allowed in. There was no hugs or kisses but both were secretly pleased to see one another. She handed him a towel to dry himself, made them both a cup of tea and they sat down to talk.

She basically told her ex, trying not to get too emotional, that both her and Eric had now moved on with their lives and were happy living down in Ramsgate. She told him that they had both made really close new friends and that Eric had settled down now at his new school and that she was not ready to move back together with him at least not for the time being.

Peter, of course, found it painful to hear as he had hoped that they would be together as a family once again in Sheffield, and one day maybe even marry, but he told her he understood why they had left him especially after everything her and Eric had been through. "At least it wasn't that she was closing the door completely on our their relationship and there was still a chance we could get back together in the future!" he said to himself, trying come to terms with it.

Ingrid was very pleased he was trying his best to conquer his drink addiction and praised him for that. He did seem like a changed man and she still loved him but it was going to take time for the wounds to heel.

"I would really like to see our son before I leave to go back to Sheffield. Even if it's from a distance!" said Peter, his eyes starting well up, showing his rare emotional side, desperate to see him again.

Ingrid then told Peter all about Eric's new hobby and how passionate he was about performing magic, and how it had really helped to make him a lot more confident. She then went on to tell him that Eric was going to be performing his magic act in the school talent show that very evening.

"The show is at St. Bartholomew's C of E School in Ramsgate and starts at 7:30 pm. Come along and poke your head in at the back of the audience and watch him perform tonight?" said Ingrid trying her best to make a compromise.

"Thanks for telling me that Ingrid. I can't wait to see him again!" said Peter smiling, very pleased he would be able to see his son at last.

"Peter, it's time for you to leave now as it won't be long before Eric gets home!" Ingrid then said slightly panicking having seen what the time was. They both got up and Ingrid went and opened the front door for him. "Ah, the rain has stopped!" she said.

"Please pass on my love to our son won't you?" said Peter as he put on his coat, still damp from the rain.

"Aye, of course, I will Peter!" she replied but at the same time thinking, "When the time is right!" not wanting to build up Eric's hopes too soon of his mum and dad getting back together again in case it didn't work out.

"It's been lovely to see you, Ingrid! Please keep in touch, the house is empty without you both!" said Peter teary-eyed as he stepped out the front door, sad to be leaving.

"Yes, okay. Take care driving back to

Sheffield! Tarra Peter!" replied Ingrid full of mixed emotions, slightly sad he was leaving, both desperately holding back the tears. Part of her still belonged to Sheffield.

"Aye, I will. Tarra love!" They did embrace one another this time, both pleased to have cleared the air somewhat. And then, Peter turned around and this time walked out of her life!

CHAPTER TWELVE

THE TALENT COMPETITION
FIRST HALF

It had been a normal school day at St Bartholomew's but there was great excitement in the air from Pupils and teachers alike in the build-up and anticipation for the talent show taking place that very evening. A lot of organising and preparation had gone into putting it all together and the day was finally here. The school assembly hall was the venue; it could hold up to four hundred people and all the tickets were now sold out! The stage was large and there was plenty of space backstage in the wings and behind the twinkling starlight curtain for the multitude of acts to prepare before going onstage and to keep all their musical instruments and props.

It was a real variety show with lots of different types of acts taking part including singers, musicians, dancers, a comedian, and a magician! The hall had been decked out with Christmas decorations and in the corner, by the stage, there was a large beautifully decorated Christmas tree with lots of empty boxes of different shapes and sizes covered in shiny paper and tied with ribbons pretending to be Christmas presents under it. On the other side hall there was a very old well-used upright piano, which if it could talk would be saying something like, "Won't you please play some other tunes other than boring old hymns for a change?" The chairs were all stacked around the hall ready to be placed into position in neat rows by the volunteers before the guests arrived.

At school closing time Eric and Jack were chatting by the school entrance gates waiting for Emily. Eric had arranged to meet Emily there so they could walk home together again.

"Ah, there's Emily over there! I'm going to get going then, Eric. Good luck tonight mate!" said Jack to his friend, patting him on the arm.

"Thanks, pal, see ya later!" replied Eric acting

cool as the two friends bumped shoulders.

"Ask her out this time!" quipped Jack as he sprinted off. Eric chuckled and picked up his school bag.

"Hiya Em!" said Eric as Emily came over to meet him.

"Good, you remembered to call me 'Em'. Hi, how are you?" said Emily smiling.

"Good thanks, you?" replied Eric smiling back.

"I hate it when it gets dark this early don't you? - Are you looking for someone?" asked Emily noticing Eric seemed a little apprehensive, looking over his shoulder occasionally.

"No, no, shall we go then?" replied Eric shaking his head slightly. Actually, he was checking to see if the two bullies were about, but he couldn't see them anywhere, "Thank goodness," he thought.

He never spoke about the bullying to Emily either. Especially not to Emily because apart from the embarrassment associated with it. - he thought she might think less of him and probably wouldn't want to hang around with him anymore. In fact, he never really wanted to admit it was actually happening to him, himself! *(It is quite normal to think in this way. But rest assured most people wouldn't think less of you, and would be sympathetic and want to help you. In fact, they would think you are brave for speaking out. So never be worried or feel ashamed and too embarrassed to tell your family and friends, and people in authority if you are being bullied. As the old saying goes, "A problem shared is a problem halved".)*

The rain had now stopped and Eric walked Emily to her bus stop so she could get the bus home to Pegwell Bay, sidestepping the swimming pool like puddles as they went. He desperately wanted to hold her hand but couldn't pluck up the courage. He wasn't sure if she liked him in the same way?

"My bus should be along any minute?" said Emily as they joined the bus queue.

"That's alright, I'll wait here with you," replied Eric wanting to ask her out but was even more nervous now than when he performed his first magic trick. "… Would you like to see a trick?" then asked Eric removing his mobile phone from his inner blazer pocket.

"Yeah, sure I'd love to! As long as it's not another card trick!" replied Emily. Eric had already shown her a lot of card tricks during the school breaks. *(It's always best not to show too many tricks and especially the same type of tricks during your performance, so as not to make it boring!)*

"I promise Em …" said Eric laughing.

"… Well, get on with it then!" joked Emily.

"Okay, well, would you like a chocolate?"

"Yes please, I love chocolates!" answered Emily delighted at the thought.

Eric searched his pockets but then said, "Oh I'm sorry Em, I thought I had one left but I must have eaten the last one!" said Eric apologetically. Emily just laughed. "But don't worry I did take a picture of it!" announced Eric grinning.

"What?" said Emily giggling? Eric then opened up the gallery on his mobile phone and showed Emily a photo of a chocolate, about the same size as a real one. Emily looked at him as if he'd gone bonkers or something.

Eric then said, "Of course if I was a real magician I would be able to take the chocolate right out of my phone and give it to you!" Eric paused for just a moment and then did just that! It looked astonishing, as he appeared to actually remove the chocolate from the screen, leaving the screen empty and handing over a real 3D chocolate! *(Learn how to do this amazing Twenty-First-Century trick at the rear of the book!)*

Emma stepped back in amazement. "What? That was amazing! That can't be?" she screamed in delight "You're like a real-life

Harry Potter!" Emily started to sniff the chocolate as if to check if it was a real one. "Well it smells real!" she said slightly unsure. Eric laughed.

"Go on eat it then," said Eric with a big grin. So Emily popped the chocolate straight into her mouth, "Um, it tastes real too!" Emily couldn't believe it as she munched away on the chocolate. It even seemed to taste better than normal. "Um, that was scrummy yummy!" said Emily with a big smile on her face. "Thank you, that was really, sweet of you Eric!" then said Emily, "Sweet of you! Do you get it?" repeated Emily laughing at her own joke as she nudged her elbow against him.

Eric then laughed having finally got the joke. He'd been too transfixed staring into Emily's eyes to notice she had cracked a joke. He had got the love bug all right!

"It's very dark without that street light on!" Someone in the queue announced. More people then joined the queue, which forced Eric and Emily closer together. They both then looked into each other's eyes and smiled.

"I really like you Eric!" said Emily quietly spoken.

"I feel the same way about you too!" replied Eric feeling more confident.

"Don't make yourself late for the

competition," then said Emily changing the subject. Both felt slightly awkward in this situation.

"I won't," said Eric letting his bag drop to the ground as he stood on his tiptoes so he could be the same height as Emily.

"Oh, I really hope you win tonight Eric!" Just as Emily said that they both spontaneously closed their eyes and pursed their lips together about to kiss. Suddenly the bus pulled up over a big puddle splashing everyone. Both opened their eyes and retracted their heads before they had a chance to kiss.

"See you at the show later!" Emily said to Eric as she moved away from him and stepped onto the bus.

"Bye Em!" Eric stepped to one side to let the others behind him, past, feeling slightly disappointed, and the two of them waved goodbye to each other through the bus window as it left.

Eric couldn't believe his luck though, even though he didn't actually get the chance to kiss Emily. "The prettiest girl in the class actually fancies me!" he thought. He ran across the road, jumping in as many puddles as he could and then all the way home with a big happy smile on his face, all chuffed with himself. He thought to himself, that even if he didn't do well in the talent competition, nothing could put a dampener on his day now!

Eric arrived home from school having just missed his dad unbeknownst to him by about twenty minutes or so.

"Hi Mum, I'm home!" called out Eric as he came bounding in through the side kitchen door and kicked off his soaking wet shoes, immediately noticing the unmistakable smell of bleach in the air. "Ergh!" thought Eric, holding his nose.

His mum was in her bedroom removing a large beaten up old suitcase from the top of her wardrobe so that Eric could put all his magic props inside to carry to school. "I'm in here love!" she answered back. Ingrid started to empty everything out she had stored away in there and as she was removing things she came across a few old holiday snaps of the three of them smiling and happy together as a family, which brought a smile to her face and as she reminisced she thought, "If only it could have carried on being that way!" Just then Eric burst in making his mum jump.

"Hiya! You look like you've seen a ghost! Are you alright Mum?" said Eric.

"Hiya! Yes, you just startled me that's all, I was miles away," replied his mum thinking, "Maybe I did see a ghost?" Certainly a ghost from her past! "Take this suitcase into your room Eric and start packing all your magic props ready for the show. This is the only suitcase we have large enough I'm afraid. I'll go and put ya tea on," said his mum as she handed Eric the suitcase noticing one of the wheels was missing.

"Hey! I've just noticed your hair is blonde again. I wondered what that horrible smell was!" exclaimed Eric, having only just realised. "I thought there was something different about you. How come then?" added Eric curious to know why she had decided to change back to her old look?

"Well, I just felt like it and besides I don't think we need to worry about anyone knowing we are here anymore. Anyroad, we need to hurry up!" His mum had been referring to his dad of course.

"Okay Mum," said Eric as he took the suitcase from her and headed straight to his room.

"Don't take too long now will you, we don't want to be late!" then called out his mum, her hair still slightly wet, starting to panic a little bit.

Eric took the empty suitcase into his room and packed all his magic props inside, double-checking he hadn't forgotten anything. Lastly, laying his black jacket with the shiny silver trim and his bow tie on top of everything. He could only just about shut the suitcase! He certainly couldn't fit his top hat into it, as it wasn't one of those collapsible types, so he was going to have to either carry it in the other hand or wear it. "I'll carry it!" he thought, laughing to himself at the prospect of him wearing it into school. Suddenly his mobile beeped, it was a text from Emily. It read "Good luck for tonight x," Eric replied back saying thanks, also putting a kiss.

The contestants had to be at the school hall half an hour before the show started to have a sound check and get ready. So straight after tea, Eric and his mum closeted themselves in their warm winter coats, scarves, gloves and woolly hats and set off for the talent competition, struggling with the large heavy suitcase of magic paraphernalia between them. On the way out Eric quickly grabbed an orange from the fruit bowl and put it in his pocket; his mum was pleasantly surprised to see that Eric had chosen fruit to eat for a change. And by the way, Eric did end up wearing the top hat after all.

It was very cold and dark outside by now and some of the streetlights were out on their estate. As they looked up into the clear night's sky they could see a myriad of twinkling stars and there was a full moon out. It certainly was a very magical night indeed.

When they finally arrived, having had to stop a few times to have a break from carrying the heavier than usual suitcase, they were confronted with a very chaotic scene, to say the least. There were the show organizers running about like headless chickens trying to sort out some last minute hitches and a singer on stage having technical sound difficulties, while other contestants with their families were milling about everywhere, not quite sure where to go!

"Ah! The amazing Fartzini!" called out Mr Potter, who had volunteered to help. "Please find a space backstage to put your things. Here is the running order for the show. Break a leg young man and remember to keep your 'Secreta, Secreto!" he said in Latin as he handed Eric the sheet of paper.

"Thank you sir!" replied Eric with a slightly blank look on his face. Eric noticed he wasn't on until the second half.

Eric was now starting to feel the pressure. "Mum, when you're nervous, why do they call it 'Butterflies'?" enquired Eric as they made their way backstage.

"Well, it's because you feel like there are lots of butterflies dancing around in your tummy tickling you. You just need to wave your magic wand and make them all disappear Eric!" said his mum reassuringly to her son. "It's known as 'Stage Fright' Eric and it's quite normal to feel in this way. You'll be great, Son! " she added. *(Having the right mindset when it comes to dealing with pressure, really helps: use pressure as a positive thing rather than a negative thing!)*

Eric smiled and placed the suitcase down on the floor by some scenery from the school production of the 'Lion King' the school had put on some time last year, then unzipped the suitcase and started to set up his props for this magic act. His mum hung up his jacket on a costume rail nearby and placed the top hat on the floor next to it. He borrowed a small round table and covered it with a tablecloth his mum had made for him, which was a shiny black material with silver stars printed on it, which she bought from the local haberdashery shop. The first prop he placed onto the table was the 'Nest of Boxes', in front of that he placed the 'Change Bag', laying his wand neatly next to it and to the side of that a can of 'Seven-Up' and the special glass for his opening trick. The cards he just put in his right trouser pocket.

Eric decided not to perform the 'Siberian Chain' escape after all as sometimes it took him longer to escape than at other times and sometimes he was even unable to release himself at all! So he didn't want to take the risk of maybe running over the allotted time or embarrassing himself.

As Eric prepared for his magic act there were also lots of other contestants backstage preparing for their acts. Some of the singers were warming up their vocal cords, while the dancers were seen to be stretching their limbs, doing the splits, and one girl lifted her leg right up next to her ear! "That looks painful!" thought Eric grimacing. A trumpet player was playing a tune on his trumpet and the comedian was pacing up and down reciting his jokes making Eric feel a bit dizzy watching him.

On stage just finishing their sound check was David's band, a heavy metal band calling themselves 'The Zombies'. They even put 'Zombie' make up on and ripped their clothes to shreds, looking quite scary as they thrashed out a 'Black Sabbath' number very loudly. David didn't need to put makeup on to be scary. He looked like a cross between a 'Zombie' and 'The Joker' villain out of 'Batman' and gelled his hair up so it was wild and spiky. By contrast, Eric put on his smart black bow tie and tails coat, keen to get ready.

"You're getting ready really early Eric? Look at me, that's better!" she said as she adjusted his tie for him.

"Alright Mum stop fussing!" said Eric, feeling slightly embarrassed by his mum.

"I'd better grab my seat before somebody else does, I'll see you in the interval darling!" said his mum as she left, trying to squeeze past warm sweaty bodies limbering up. The band stopped and the front of house curtains started to close as guests started to come in to take their seats.

Just then one of the girl dancers handed Eric a note on a small scrap of paper. "I was told to give you this," she said. The note scribbled in big letters read: *Watch your back tonite, David has got something bad planned for ya!'* Well, there was only one 'David' that Eric knew and it immediately made him start to feel ill at ease. There wasn't much more room left to write anything else on the scrap of paper except just squeezed in, there was the word 'Sorry' written?

"Who gave you this note?" Eric called out to the girl as she left, perplexed as to who it might be? "Whoever it was that wrote it is not very good at spelling," thought Eric.

"I think his name is, erm … Gary?" replied the girl who then went off to join her dance troupe.

"Gary?" Eric said to himself. Trying to think

of the Gary's he might know. Then it dawned on him, 'Hamburger'! But why would 'Hamburger' warn me about this?" Eric thought even more baffled. The truth is, 'Hamburger' no longer wanted to be David's friend and was sorry for all the horrible things he had done to Eric and so wanted to warn him.

"Please take your seats, Ladies and Gentleman. The show will be starting in approximately ten minutes!" A voice was heard over the P.A system. The compère for the evening was the Deputy Head, relieved that the sound system was finally working.

The band switched off their amps and left their musical equipment where it was 'Upstage' and headed off into the 'Stage Left' wings messing about and pretending to walk and groan like scary 'Zombie' characters as they did. 'The Zombies' were down to close the show so had some time to waste and as David made his way through some of the acts waiting in the wings ready to go on stage and perform, in the distance to his left above the heads of the mass of dancers, he could see someone wearing a top hat?

He barged past a few of the acts to get a closer look. Some girls gave out a scream seeing him in his 'Zombie' makeup for the first time, nearly tripping over a girl's legs who was doing the splits. And then noticed, it was Eric Fartz. "What's he doing here? Oh no!" he thought to himself, very surprised to see him having hoped that he had put him out of action on the rugby pitch.

For a moment David just stood there motionless giving Eric the 'Death Stare'. He then turned back barging his way past pupils again, and angrily walked through the already open backstage exit door, which lead to outside the building, leaving it slightly ajar again. "Time to put my original plan in action and stop him entering the talent show once and for all!" sinisterly thought David.

The three other band members of 'The Zombies' were already outside by the dilapidated bicycle sheds nearby, joking and messing about, and drinking cans of high-energy drinks; one had lit a cigarette.

"If we get caught smoking it won't matter because with all this makeup on the teachers won't recognize us!" joked one of them as he took a puff on the cigarette and passed it over to one of his mates. David went over to join them.

"That magician Fartz is here!" said David sounding bothered and angry.

"So what!" said one of the band members

wondering why David was so bothered.

"Yeah, don't worry about him, he is good but were much better!" boasted another.

"I ain't bothered about that talent-less nobody in the faintest!" snapped back David, jealous and clearly agitated by seeing Eric backstage.

"You do seem bothered?" argued one of the band members.

"I told ya, I'm not bothered, now shut it!" said David getting even more agitated.

"Anyway, I thought you said your dad was gonna have a word with one of the judges?" enquired one of them.

It's true, his dad the governor had persuaded one of the judges he knew to give the other acts low marks and mark his son's band with high marks by offering him a financial incentive. Therefore giving 'The Zombies' an unfair advantage!

"He *has!* Now drop it all right! Give us a puff!" said David reaching to take the cigarette.

"There's a teacher, put the cigarette out quick!" said one of the lads noticing a teacher opening the stage door and triggering the security light as they pocked their head outside to have a look round wondering why the door was open?

"Hide behind these bikes!" said David as the

four 'Zombies' only narrowly missed getting caught. The teacher shut the fire exit door.

"Oh great, now we're locked out!" exclaimed one of them.

By now the audience had all taken their seats and there were even a number of people standing at the back who had not been able to get tickets but Eric's dad was not among them. Ingrid turned her head around a few times looking for her ex and was a bit disappointed that he had not turned up. Eric made his way to the wings and peeked through the stage curtain to see where his mum and Emily were sat. He could see his mum was sat a couple of rows back in the centre and Emily was sat nearer the back with her mum and dad.

"You can't stay there!" then said a slightly grumpy stage manager indicating for Eric to move away. So Eric went back to where he had left his magic props to find a couple of the dancers nosing around, lifting things up and trying to find out his secrets. "Come away from there!" Eric told them in an assertive manner and then straightened up the props on his table again.

"Five minutes till curtains up!" announced the stage manager to the acts nervously waiting backstage. It suddenly went very quiet backstage, except for a few contestants whispering to one another and the occasional nervous giggles heard. Then after what seemed like a long five minutes the stage curtains opened revealing a table 'Stage Right' with three shiny handsome trophies sat on it, one bigger than the other, with the biggest one in the middle for the winner.

The Deputy Head then walked out on stage smiling, carrying a radio microphone in his hand. Sat along the front row were David's dad the school Governor, the Head Teacher and some invited guests.

"Testing One, Two, One Two. Good evening Ladies and Gentleman, Boys and Girls and welcome to St. Bartholomew's Got Talent on Friday The Thirteenth!" announced the Deputy Head in an overly theatrical voice. "Oooh, spooky!" quipped the Deputy Head making light of it. The audience joined in making an 'Oooh' sound. "Now before we get started introducing the acts, I'd like to, first of all, introduce to you the judges for tonight's competition. So please will you give them a big hand as they make their way to the judge's table. They are Mrs Sharp who runs the local Stage School 'Twinkle Toes', Brian Hobbs a local businessman and lastly but by no means least our Head of Dance and Drama Miss Hopkins!" The audience applauded as the three judges made their way to their seats at the judge's table in the centre of the hall.

"Also, I would like you to give a warm welcome if you would please to the Deputy Mayor of Ramsgate, Bill Turner who very kindly has stepped in at the last minute for The Mayor, who I am very pleased to say is making a remarkable recovery!" then announced the compère. The audience applauded loudly as the Deputy Mayor got up, twisted around and waved his hand in the air in acknowledgement.

After clearing his throat a couple of times the Deputy Head then said, "Now, unlike the real 'Britain's Got Talent' on T.V. - in *our* talent competition, we don't have a Mr Nasty Simon Cowell-like character or any buzzers to buzz acts off, and there are no advert breaks, thank goodness." A cheer went up as he said that. "This will be a fair and honestly judged competition, filled with great entertainment, performed for you tonight by our very talented lower school pupils!" Another even louder cheer was then heard. "But, of course, Ladies and Gentleman, this is a competition and there can be only one winner and this will be up to the judges to decide who that winner will be to receive the top prize of £100.00!" The audience cheered again as the prize money was announced. "There will also be cash prizes for the runners-up in second and third place!" This statement was followed by yet another loud cheer.

They certainly were a lively crowd with many of the acts families making up the audience. "The marking will be determined on an acts talent, presentation and entertainment value. The highest mark for each being ten," continued the Deputy Head, sweating slightly under the bright spotlight.

The Deputy Head was then handed a note from one of the teachers, "I have just been handed a note to inform you that a couple of the acts listed in the programme have pulled out, so there will now be a total of sixteen acts in the competition! Anyway enough of my waffling and without any further ado, it gives me great pleasure to introduce to you the first act on this evening, one of Seven dance troupes, so please put your hands together and give a warm welcome to … The Blasting Rockets!" The Deputy Head announced, reading the name of the act from a slip of paper, thinking as he made his way off stage, "Oh dear, did I just swear then?"

Their music started and to loud applause and cheers all twelve of the female dancing troupe, six from each wing came bounding on stage dancing the Charleston to start the show off with. All wearing dresses from the 1920's era, sequins flying all over the place! One dancer almost accidentally bumping into the Deputy Head as he attempted to exit the stage, causing him to dance awkwardly and embarrassingly out of her way. He was clearly not used to doing this sort of thing.

"Shh!" said the Deputy Head as he finally made it off stage, putting his forefinger to his lips to quieten down some of the other noisy entrants waiting to go on in the wings.

Eric was still backstage by his magic props practising, he dared not leave his props unattended again in case some of the other contestants become nosy and wanted to try and discover his secrets like before.

The music ended and the audience clapped and cheered as the dancers all took a bow and then made their way off stage and into the wings. The show had got off to a good start and the next act to be introduced, was a female singer called Sara Pilkington wearing a long flowing dress singing 'My heart will go on' from the film 'Titanic'. She sang really well and if it hadn't of been for the stage prop, in the form of the bow of a ship, collapsing as she leaned against it singing the last note, it would have been even better! "That wasn't supposed to happen, was it? Poor girl!" A lady on the second row was heard to say. "I don't remember that happening in the film?" said another.

The Deputy Head quickly came rushing on and helped her up. She was all right apart from some tell, tell signs of embarrassment, running off stage with her hands covering her face sobbing. The slightly embarrassed Deputy Head then quickly introduced the next act.

"Ladies and Gentleman moving rapidly along, this next act doesn't need an introduction because he can blow his own trumpet and that's exactly what he's going to do for you now. So would you now please put your hands together for a fine musician called Robert Wiśniewski!" announced the Deputy Head, reading from a slip paper what he'd written down, struggling to pronounce his last name.

Meanwhile, David and his band were knocking as loud as they could on the stage door, competing with all the even louder noise inside, desperately trying to get back inside.

Open the door! It's freezing!" called out David, alternating knocking at the door with blowing inside his fists to try and keep warm.

"Open the door and let us in!" All four of them now shouted in unison. Not just because it was cold outside, but also because someone hiding in the dark had now started throwing 'Fun snaps' and firing a spud gun towards them. Bangs and explosions went off and could be heard to splatter against the wall and the door.

"Ouch! My butt!" yelled one of them, clutching his sore backside.

"It's no good, we'll have to go around to the front!" called out another.

"We'll get told off if we do that Einstein," said another sarcastically. Just then the door opened and one of the dancers let them in, getting the fright of her life as four 'Zombies' came rushing in groaning and moaning. Mainly from becoming cold outside and being shot at by some crazed mystery 'Zombie' hunter. The crazed mystery 'Zombie' hunter in question was 'Hamburger', who had left his mum inside and sneaked round to the back, armed with a spud gun and box of 'Fun Snaps' to play a prank them, and with still the need to get his fix shooting at 'Zombies'!

The band, still wondering who the devil that was outside, mixed in with all the other entrants and luckily for them were not spotted by any of the teachers or stage crew who were very busy trying to run the show.

"I bet that was one of the bullies from the year above?" thought David feeling relieved to be inside. David left his other band members and walked in the direction of Eric who had his back turned not realizing David was fast approaching.

By now a few more acts had been on and off stage performing to a very supportive audience and the judges were busy giving each act their marks and consolidating with each other after each act had finished. "Your marks are a bit stingy?" said one of the judges to the other, noticing that they had marked all the acts so far with low marks. The judge who gave these very low marks, who was a slippery looking character with a slightly crooked moustache, didn't reply but just turned their head away ignoring the comment and promptly shielded his marks from the other judge's view.

The compère then introduced the next act who was a comedian and a welcome change from all the dancers and singers that had been on so far.

Ingrid quickly looked over her shoulder but there was still no sign of her ex at the back of the room, "Where could he be?" she thought to herself.

"Ladies and Gentleman would you now please put your hands together and welcome on stage a very funny lad who I'm sure is going to make you laugh. Give it up for Billy

Mathews!" The audience clapped and cheered as the young man came bounding onstage smiling his head off. "Remember to keep it clean young man!" stage-whispered the Deputy Head as they passed each other on stage.

The cheeky comedian stepped up to the mic and cracked his first joke. The audience laughed and the Deputy Head cringed and the young comedian then told one quickfire joke after another. The audience was really enjoying his act.

"Boo!" shouted David in Eric's left ear as he made his way around to face him. It made Eric jump and as he moved his head away quickly to see whom it was, he soon realized it was the bully David. "… What are you doing here then? I thought they only allowed good acts to enter this competition!" sniggered David looking down at little Eric, mocking him.

"I could say the same thing to you!" replied Eric bravely not letting the bully get the better of him.

"Oi, watch it *Fartz!* Magic's boring anyway and you don't stand a chance of winning against my band!" snarled David, slightly taken aback with Eric's comeback line, not expecting him to answer back.

"You don't frighten me! Why don't you just go away and grow up!" said Eric standing up to the bully. Something he didn't have the confidence to do a little while back.

Angry, David then reached over and grabbed Eric's magic wand off of his table and snapped it in half over his knee! But instead of an upset response from Eric that David was expecting, Eric burst into laughter? He laughed so much he fell on the floor holding his sides and just couldn't stop laughing. Some of the dancers nearby were looking at Eric thinking, "The comedian's not that funny?"

"Why are you laughing?" demanded David, cross that it was him for a change that was being laughed at. What David didn't realize, that Eric found so funny, is that he had picked up the comedy collapsible wand that is meant to appear like it's broke but it's not really broken!

The interesting thing about laughter is, it is infectious and the sight of Eric rolled up on the floor laughing caused others around him to also join in the laughter, not even knowing what they were laughing about. So with that, David promptly threw the apparently broken wand down on the floor and stormed off.

Eric got up and picked up his wand, straightened it again and put it back in place on his table. "Buying this wand was money well spent!" thought Eric relieved that David had left, and hoping that was the end of it. "That wasn't 'bad'" Eric then thought to himself, thinking about what was written on the note. But, this still wasn't what David had in store for little Eric!

It was now the turn of the last act on before the interval. "Oh no, not more dancers!" thought the Deputy Head. So this time he thought it wise to introduce them from off stage, especially after the near collision the last time.

Out they came, dancing to a hip-hop track this time, which really energized the audience who clapped along to the track as the dancers, a mix of four boys and four girls strutted their stuff, body popping and break dancing all over the stage. This was the troupe that Emily's sister was in.

"Let's hear it for Streetz Ahead Ladies and Gentleman! Streets spelt with a letter z apparently? The audience gave them a really big round of applause and cheers, especially Emily and her mum and dad of course.

"I must have a word with their English teacher!" joked the Deputy Head. "Well I wonder if the judges have put them *Streets Ahead* in the competition so far?" then said the compère to a few groans from the audience, trying to be witty again as the dancers left the stage. "It's now the interval Ladies and Gentleman. Refreshments are being served at the back of the room and the second half will recommence in twenty minutes time, thank you!" The curtains closed and the house lights came on.

Ingrid looked behind her again noticing that her ex, had still not arrived? Backstage there was a hub of activity as the acts appearing in the second half got changed and prepared to go on stage. Eric put on his jacket and apart from putting on his top hat he was ready and raring to go.

"Will you show us some magic?" asked one of the dancers stood near to him.

"Sure!" said Eric confidently and performed an amazing trick he'd learnt from his magic book. Eric borrowed a shiny new penny from the girl and asked her to hold it tightly in her hand. By now a small crowd had gathered to witness what was going on. He told the slightly excited girl to concentrate and then after a little while to slowly open her hand. Upon opening her hand the girl shrieked out loud and everyone's jaws dropped! "OMG!" slowly said the girl, totally amazed! Her penny was now bent! *(Find the secret to this astonishing trick called 'The Bent Penny' at the rear of the book!)*

CHAPTER THIRTEEN

THE TALENT COMPETITION
SECOND HALF

"The second half of the show will be starting in five minutes Ladies and Gentleman if you would like to please take your seats!" The Deputy Heads voice was heard saying over the P.A system. Upon hearing this, the audience finished their drinks and started to sit back down again. Eric's mum was outside having a quick look around to see if her ex was there, but there was no sign of him there either. She did notice an open half-filled can of larger on the floor near the entrance though, and it did cross through her mind, "I wonder if that was Peter's?"

Ingrid quickly went back inside and just before the second half got underway, popped through the stage door by the side of the stage, climbed up some steps and made her way past all the contestants to find her son backstage.

There he was in the same spot still surrounded by a number of the other contestants admiring his magic. Eric's confidence was just growing and growing!

"Shuffle the cards," Eric was heard to say. He then took back the thoroughly shuffled pack and held it behind his back. "I shall now attempt to locate the four Aces behind my back, sight unseen by feel alone -"

"Break a leg love, you'll be fantastic!" called out his mum quickly to her son, interrupting him for a moment. Eric acknowledged his mum with a nod and carried on performing the card trick as she then went to take her seat to watch the second half.

"There's the Ace of Diamonds!" Eric announced dramatically as he brought the Ace into view from behind his back. The onlookers started to applaud. "Wait! I still have three more Aces to find!" Eric announced as he fumbled behind his back in search for another Ace. "Ah, here it is!" said Eric looking pleased with himself as he brought forth yet another Ace. Then as a finale, Eric impressively produced the last two Aces at once! The group around him applauded making too much noise. *(Learn how to perform this skilful-looking trick called 'The Easiest Four Ace Trick in the World' along with all the other tricks in 'Eric's Magic Secrets' at the rear of the book!)*

"Quieten down!" called out the Deputy Head who was in the wings waiting to go back on stage at any moment. Eric thought he'd better stop performing and the group dispersed. Eric wasn't on until towards the end of the show and had got a bit bored with all the waiting around.

David wasn't anywhere to be seen and even his bandmates had wondered where he was? What was he up to this time? What was he planning to do to poor Eric!

Two of the judges took their seats again; one of them was still talking with the School Governor and quickly then joined the others at the table as soon as he heard the microphone being tested.

"One, Two, One, Two," was heard over the P.A system. The house lights went dim; the curtains opened and out walked the Deputy Head to centre stage.

"Well, Ladies and Gentleman I hope you are all refreshed and ready to be entertained by all our wonderful and amazing pupils in the second half of the show?" The crowd cheered loudly answering that question. "So then, Ladies and Gentleman without any further ado, to open the second half of the show we have another street dance troupe for you, so will you please put your hands together and go wild for The Streets!"

The music started, the audience applauded and the Deputy Head headed quickly for the wings as the high kicking, arms flinging, hip gyrating dancers came strutting out on stage.

"It's dangerous out there! There are limbs flying everywhere!" said the Deputy Head glad to be off stage and out of harm's way. "... Didn't they perform in the first half?" then casually asked the Deputy Head to the stage manager looking very confused.

"No that was Streetz Ahead ... different troupe," replied the stage manager.

"Oh, they all look the same to me!" said the Deputy Head as he picked up his cup of half-drunk coffee, smelling as if something stronger may have been added to it?

The next act to go on after the dancers was a girl originally from Hong Kong called Victoria Wang. A virtuoso violinist who everyone thought would probably win the competition but as she went to pick up her violin she was suddenly heard to burst into tears and was very upset. The Deputy Head went over to her to see what was the matter, as did some of the other pupils who gathered around her. He didn't need to ask her because he could instantly see what had happened. Someone had purposely cut all the strings on her precious violin!

One of the female teacher's, who was also backstage helping, came to consul her but the poor girl was inconsolable and wept and wept.

"I not can play now!" The Chinese girl tried to say, sobbing after every word in a broken English accent.

"Do you have spare strings?" asked the teacher trying to be of help.

"No, not enough! Someone sabotage my act!" replied the virtuoso still very upset and now angry.

The Deputy Head left the teacher to deal with it, as he then got ready to take the dancers off stage, desperately trying to think of what to say to the audience about the crisis unfolding backstage.

"Are you ready to go on now instead?" The Deputy Head quickly asked the solo male singer. Panic clearly heard in the Deputy Head's voice.

"Errrm, yes s–s-sir," replied the singer with a nervous stutter, licking his dry lips and now panicking at the thought that he had to go on next and sing for the first time in front of a live audience. His hands were slightly shaking and his legs felt like jelly: all wobbly. The poor lad was consumed with 'Stage Fright' and got himself into a right tiswas!

"Are your parents in the audience?" asked the teacher to the violinist.

"Yes!" she replied very disappointed that she would not be able to take part in the competition.

"Come with me and I will take you to them now," said the teacher escorting her out.

"Okay," The violinist reluctantly agreed, clutching her unusable violin, strings dangling down and swinging about tuneless as they both left.

The dancers finished their spot and the audience cheered and applauded them as they left the stage. "Let's hear it one more time for The Streetz! ... Now, unfortunately, Ladies and Gentleman, due to a technical problem our next act, Victoria Twang, I mean Wang, will not be able to perform tonight!" embarrassingly announced the Deputy Head.

A big sigh of disappointment was heard in the audience. "But we have a wonderful singer for you now, who is going to sing a song by Robbie Williams, called Let me entertain you," said the Deputy Head, reading the singer's intro direct from his notes for the first time since he'd scribbled it down earlier. "He's a bit nervous so please put your hands together and give a warm Bartholomew welcome to …" There was an awkward pause. "Now where's his blooming name?" The Deputy Head was accidentally overheard saying under his breath on the mic, as his eyes desperately searched for it on his crumpled up sheet of paper. "… Oh yes, sorry! John Edwards!" he finally announced.

The audience applauded loudly as the nervous boy entered the stage.

"Oh, God! The violinist's parents aren't going to be very happy!" thought the Deputy Head as he quickly exited the stage even sweatier than before.

The Chinese parents of the violinist had by now been reunited with their daughter and upon hearing the announcement turned to each other shocked. The father become very animated and was heard saying something in Mandarin, which translated was something like, "Is the Deputy Head taking the Mick?" They all got up in disgust with their arms around their daughter who was still sobbing and promptly started to leave.

Several people turned around to see what the

commotion was including Ingrid, who was also looking to see if she could spot her ex. Alas, he was not there!

"Will you stop keep turning around!" said an irritated older female member of the audience, sat behind her, in a snobby voice as Ingrid turned around again for the umpteenth time.

"You mind your own business!" snapped back Ingrid in her strong northern, 'Don't you mess with me' accent. The quarrel was starting to get quite heated! At one point it looked as though a fight might break out! The music started and Ingrid turned back around to continue watching the show.

The singer slowly and anxiously reached the mic stand somewhat dazed by all the lights, forcing a smile, clearly still very nervous and as he opened his mouth to sing, nothing came out! He, unfortunately, forgot the first line of the song but then suddenly remembered and starting singing, but he was now out of sync with the music! It sounded awful! Everyone in the audience felt for the poor lad.

"It's turning out to be a disaster!" said the Deputy Head to the stage manager, peering out from the wings. But the singer soon managed to get back in time with the music once his nerves had calmed down and sang the rest of the song really well, much to the delight of the audience! "Let's hear it for John Edwards." requested the compère. The audience gave him an extra big round of applause and a cheer for not giving up and carrying on, and a much more confident boy exited the stage. "Well done lad!" said the compère thinking to himself, "Only a few more acts left to go thank God!" The Deputy Head hadn't realized just how stressful being the master of ceremonies could be, having to get everyone's names right and deal with unforeseen technical difficulties and so on. *(Just picking up on how brave and determined the singer was in the story by entering the talent competition in the first place despite being very nervous and frightened, and carrying on and not giving up after forgetting the first line of the song.*

Many people from all walks of life have confidence issues for a number for different reasons and it's usually only fear that stops people from doing what they truly want to do!

So be brave and determined like Eric and the singer in the story by not letting fear stop you doing whatever it is you want to do or being whoever you want to be, and don't worry about what other people may think of you! You will feel a lot better about yourself and achieve a lot more if you don't let your fears get in your way! Just go for it!)

David suddenly showed up backstage and went over to join his band.

"Where did you get to?" asked one of the band members.

"Oh, I sneaked outside again to get some fresh air and a quick smoke. It's very stuffy backstage!" It was very stuffy backstage with so many bodies about but was there another reason why David went outside?

"We thought we might have to become a trio instead tonight!" joked one of them.

"What and miss winning the competition. No way!" bragged David cockily.

The show progressed with yet another dance troupe followed by a girl reciting poetry and the judges were busy writing down their marks. Then the compère introduced another female singer who made her way onto the stage singing a lively number to an up-tempo beat.

Eric's mum was sat, anxiously waiting in her seat for her son to come on stage next after the singer, fingers tightly crossed. Backstage, Eric started to feel the nerves again, his heart was beating even faster than the beat of the music he could hear on stage, but he remembered some advice his mum had told him, which if you feel nervous count backwards from ten to one and this will help you focus and so this is what he did and sure enough it did help a lot.

His top hat had been on and off his head numerous times and once again Eric picked it up and put it on his head so he could use both hands to carry his table full of magic props over to the wings ready for the assistant stage manager to set it in place on stage as soon as the singer finished her song. All he had to do now was navigate past all the other performers still backstage, which was no easy task.

"Excuse me please!" said Eric as he tried to get past people. But as he was carrying the table the motion caused the slightly oversized hat to slip over his eyes as he was walking and he couldn't see a thing. "Sorry! He said as he bumped into someone. Just then someone snatched his top hat off of his head and started to run off with it. It was David, who had waited for this opportune moment to carry out his devious plan. David pushed open the backstage fire exit door and ran outside with Eric's hat. Eric was slightly taken aback at first, but then quickly realized who this scary Zombie was and promptly put his table down and bravely gave chase.

"Hey! Come back here with my hat!" Eric called out as he followed David out through the door. The music was playing loud and the Deputy Head and the stage management were too busy running the show to notice the commotion going on behind them and the other pupils just thought it was a prank.

"I thought it was zombies that were supposed to do the chasing, not the other way round?" joked one of the other pupils to their friends standing nearby.

Eric needed his hat for his magic act and was desperate to get it back. The security light had automatically come on but David was nowhere to be seen? So Eric rushed to have a look over by the bicycle sheds and noticed his hat lying on the ground. But as soon as he reached down to pick it up, David who'd been hiding behind a row of bikes suddenly pounced on Eric from behind, forcing him to the ground. David had tricked Eric into following him!

"Get off me!" Eric screamed, powerless against the bully's sheer size and brute strength. David looked scarier than ever with his make up on. It was like a 'Zombie Horror Film' and what nightmares are made of, only this was for real! "Let me go, why are you doing this?" then angrily shouted Eric.

"Shut it! Make another sound Fartz, and I'll punch you hard!" threatened David as he grabbed hold of a longish chain from the ground nearby, which he'd planted there earlier.

"I'm on stage next, let me go!" then pleaded

Eric, desperately struggling to get away, realizing he was going to miss his chance to perform!

"That's what you think! Now shut it or else!" said David, trying to keep his voice down.

"Ouch!" screamed Eric as the nasty pitiless bully wrapped the freezing cold steel chain several times around Eric's puny wrists, making them sore. David then unsympathetically grabbed poor Eric's nice new stage jacket, ripping part of the silver ribbon away from the lapel as he dragged him a little distance to where there was a metal roof support at the desolated far end of the bike shed.

There, David continued to tie him up - hurting Eric as he wrapped the chain tightly around his frail little body and the roof support – taking out his own frustrations on him. "This is a lot tighter than I'm used to!" thought Eric.

David then quickly reached into his trouser pocket, his fingers desperately fumbling around in the dark amongst lots of coins from the day's plunder and other bits and bobs in search of the padlock. His fingers finally located the padlock and as he removed it from his pocket a pair of sharply pointed scissors accidentally fell out onto the ground. Eric desperately cried out for help, fearing the

worst. "Shut it or else!" snarled the big brute.

Eric then put two and two together and deduced that there was a very strong possibility that they could have been the very same scissors used to cut the strings on the violin! He had noticed David earlier, hanging suspiciously around near to where the violinist had left her violin, and wouldn't have been at all surprised or put it past David to do such a horrid and spiteful thing.

David carried on further tightening the chain around poor Eric in a crazed state of mind, pinching his skin as he fastened the padlock securely through the links of the chain. It all happened very quickly and Eric's hopes of entering the talent competition were looking very bleak just like the weather, which had now turned bitterly cold.

"Now try and perform your magic tricks, loser!" said David, as cold as the steel chain he used to tie Eric up with. David rose up from his crouched over, domineering position and started to move away, his cold heart racing, feeling a massive adrenalin rush.

"I'm going to report you!" said Eric as he continued to struggle.

"You' better not! Nobody would believe you anyway!" replied the horribly jealous and insecure bully, and quickly kicked the gleaming suspect scissors away from the beam of light and into the dark.

"HELP! HELP!" screamed Eric out loud, starting to panic as he tried to wriggle his way out of the chain to no avail, thinking to himself, "I'm never going to escape from this chain!"

"No one's gonna hear you out here! You're wasting your breath. Don't worry I'll come and release you when I've won the competition!" boasted David as he hurriedly left Eric all alone shivering in the freezing cold, laughing as he did at his victim's predicament! It was the sort of cold one could die from if exposed to it for too long!

Eric then suddenly heard the magician's voice from the Christmas fair in his head again, which he hadn't heard in a while, hadn't needed to, but he certainly needed all the help he could get now. As he listened, he started to pull himself together, no longer panicking and screaming and thought to himself, "You know what, that's the only and best advice that bully David has ever given to me!" Eric then remembered reading one of 'Harry Houdini's' secrets of escape was to be relaxed and be calm, which made it easier to escape.

So despite deciding not to perform a chain escape that evening, he now had no choice but to try and escape, determined not to let the bully beat him, and still enter the talent show. But this time it was going to be a real challenge, as the security light had just switched off and David had fastened the chains very tightly indeed!

David sneaked back inside the hall, still slightly out of breath and joined his bandmates again. The singer had just finished her song and the compère went on stage to take her off.

"Where's the next act? What's his name? Where's my running order? … Oh yes, The Amazing Fartzini, that's it! Why isn't he here ready to go on?" said the stage manager to one of the stagehands in the wings, slightly panicking and annoyed.

"Oh, I don't know?" replied the stagehand and went off looking for him.

"He must have disappeared sir!" said David overhearing the conversation, trying to be funny, giggling along with his bandmates after he said it. Knowing full well where his main rival, as he saw him, was.

The stagehand came back to where the stage manager was by the wings carrying Eric's table of magic props. "I found his table, but there is no sign of the boy!" said the stagehand putting the table down, not knowing what to do next.

"He must have got too nervous and decided to leave? I see it happen all the time!" said the stage manager to the stagehand and quickly scribbled something down on a slip of paper.

The Deputy Head unawares that something was amiss took the singer off and started to announce the next act. "Do you like magic ladies and gentleman? ... Well, this next act is a magician who is going to amaze you all. So will you please put your hands together and welcome on stage 'The Amazing -'"

Just then before he could finish what he was saying, one of the stage hands came rushing on interrupting him and handed him the note. The Deputy Head apologized and quickly read out what was written. "Ladies and Gentleman the magic act that was due to go has unfortunately decided to pull out of the show so there won't be any magic after all!" Eric's mum's heart sank upon hearing the disappointing news. "Sorry about this ladies and gentleman. Just a moment please," then said the Deputy Head, completely unaware as to the real reason why Eric was not there and went over to the wings to speak with the stage manager.

The judges all crossed out 'The Amazing Fartzini's' name as they prepared to judge the last act on the show 'The Zombies'.

"Are the band ready?" asked the Deputy Head in a bit of a panic again.

"Yes, they are," answered the stage manager, having quickly looked around to check.

"Okay, tell them to get on stage quickly and turn on their amplifiers and instruments!" The Deputy Head then quickly rushed back on stage.

Eric had just faintly heard the compère announcing him on stage as he still struggled to escape in the dark. He managed to get one hand free and immediately reached for his mobile phone in his inner jacket pocket, but it wasn't there! Eric had left it in his school blazer pocket by mistake so he couldn't even try to ring someone for help. Time was running out fast for the would-be escapologist!

His mum was sat in the audience wondering why her son had suddenly changed his mind about going on stage. She couldn't understand it? She couldn't go backstage to speak to him and find out what was the matter because when the show was on, no one is allowed backstage. Emily and Jack and a number of his other friends were also surprised and very disappointed that Eric was not going to be performing.

The band, looking appropriately menacing as 'Zombies' made their way over to their instruments and switched on their amps and mic, causing a horrible feedback sound. David sat down at his drum kit with a sly smirk on his face. The two guitarists, one bass and one electric strapped their guitars to them and the lead singer stood by his mic stand ready. "Let's blow the roof off this place!" said the lead guitarist as he cranked up the volume on his amp.

"Well, ladies and Gentleman, despite the show being a little bit shorter than planned, hasn't it been a wonderful show!" announced the Deputy Head. The audience agreed and cheered and applauded. "But we still have one more act to go in the competition. I'd now like to introduce you to our closing act, four nice lads who are an asset to our school and I believe only formed the band this term. So Ladies and Gentleman without further ado, would you please put your hands together and give a warm St. Bartholomew's welcome to ... The Zombies!"

As the band started up the slightly rosy-cheeked Deputy Head headed off into the wings for another sip of his much needed special blend of coffee, thinking, "The band's rather loud!" and feeling relieved that his compèring duties were almost over.

The singer screeched into the microphone some undecipherable lyrics only the band seemed to understand, causing the front row to immediately place their fingers in their ears and the plastic cups of water on the judge's table to vibrate while the guitarists jumped up and down and nodded to the beat of the drummer. Eric certainly had no chance of being heard now!

The unscrupulous judge in the Governor's pocket gave David's band top marks for everything before they had even started their performance and had marked all the other acts very low, which probably meant 'The Zombies' were sure to win!

The band, now very sweaty looking with their make-up running and smudged from all that jumping around finished the song with a loud crescendo and David in a frenzied state acting like a rock star pushed over one of his cymbal stands, which went crashing to the floor! The Governor was the first to start applauding his son's band and started to stand up, then quickly sat back down realizing he was the only one giving a standing ovation.

"Aren't these seats uncomfortable!" The Governor said to The Deputy Mayor next to him as if to give a reason why he got half way up from his seat. The front row of dignitaries smiled at the Governor and joined in the flattering applause, more out of respect for the Governor than for the band. The rest of the audience wasn't very impressed either and only gave a look warm response with their applause.

The Deputy Head came back on stage looking even more wobbly after finishing his drink and took the band off … "Ladies and Gentleman please put your hands together one more time for the 'Zombies'! Weren't they fantastic!" announced the Deputy Head very enthusiastically, slurring his words and sounding a little incoherent.

Only the front row though seemed to agree however and after taking another bow 'The Zombies' exited the stage confident they would win whatever.

"Well, Ladies and Gentleman the judges will now begin to tally up their scores and we will very shortly have the results of tonight's winner!" The compère was suddenly interrupted by a commotion at the back of the room.

"Let me through, let me through please!" a voice was heard. The spotlight moved from the stage on to a slightly bedraggled figure running down the centre aisle. The figure turned around in the middle of the audience, put on his top hat and announced with gusto, "Good Evening Ladies and Gentleman … My name is The Amazing Fartzini and I am a magician! Would you like to see some magic?"

Well, the crowd went wild thinking it was all planned and part of the act and shouted, "Yes!" with excitement. Eric had managed to triumphantly escape from the chains defying the bully!

The compère was speechless for a change and the judges all looked at one another not knowing what was going on or whether he would be allowed to perform now or not?

The room was filled with anticipation and there was a momentary silence as the Deputy Head came to the front of the stage and leaned over to speak with the other organisers.

"We can't let him go on now surely?" protested a biased and disgruntled school Governor.

"Let him perform!" shouted Eric's mum from the audience. Emily and Jack also then joined in, as did others. And despite the Governor's protests the Head Teacher intervened and overruled saying, "Listen to the audience, we'll have a riot on our hands if we don't let him perform. There is still time and besides everybody like's a bit of magic!" The Governor kept silent holding his annoyance and anger in and begrudgingly smiled and nodded in agreement with the others.

The compère stood up and called over to the stage manager in the wings. "Bring the boys table of props on stage please!" So, one of the stagehands brought on Eric's table of magic props and set it at the front of the stage as Eric made his way up the steps and onto the stage to cheers from the crowd.

"Ladies and Gentleman the decision has now been made to allow this young man to perform. So, without any further ado for the second time will you please put your hands together for The Amazing Fartzini!" The audience clapped and cheered as Eric walked across the stage taking the radio microphone out from its stand.

Backstage, David was in shock and couldn't believe it when he heard his name announced, and wondered how on earth Eric could've escaped.

"Thank you very Much!" said Eric as he picked up a glass and can of 'Seven-up' from his table. He started to pour himself a drink and suddenly as the liquid was still pouring into the glass, Eric let go of the glass to look at his watch and to everyone's surprise and amazement the glass remained suspended, floating in midair! "Oh, is that the time! I'd better get on with performing some magic!" The audience laughed and applauded instantaneously as Eric then re-gripped the glass and proceeded to drink from it. His mum, of course, applauded the loudest, very proud of her son. Even 'Hamburger', who was sat near the front of the stage with his mum, was clapping hard. 'Hamburger' secretly enjoyed watching Eric perform magic.

Eric put the glass and can back down on his table and removed his top hat, placing that also on his table thinking what a lovely audience they were, pleased that his opening trick worked out well.

Eric then said to the audience, "I went to see a magician the other day and he performed this amazing trick where he counted six cards," Eric counted the six cards out aloud clearly showing he had only six. "He then threw away three cards but to everyone's amazement, when he counted the cards again he still had six cards left!" Suiting the actions to the words he tossed three cards one by one into his upturned hat and then showed to the even more astonished audience that he still had six cards left in his hand?

He didn't stop there either because in this incredible trick the magician repeats this sequence several times and each time Eric threw three cards into his hat and counted them again, sure enough, he still had all six cards left, and each time the audience applauded louder and louder! Eric counted the cards one final time to the loudest applause yet,

"One, two, three, four, five, six cards left!" Eric's top hat was now filled to the brim with playing cards! What an amazing trick everybody thought, well except David of course, who was giving him the evil eye from the stage wings.

"Thank very much Ladies and Gentleman ... It's very hot up here under these stage lights!" said Eric as he pulled a red silk hankie out of his pocket and wiped his brow. But then as he casually pulled the hankie through his hand, to the audience's amusement the hankie, changed colour from red to green! Eric pretended he hadn't noticed and just placed the hankie back into his pocket, which made it all the more amusing getting some laughs and applause around the audience.

Eric's mum by now had given up expecting her ex to show up but thought she would have one last quick look and when she turned her head around to her pleasant surprise, there he was standing at the back amongst a crowd of people, smiling and thoroughly enjoying watching his son perform! Ingrid turned back around with a big smile on her face really pleased he did make it after all.

"For my next trick I need a volunteer!" asked Eric eagerly. People on the front row immediately shrunk down in their seats hoping it wouldn't be them being picked! Eric asked one of his teacher's, Mr Johnston his Geography teacher sat on the front row to assist him on stage and reluctantly he joined Eric up on stage to a round of applause.

Eric then went on the perform the 'Change Bag' routine that he had so much enjoyed watching the magician at the Christmas fair perform to him. After showing the bag to be completely empty, Eric asked the volunteer to wave the magic wand in the air, but as Eric handed the wand to them the wand collapsed much to the hilarity of the audience. The audience were in fits of laughter!

Eric then proceeded to reach into the bag and much to the surprise and delight of the audience pulled out one handkerchief after another, all different colours, getting faster and faster as he tossed the handkerchiefs into the air. What a spectacular sight it was too! The last handkerchief he pulled out was a gigantic one and when he opened it up, written on it in big letters were the words 'Applause Please'. The audience thought that was very amusing and burst into instantaneous applause! Eric thanked the volunteer and he went and sat back down again to more applause.

Eric's act was going down very well with the audience and you could see that he was enjoying himself. *(You see when you perform it is so important to enjoy what you are doing because if the audience sees that the entertainer is confident and relaxed and enjoying themselves, they will themselves relax and enjoy the show!)*

"And now Ladies and Gentleman for my last trick I need to borrow somebody's finger ring!" Announced Eric as he looked around the room for someone to loan him their ring …

The Deputy Mayor then offered to lend Eric his ring and after struggling to remove it from one of his chubby little fingers he finally removed it holding it aloft. "Here you are," he said slightly apprehensively. Eric went down into the audience to collect the ring, the spotlight following him. "Take care of it won't you, it's worth a lot of money!" he then added, laughing but slightly nervous to be handing over his precious diamond-encrusted gold ring to the young magician.

"Don't worry, I will wrap your ring in this handkerchief for safekeeping!" said Eric with a glint of mischievousness in his eye.

Eric carefully wrapped the ring inside his hankie and asked someone else on the front row a few seats away to hold it up in the air. Eric then removed an orange from his pocket and gave it to the Deputy Mayor to hold in the air also, announcing, "On the count of three the ring will disappear and reappear inside this orange!" Everyone's eyes flitted back and forth between the handkerchief and the orange not wanting to miss a thing. "Are you ready? … One ... two ... three!" Eric suddenly whisked away the handkerchief and the ring seemed to have just disappeared!

"Ladies and Gentleman. Prepare to be amazed!" said Eric as he put the hankie back in his pocket hoping that he didn't mess his finale trick up! "Now sir, would you please peel the orange ..." The tension in the room was building and the room suddenly went silent, except for an odd cough or two, in anticipation of the ring ending up inside!

Eric's mum looked on slightly worried too, as Eric hadn't practised this trick very much and the chance to win the competition possibly hinged on this last trick! Or so she thought?

The Deputy mayor started to peel away at the orange bit by bit, but there was no sign of his ring? Eric looked worried; not as much as the Deputy mayor though. Once all the peel was off, he broke open the orange but the ring was definitely not there! The school Governor looked on with glee as it looked like 'The Amazing Fartzini' was not all that amazing after all.

"Oh, I am terribly sorry the trick must have gone wrong!" said Eric as he made his way back up onto the stage looking disappointed and shaking his head. The Deputy Mayor was not looking very happy at all and was starting to get worried. "But don't worry! As a way of compensation I have a present for you!" said Eric, drawing everyone's attention to the large wooden gift box on his table, which was nicely wrapped with brightly coloured ribbon and tied on the top in a bow that had been sitting there in full view since the beginning of his act.

Eric picked it up, brought it to the front of the stage and leaned over and handed it to the Deputy Mayor. Everyone wondered what could be inside the box? "This is for you, please open it," said Eric, now hurrying things along, realising his allotted time was fast approaching and not wanting to be penalized.

The Deputy Mayor smiled and went along with it in good sportsmanship fashion, but thinking, "I'd rather have my ring back!" He untied the ribbon and opened the box, but inside the box was not his ring but yet another box secured with ribbon? The audience became more and more curious and found it highly amusing that every time he was expecting to find something inside, all there was, was another box?

The Deputy Mayor had opened three boxes each one getting smaller and smaller before he finally came to a very small box, securely locked with a padlock. Eric then handed him a key and he was instructed to open it. Surely his ring was not inside there? That would impossible!

The Deputy Mayor unlocked the tiny box and slowly raised the lid and looked inside ...

"Does that look familiar?" announced Eric into the mic with a big smile on his face.

"There's my ring!" shrieked the Deputy Mayor all excited like he was a child once again. He couldn't believe it; he reached inside the box, picked up his ring and held it high in the air, waving it about relieved he got his ring back, completely flabbergasted! The audience gasped and burst into rapturous applause! What an amazing feat of magic that was!

But Eric's most amazing feat of all was changing from a shy and quietly spoken boy into a now confident and popular boy! (*In case you were wondering what the old magician at the Christmas fair had whispered to Eric, which helped him to overcome his shyness and become more confident. It was simply "The real magic is within you! All you have to do is summon it up and then you can do almost anything!" This one sentence gave Eric a lot of inner confidence and self-belief he never thought he had. In other words, we all have the capability to do amazing things, if we believe in ourselves!)*

"Thank you very much Ladies and Gentleman!" said Eric taking a bow and smiling from ear to ear overwhelmed by how well his act had gone down with the audience.

"Ladies and Gentleman please put your hands together for The Amazing Fartzini!" announced the Deputy Head as he came on stage to take the young magician off.

Eric walked off stage to even more applause and a lot of the audience were even chanting his name, "FARTZINI! FARTZINI! FARTZINI!" How nice it was for Eric to hear his name called out in praise for a change. Eric had given a flawless performance but now it was up to the judge's scores! He then joined all the other acts now gathered in the wings eagerly awaiting the results as the judges counted up 'The Amazing Fartzini's' scores and determined who the winner and runners-up were.

An argument could be heard at the judge's table between the corrupt judge and the other two judges?

"Please bear with us Ladies and Gentleman while our judges determine who will be the winner and who will be the runners-up of 'St Bartholomew's got talent'! Thank you," announced the Deputy Head. The audience all chatted among one another discussing which acts they thought should win? There was a lot of excitement in the air!

Ingrid turned around again smiling, expecting to see her ex at the back of the room still, but he was not there! He had disappeared like one of Eric's magic tricks! Ingrid was disappointed but thought it was good he had come along and got to see their son perform. Her mind was then distracted from such thoughts as the compère came back on stage carrying three envelopes.

Who could be the winner? Did Eric score enough marks to win or be a runner-up even, despite one of the judges cheating?

You could feel the tension in the room. The room then went silent in anticipation as the compère spoke into the mic.

"Well, Ladies and Gentleman hasn't it been a wonderful evening of entertainment! Have you enjoyed yourselves?"

"Yes!" shouted the audience.

"The judges have all said how difficult it's been to judge with so many good acts in the competition! Well, it's now time to announce the results! Will you please put your hands together and welcome on stage, The Deputy Mayor of Ramsgate, who will hand out the prizes," said the Deputy Head.

The Deputy Mayor then made his way up onto the stage and over to the trophy table carrying three envelopes'. "Okay Ladies and Gentleman in third place winning a cash prize of £25.00 is ..." The compère paused from speaking as he opened the envelope and removed the card to see who's name was on it? "... The comedian Billy Mathews!" announced the Deputy Head.

The audience applauded and cheered as the young smiling comedian made his way out onto the stage, squeezing past all the other anxious contestants backstage. "Congratulations!" said the Deputy Mayor as he shook his hand and handed over his trophy and prize money. "If you just go and stand over there to one side please," said the Deputy Mayor to the chuffed boy.

"In second place ..." the compère announced ripping open another envelope and removing the card, "is ... Streetz Ahead!" The audience applauded and cheered loudly, especially Emily and her mum and dad, as the stage suddenly filled with outstretched limbs of noisy and excited dancers. It was a fantastic display of dancing they had put on for everyone!

Eric's mum by now was even more nervous than Eric was earlier, sat on the edge of her seat, anxiously waiting in anticipation to hear if her son's name was going to be called out?

Backstage the cocky and arrogant David was standing with his Zombie bandmates bragging again. "We've got this in the bag boys!" said David positive they were going to win.

"And now Ladies and Gentleman, it gives me great pleasure to now announce the winner of 'St. Bartholomew's Got Talent', who will receive this wonderful trophy and a cash prize of £100.00!" announced the Deputy Head as he gestured towards the shiny trophy being held up by the Deputy Mayor.

Who could the winner be? Eric and all the other acts waited nervously backstage hoping it would be their name called out. The Deputy Head then opened up the final envelope and slowly removed the card with the name of the winner on it, pausing to build up the suspense like on the T.V. before making the announcement. "... Ladies and Gentleman the winner of St. Bartholomew's Got Talent is ... The Amazing Fartzini!"

THE END.

ERIC'S MAGIC TRICK SECRETS

Written by Shane Robinson
&
Illustrated by Alexandra Stone

CONTENTS

The French Drop

To make coins disappear as Eric did in the story, you need to learn a basic sleight of hand technique called the 'French Drop'. This is a very useful and versatile technique to vanish a coin or coins or in fact any small object!

Hold a coin/s in your palm up left or right hand by its edges between your first and second finger and thumb, displaying the coin to the spectators. (Figure 1. Exposed Magician's View)

Figure 1

Let's assume you are holding the coin in your left hand. Your right-hand approaches the coin palm downwards as if to take the coin but as the fingers shield the coin momentarily from the spectator's view, your left thumb releases its grip on the coin to allow the coin to drop, hence the name, and fall into a finger palm position out of sight. (Figure 2. Exposed Magician's View)

Figure 2

In a continuous action, you pretend to grip the coin between your right fingertips and thumb and carry the coin away as if it has the coin, closing this hand into a loose fist and holding it up slightly, looking at your hand to draw attention to it. It is important that your left-hand remains motionless as the coin is seemingly taken away so the spectators will see an empty space where the coin was seen moments before, which adds to the deceptiveness. You then casually relax your left hand and let it fall naturally to your side or relax on the table if you're sat down. Now to vanish the coin, act as if you are squeezing the coin or crumpling the coin and then slowly open your right-hand palm upwards to show the coin or coins have vanished.

If you wish to vanish a few coins, just have the coins stacked together and as you pretend to take them, release all of them into your finger-palm position and the sound they make as they drop will sound the same as if you did take them in your right hand.

You could practice this technique in front of the mirror to check you are performing it correctly. The important thing is to make sure it looks natural and if you believe you really have taken the coin/s then so will the spectators!

Now in the story, Eric showed both his hands empty, which really fooled David and 'Hamburger' and one effective way to do this, is as follows.

Being at school Eric wore a blazer but you could wear any type of jacket, coat or a hoodie for instance, as long as it has side pockets. Now once you have performed the 'French Drop' and supposedly taken the coin/s away into your right hand. Focus all your attention upon your right hand while your left arm moves across your body to pull up your right sleeve from underneath, near the elbow using your left thumb and forefinger, apparently to show that there is nothing up your sleeve. However, craftily in the action of doing so, as your left hand nears the opening of your right side jacket pocket, you secretly allow the coin/s to drop unseen into the pocket. Sneaky huh! You then move your left hand away allowing it to relax and vanish the coin/s as above. You can now show both hands empty!

If vanishing more than one coin, shake your right- hand fist as if shaking the coins, to cover the noise of the coins falling into your pocket. Also, make sure there is nothing in your pocket that will cause a noise when you drop the coin into it! You could place a handkerchief or something else soft into the pocket to help keep it open, which will make it easier for you.

Another good way to completely vanish the coins if you are sat down at a table, is to perform the technique as above and as you draw attention to your right hand, casually relax your left hand, bringing it to a position overhanging the tables edge and drop the coin/s onto your lap, (This technique is called 'Lapping') where you leave the coin/s behind. Then after a few moments bring your left hand above your right hand and make a magic gesture and open your right hand to show the coin/s has vanished and both your hands are seen empty!

If you wish to reproduce the coin/s, keep the coin/s hidden in your left-hand finger-palm position and after you have performed the vanish, simply reach into the air or behind someone's ear for instance and pretend to make the coin/s re-appear by pushing the coin/s up into view at the fingertips. This way you won't have to dispose of the coin/s hidden in your left hand.

The Transformation of One Object to Another

It is very useful to learn how to switch one small object such as a coin for another and in the next incredible trick I am going to teach you how to do just that. It is known as the 'Bobo Switch'.

To switch one coin for another, for example, hide the coin to be switched in your right-hand finger-palm position. Using the right hand first two fingers and thumb, with the back of your hand towards the spectators the whole time, pick up a different value coin and display it casually at your fingertips, being careful to keep the palmed coin hidden from view. (Figure 3. Exposed Magician's View)

Now toss the coin over into your waiting palm up left hand, which catches it and immediately closes over the coin as it does. Then open and repeat this action once or twice more. This is to condition the audience into accepting this as a normal action so they are not suspicious when you do make the switch. Now without looking at your hands, the third time you go to throw the coin over to your left hand, two things happen at once. You maintain your grip on the visible coin, and instead of throwing this coin, you release the finger palmed coin instead, by extending your right fingers slightly, which immediately cover and hide the switched coin from view. (Figure 4. Exposed Magician's View)

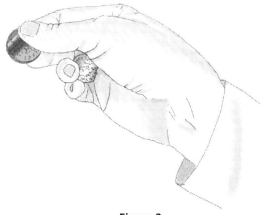

Figure 3

As before you should immediately close your left hand over what is assumed to be the same coin to conceal it as your right hand casually drops to your side, finger palming the coin. Then blow on your hand or however else you wish to present it and open your left hand to reveal the object has been transformed! When the switch is performed properly the spectators will not notice a switch has been made! It should be performed casually on the offbeat.

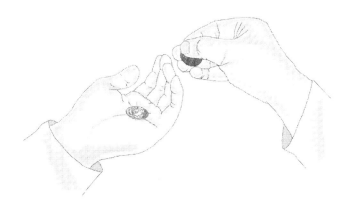

Figure 4

You can use this switch with a number of small items. For instance, as well as changing one coin into a completely different coin, you could magically change a coin into a sweetie or a chocolate! Magicians often use this switch when they need to switch a regular coin for a gimmick or gaff coin.

The Bent Penny

Well, now that you have learnt how to switch one coin for another you are ready to learn this next amazing trick! In the story, Eric amazed his fellow contestants backstage by causing a penny to become bent! This is one of those tricks where it is the presentation that makes all the difference between people thinking they have witnessed a mere trick or a miracle. Really!

To perform this trick you will need to, first of all, make only a slight but noticeable bend in the penny. The easiest way to do this is to acquire two pairs of pliers and gripping the coin between the pliers on either side bend the coin so it becomes sufficiently bent. I recommend bending several pennies at a time because in this trick it is more impressive if you borrow a penny from someone and at the end of the trick return the coin to them in a bent condition so that they have a memento of your performance. It is also more impressive if the coin is seen by the audience to be only slightly bent, rather than if it has a huge bend in it, as it will be less believable. Of course, you can use other coins as well if you wish.

Before you are about to perform the trick, finger palm the bent penny in your right hand. Ask to borrow a penny from the audience, making sure it resembles the one that you have finger palmed and display it at your right-hand fingertips. Now look around as if looking for a suitable volunteer saying, "For this experiment I need a volunteer," and while you are talking casually toss the borrowed penny into your palm up left hand, immediately closing your left hand as you catch it and repeat this once or twice more, finally making the Bobo switch as explained in the previous trick.

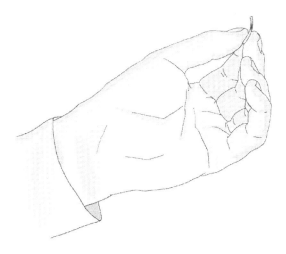

Figure 5

Now because in this trick you are using two coins of the same value and it is only a slight bend in the coin, you can even push the coin up to your left fingertips to display part of it as if it's still the same coin but making sure the bend is hidden from view. (Figure 5. Exposed Magician's View)

To make it even more convincing you can even toss the coin up into the air and catch it without the bend in the coin being noticed. Remember the audience at this stage do not know what you are about to do so they are not looking out for it!

Then ask the spectator to hold out their right hand, and here if you wish you could demonstrate to them how you want them to hold their hand by turning your right-hand palm upwards but still hiding their switched coin behind your curled fingers. This is very deceptive because it looks to the audience that the hand is empty and being a small coin it is easy to hide.

Now place the bent coin onto the palm of the spectator's right hand keeping the bend in the coin concealed and tell them to close their hand over the coin saying something like, "So no one can get at it!" Once this is done, as a safety measure, ask them to turn their hand over palm down, so they are less likely to open it prematurely.

The spectator won't be able to tell that the penny is bent when it is in their closed hand since the coin is only slightly bent! Dispose of the switched coin in your right hand by casually dropping it into your pocket when it is convenient.

Now the work is done, it's now just down to presentation and how you sell it so to speak! Turn the conversation round to the paranormal and how some people can somehow harness unseen energy and bend metal with their minds! Ask the spectator to grip the penny tightly and after a little while say to the spectator, "Focus on the coin in your hand," and ask them if they can feel the metal getting warmer. More times than not they will confirm this is true as it will naturally get warmer in their hand anyway. Now say to them, "Try to use the power of your mind to cause the penny to change its molecular structure," or words to that effect.

To finish ask the spectator to very slowly open their hand! Then be prepared for the screams as people freak out just like the spectator in the story!

You could even have the spectator apparently initial their coin with a permanent marker pen, but in reality, you have them initial the bent penny once the switch is made and while you are still holding the coin at your left fingertips, hiding the bend. The coin is then placed into their hand as above. The effect is even stronger this way!

Congratulate the spectator on their amazing paranormal ability and leave them with the bent penny to remind them of this incredible experience.

The Rubber Spoon

To perform this fun and surprising trick all you require is a metal teaspoon. It is an ideal trick to prank your friends and family when you are out and about in a café or restaurant or having a cup of tea around someone's house, as Eric did at his mum's friend's house.

Figure 6

To start off with pick up a teaspoon in your right hand and hold it vertically by the handle in a loose fist with the bowl visibly facing outwards towards the spectators, fingers wrapped around the front of the spoon with the pad of the thumb pressed against the top rear part of the handle. (Figure 6. Audience View)

Now bring your left hand over and clasp the right hand, covering the right-hand fingers and the tip of the spoon handle completely, as if to get a good grip on the spoon with both hands to seemingly use force to bend the spoon against the table. As the left-hand covers and conceals the right-hand fingers, the right little finger repositions itself behind the handle by the bowl to act as a hinge. This is where your acting skill now comes in because you now need to make it look as if you are actually bending the spoon against the table.

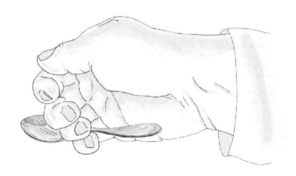

Figure 7

To do this place the bowl of the spoon against the table or against your knee and tilt your hands forwards, using some shoulder movement as if you are forcibly bending the spoon in half but in reality allowing the handle of the spoon to secretly lower, concealed by your hands. The illusion of the spoon being bent is perfect! You could say as Eric did in the story that the cutlery must be made of rubber, which the audience will find amusing. (Figure 7. Exposed Magician's View)

Once you have seemingly bent the spoon in half, keeping the state of the spoon concealed from the spectators, cover the spoon with both hands, with one hand overlapping the other and wiggle the fingers as if making a magical gesture and then after a moment remove your hands to reveal the spoon is fully restored! Much to the relief of whoever's spoon, it belongs to! Practice this fun trick to make it look realistic!

The Centre Tear

This trick will make people think you have genuine mind-reading powers! In the story, Eric asked a spectator to write down the name of a famous person on a small piece of paper and fold the paper into quarters to hide what they had written. The paper was even torn up to destroy evidence and yet Eric was able to read the spectators mind and name the person she was thinking of correctly?

To perform this astonishing feat all you need is a slip of blank paper approximately 8 centimetres square and a pen or pencil. Ask a spectator to think of the name of a famous person as Eric did in the story or something else if you prefer. While they are doing that draw a large circle approximately 4 centimetres in diameter in the centre of the paper and tell them, "So as to get a strong mental image of the person in your head, please write down the name of the person in the circle." (Figure 8.)

Turn your head away from them as they do this. Then instruct them to fold the paper in half and then into quarters, saying, "So I can't see what you have written". When they have done that, take the folded paper back from them with your right hand, holding the paper so that the folded edges are at the top right-hand corner. (This is the area that contains the name and why you ask the spectator to write in the circle) Now without hesitation and without looking at your hands, rip the paper in half vertically placing the left-hand piece in front of the right. Then in a continuing action turn the pieces horizontally to the right and tear the paper once again into quarters, placing the left-hand pieces in front of the right again. So as to seemingly destroy any evidence of what they wrote.

Figure 8

You are now going to secretly steal away the piece of paper closest to you, which has the information written on it, so you can secretly read what it says. As soon as you finish ripping up the paper, take the pieces from your right-hand fingertips with your left-hand fingertips, but as you do your right thumb simply pulls back the top folded piece and retains it in the right hand, secretly hidden behind the fingers. (Figure 9. Exposed Magician's View)

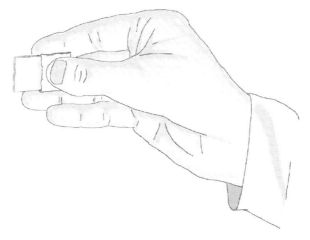

Figure 9

Now throw away and discard the pieces of paper in the left hand as you ask the spectator to concentrate on the name of the person they are thinking of, while you attempt to read their mind. As you tear up the paper and discard the pieces act as if it was not important.

All you have to do now is to secretly open up the piece of paper and read the information written on it. There are a number of ways you could do this. For instance, when you place the pen back into your pocket you could unfold the paper using one hand by pushing the folds open with your thumb assisted by your fingers, and then casually bring your hand out of your pocket with the slip of paper concealed in your hand. Then simply glance at what is written as you raise your hand to place your first finger and thumb against your forehead for dramatic effect as if concentrating as Eric did in the story. Then finally, name the person they are thinking of, to everyone's amazement!

But one of the easiest and best ways is to pick up a small pad, which you tore the piece of paper from initially and use this as cover to secretly unfold the paper behind it and keep it hidden from view, all the while pretending to read their mind, writing down one letter at a time on the pad in your attempt to divine the name of the person they are thinking of before finally naming the person correctly!

If you are sat down at a table you can secretly open the folded paper on your lap. Then with your eyes clearly seen closed, place both your hands against your forehead as if concentrating. Then under the cover of your hands, which shield your eyes from view, simply glance downwards and read what is written!

Lucky Thirteen

This is a strange and spooky card trick, which I created myself and it is really baffling and surprising!

Thirteen is supposed to be an unlucky number but in this trick, it proves to be lucky. A card is selected and returned to the pack and despite the pack being cut thirteen times when the pack is spread all the cards are now shown to be in numerical order in their various suits, except for the chosen card which is the only card out of position. But as if that wasn't strange enough - The chosen card is seen to be in the thirteenth position from the top of the pack! Now that's lucky!

To perform this very surprising trick first of all you need to secretly arrange the cards in their four suits and in numerical order - Ace through to King (Ace being at the top of the face down pack) Just remember, which King and suit is on the bottom or 'Face' of the pack. Herein lies the main secret to the trick.

At the start of the performance if you are able to give the pack a 'False Shuffle' retaining the complete order, then do so, but it is not necessary. Spread the cards out face down between both hands and ask a spectator to remove a card, remember it and show it to some other spectators.

Then, when they are looking at the card and showing it around to others, secretly count twelve cards from the top of the pack and separate your hands at this point to have the chosen card returned to the top of your left-hand cards, placing your right-hand cards on top so their card will be in the thirteenth position from the top of the pack unbeknownst to the audience. I turn my head away as the card is returned to suggest everything is fair.

Now once the card is returned, square the pack and set it down on the table in front of the spectator. Talk about superstitions and that the number thirteen is supposed to be an unlucky number, but for you, it's a lucky number! Then offer to show them.

Tell the spectator who chose the card that you would like them to cut the pack and complete the cut twelve times to mix up the pack and lose their card, but you will cut the pack the thirteenth time. Count out loud as each cut is made. (Figure 10.)

Once the pack has been cut twelve times, you remind them you will cut the pack one final time making it thirteen cuts in all. Now to return the cards to their original order and re-position the chosen card thirteenth from the top, all you have to do is simply cut pack bringing the King which was the original bottom card back to the face of the pack, because no matter how many times the cards are cut it will not affect the original order otherwise.

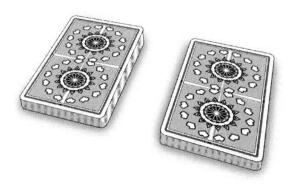

Figure 10

The easiest way to do this is to casually pick up the pack and with the card faces towards you simply spot the King card and cut the pack bringing it to the face of the pack, counting thirteen. (There are a number of other ways to achieve this including using a 'Short Card', a 'Thick Card' and the method I use, which is using a 'Crimp Card'. For a brief explanation refer to the 'Glossary'.) Say to the audience that despite the cards being well and truly mixed up, you will attempt to locate their card. The pack is then spread face up on the table showing to everyone's surprise and amazement the cards are now in numerical and suit order, except the chosen card which is the only card not! At this point act as if the trick is over and then after a short pause, point out that not only that but also their chosen card is located at the thirteenth position in the pack! Proving that the number thirteen is a lucky number for you!

As regards to secretly counting twelve cards from the top of the pack; if you prefer a much easier way is to put a light pencil dot on the back of the diagonally opposite upper left-hand corners of the Queen card so that you can easily spot the position of the twelfth card in the spread.

It is recommended to have two matching packs, with one of them pre-arranged as above and hidden in your pocket, for instance. You perform one or two card tricks with the other pack showing the cards are clearly all mixed up. You casually put the pack away in the same pocket as the pre-arranged pack and perform some other type of trick. Then as you offer to show them one more card trick you simply bring out your pre-arranged pack and perform 'Lucky Thirteen'. It is an ideal card trick to finish on!

The Penetrating Rubber Bands

This is the trick, which Eric performed in the story for his friend Jack, on their way to school, where two rubber bands link and unlink in a most mysterious way. For this amazing little trick, all you need are two thin rubber bands, ideally size # 19 (1.6mm thickness and 88.9mm diameter) or a similar size. Whatever size is best for your size hands really.

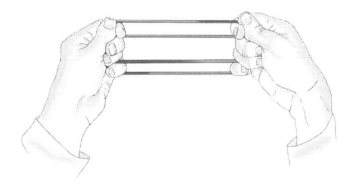

Figure 11

To perform the trick, have the bands examined and once that's been done, take them back and grip and display one of the bands stretched out between the curled forefingers of both hands and the other band by both your curled little fingers. (Figure 11. Magician's

View)

Now in order to make it look like the band's link and unlike with one another, first you must secretly swap the two middle strands around one another.

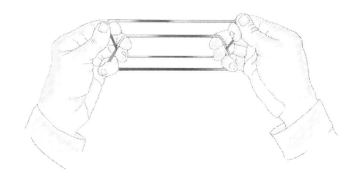

Figure 12

To do this, after holding the bands up at chest height displaying the bands to the spectators, casually lower your hands to about waist height relaxing the tension on the bands and as you are talking to them and taking attention away from the bands, casually swap the two middle strands around using the thumb of the right hand and the middle finger of the left hand, wrapping the bands completely around one another and insert the middle and third fingers of both hands inside the loop thus formed, and re-grip the bands by curling these fingers inwards. (Figure 12. Exposed Magician's View)

To cover this action, you could casually stretch the bands back and forth a couple of times, the bigger motion concealing the smaller motion. Now bring you're your hands up to chest height again and stretch the bands out. To the audience, the bands will look exactly the same as they were before.

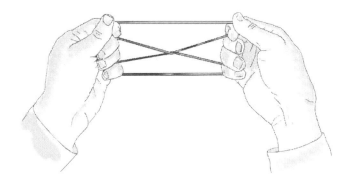

Figure 13

Now ask a spectator stood opposite you, to gently rub the two middle strands together using their thumb and forefinger, and as if to illustrate extend the middle and third fingers of your left hand and rub the bands together yourself for a moment, afterwards curling your two fingers inwards again. After they have rubbed the bands a couple more times, say to them, "Now slowly re move your fingers. Look, you must have magic powers! You have caused the two bands to link together. That's incredible!" When they remove their fingers it will look like the two bands really have linked together. (Figure 13. Magician's View)

Now using your right thumb, you can push the bottom strand of the top band downwards to really emphasise this! Now all you have to do is ask the spectator to rub the two middle strands together again and as they do simply move your middle and third fingers of the right hand unnoticeably and release the bands. When the spectator removes their fingers the bands, to everyone's astonishment, will now be seen separated. A miracle! No wonder Jack was so amazed!

The Glass Through the Table

This trick is a showstopper and well worth the time and effort to practice and learn it! It is also an excellent lesson in misdirection. A solid glass penetrates through a solid table! A classic trick that always gets gasps! This is an ideal trick to perform anywhere where you are sat down at a table having a meal or a drink.

All you require is a small glass tumbler, a paper napkin and a coin. Oh yes and a table of course! You need to be seated with your legs together allowing some space between you and the tables' edge. With the props already on the table tell your audience that you are going to cause the coin to penetrate through the solid table. You could tap the coin against the table to prove it's solid. Place the coin on the table, about 30cm directly in front of you and then turn the glass upside down and place it over the coin. Now you need to create a mold for the glass using the paper napkin. So unfold the paper napkin and place the centre of the napkin over the top of the glass so the glass will be completely concealed and mold the napkin to the shape of the glass. (Figure 14.)

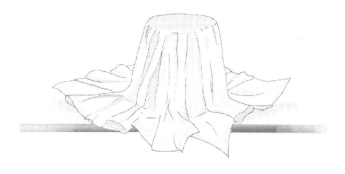

Figure 14

If you were to remove the paper mold or shell it should still maintain its shape like as if there could still be a glass under it, which is a large part of the secret.

To give a reason to cover the glass with the napkin you could say, "I shall cover the glass with the napkin so as to shield the secret in mystery!" Now lift the napkin covered glass up with your right hand, fingers wrapped around the front side with your thumb at the rear, to show the coin is still on the table and place your left hand under the table as if to catch the coin. Now say, "On the count of three the coin will pass right through the solid table! One, Two Three!" As you say "three", lift the glass and bring it back towards you, resting at the edge of the table with the rim of the glass just below the table, acting surprised and a little disappointed to see the coin is still there. What you are doing is conditioning the audience into thinking this is a natural and innocent action, because the next time you do that you are going to secretly release the glass out of its paper shell so it falls onto your lap unbeknownst to the audience. (Figure 15. Exposed Magician's View)

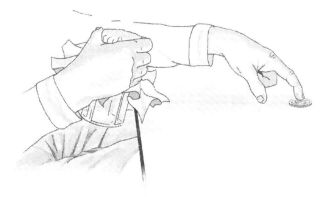

Figure 15

Say something like, "Oh dear! The coin should have gone through the table? Let's try that again." Suiting the actions to the words, proceed to cover the coin with the glass again making a noise with the glass against the table as you set it down. Count to three and once again lift the glass, bringing it back to the table's edge as before. But this time drop the glass out of the paper shell and onto your lap, drawing all the attention to the coin on the table as you do, saying to the audience, "The trick seems to have gone wrong? One last try!" Make the audience think it really has gone wrong. This is misdirection.

Now without hesitation bring your right hand forwards to cover the coin with the paper shell, the audience will believe the glass is still under it, and the same time, place your left hand under the table and on the way secretly pick up the glass and bring it directly under the same spot as the coin is on the table. Now as you place the paper shell down onto the table to cover the coin, knock the glass against the underside of the table so it will sound like it is still above the table. This helps to make it convincing and is very deceptive!

For the finale, say, "I have confidence this time. On the count of three! Three!" Just say the word "three" and suddenly slam your palm down right down on top of the paper shell and squash it flat against the table. The audience will be taken by complete surprise and it will really look as if the glass has penetrated right through the table. Pause for just a moment to let this amazing effect sink in with your audience and acting as if you caught the glass, bring your left hand into view from under the table showing the glass mouth downwards and finish by saying, "Oh look! The glass has gone through the table instead!"

I recommend that you use a good quality paper napkin or serviette, the stiffer the better, when performing this trick so the napkin holds the shape of the glass better. When holding the napkin covered glass, to help maintain the shape after the glass is secretly removed, I pinch or clip a small part of the paper near the top edge of the glass between my first and second fingers.

After witnessing this trick, just like those who watched Eric perform it in the school dining room, your audience will be amazed too!

The Vanishing Pen Cap

This is a very surprising and fun trick to perform and another excellent example of how to apply misdirection in your magic routines. All you need to perform this amazing trick is a pen with a cap. You misdirect the audience from the start in this trick by telling them that the pen cap will disappear when actually it's the pen that will disappear! But then finally the pen cap does disappear using more misdirection naturally built into the routine.

As in the story when Eric amazed the school receptionist, remove the cap from the pen and show the cap resting on the open palm of your left hand at waist height and tell the spectators that you are going to make the pen cap disappear on the count of three. Pick up the pen and hold it by the nib end, saying to your audience the pen will act as a magic wand.

Now for this trick to be effective you need to turn your body about a 45-degree angle to your right, so your right side is shielded from the spectators view in front of you. Now raise the pen close to your right ear and then in a continuous action lower it and tap the cap with the pen as you say, "One!" Raise the pen again up near your ear and bring the pen downwards again counting, "Two!" Now this time when you bring the pen upwards by your ear, stick the pen behind your ear and leave it there, and without hesitation bring the right hand back down again as if it still held the pen, continuingly looking at the cap in your left hand the whole time during the counting to focus the spectator's attention on it. Count, "Three!" as you go to tap the cap again, acting surprised that the pen has vanished instead of the cap! (Figure 16. Exposed View)

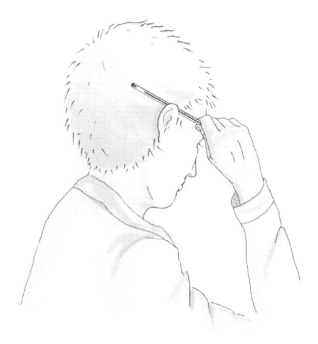

Figure 16

Now what you are going to do is very sneaky. Say "Oh dear! The cap was supposed to vanish, not the pen! Where's the pen gone?" Casually close your left hand over the cap and first look around towards your right as if searching for it and then turn your body around to look to your left, so your left side is now facing away from the audience and as you do the audience will see the pen is behind your ear as if it's reappeared there! Normally they laugh at this point, as it's a very funny sight! Now as soon as the audience spot the pen and react, simply drop the pen cap into your left side jacket or trouser pocket. Quickly close your hand again as if you are still holding the cap and as you swing back round to the front everything will look the same as before.

Now remove the pen from your ear as you say, "Let's try that again! On the count of three!" With your left hand still closed, raise your right hand again and this time don't count to three but as soon as you bring the pen downwards open your left hand fully and hit the pen against your palm counting, "Three!" The cap has vanished!

To make the trick deceptive it is important to make your actions look smooth and natural, especially during the counting when you are placing the pen behind your ear!

This trick is normally performed using a coin and a pen or pencil, so you could also perform the trick that way. Or make any small object disappear you like, perhaps a sweetie for instance. You could secretly hide a duplicate sweet in your mouth just before you start the trick and when the sweet vanishes at the end of the routine you then display the duplicate sweet on your tongue or between your teeth as if it has re-appeared in your mouth!

The Ubiquitous Pen Caps

Here is a fun thing to do with a pen cap, which can be combined with the previous trick. The magician removes the cap from the pen and places it in his pocket only to discover that the cap has re-appeared in his other hand! Once again the pen cap is removed but this time another pen cap appears! This is repeated again and again as pen caps keep appearing much to the surprise and annoyance of the magician!

To perform this all you require is one matching pen cap. Have the pen with the cap on it along with the matching cap in your left jacket or trouser pocket. To start the trick, reach into your left side pocket with your left hand and pick up the pen and the matching cap, secretly hiding the matching cap from view as you bring your hand out from your pocket. (Figure 17. Exposed Magician's View)

Now casually remove the cap from the top of the pen with your right hand and place it in your right jacket or trouser pocket. At the same time casually toss the pen down onto the table or give it to someone to hold for a moment, secretly retaining the matching cap in your loosely closed left-hand finger-palm position.

Figure 17

Now two things should happen at the same time. You casually look at your left hand and act surprised as you open your hand displaying the pen cap to have suddenly re-appeared, while you only pretend to leave the cap in your right-hand pocket but retain it secretly hidden in a thumb palm position as you remove your hand from your pocket. (To 'Thumb Palm the cap, simply close your hand into a fist and grip the cap between the crux of your thumb and forefinger. The thumb palm allows you to open your fingers slightly giving your hand the appearance of being empty and will help facilitate this trick. The focus should be on your left hand! (Figure 18. Exposed Magician's View)

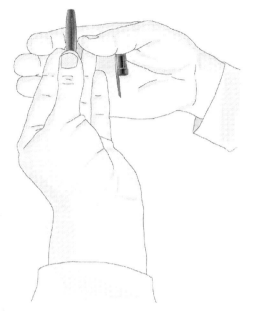

Figure 18

You are now going to perform what is known in magic as the 'Put and Take Move'. Basically, as you remove the cap from your left-hand fingertips you replace it with the cap secretly held in the thumb palm position.

So after the cap is shown to have re-appeared in your left hand, display the cap, now holding it between your left first and second fingertips and thumb, with the top of the cap pointing upwards. The right hand with the other cap hidden in the thumb palm approaches the left hand and the right first finger and thumb grip the cap in the left hand towards the bottom and removes it in an upwards direction and at the same time deposits, the thumb palmed cap in exactly the same position where the other cap previously was a moment ago. It looks like as you remove the cap from the left hand another one magically appears in its place!

As you remove the cap from your left hand and place it in your right-hand pocket pretend at first not to notice another cap has appeared. But as before you re-palm the cap into the 'Thumb palm' position and remove your hand from your pocket. Now noticing another cap has appeared, I usually do a 'double take' and act surprised and slightly perplexed and then continue repeating these antics several times, using the same method explained above. Placing the caps in my pocket as they keep appearing and doing it faster and faster as I act more and more flustered and bothered as if it is out of my control. It looks very comical to see!

For a surprise ending place a pen cap of a different colour or an entirely different small object in your right- hand pocket from the start and the last time your right- hand goes to your pocket to supposedly deposit the cap, this time actually release it and thumb palm the other object and make that appear instead!

Also because you are only using two pen caps another climax would be to show all the pens caps you have produced have vanished! This way you get an additional effect. Simply pretend to place the last cap in your pocket but secretly retain it and then show your pocket empty.

As already mentioned this trick makes an ideal lead in to 'The Vanishing Pen Cap Trick'. You decide that the only way to stop the caps from keep appearing is to make them disappear!

The Cut and Restored Earphones

This trick is sure to get your audience's attention! Although this trick it is very easy to do, you will get great reactions just like Eric did in the story when you perform this surprising trick. If you remember, he borrowed someone's earphones and cut the wire in half and then miraculously restored it, much to the boy's relief. It is a fun trick that certainly has the shock factor!

Lots of people wear earphones to listen to their favourite music on their music devices so there should always be someone about whose earphones you could borrow to perform this amazing quick trick.

This trick is most effective if you borrow someone else's earphones and act as if it had not been planned and that you decided to perform this trick on the spur of the moment. It is also best to perform this phase quickly so once you've cut the wires and show them to be apparently separate, you immediately restore them! So you have the shock value but also so the audience doesn't have a chance to think too much about how it was done!

To perform this trick you are going to need a supply of the same type of black or white wire used with most earphones sets, plus a pair of scissors. To prepare cut off a length of approximately 12 centimetres and simply fold the wire in half. We will refer to this wire as the gimmick. Place the wire with the loop pointing forwards and the scissors together in your left side pocket or rear trouser pocket and you are now set to create a stir!

First, make sure the earphones wires you intend to borrow match your gimmick closely enough. Then ask them if you may borrow their earphones for a sec so you can show them an amazing trick. As you ask them this, remove the scissors along with the gimmick with your left hand so the loop is uppermost and put the scissors on a table or somewhere convenient for a moment keeping the gimmick secretly hidden from view in your loosely closed left hand. Take earphones from the spectator, holding the middle of the wire so as the earphones hang down and the wire is doubled in half forming a loop. Now what you are going to do is switch the loop in your right hand for the gimmick loop in your left hand.

Very casually, whilst looking at the spectator and talking to them, just simply bring the right hand loop up from under the left hand, leaving it behind in the lower part of your left hand, holding it in place with your left little and third fingertips and in a continuous movement and without hesitation, pick up the gimmick loop and bring it up into view about 3 or 4 centimetres above the left hand. (Figure 19. Exposed Magician's View)

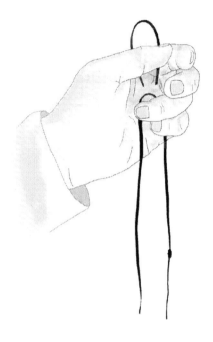

Figure 19

Now pick up the scissors with your right hand and cut the gimmick loop in half. To the audience, it should look like you just transferred the earphones wire from one hand to the other so you can pick up the scissors with your right hand to cut the wire. The audience will be shocked by the fact that you have cut the wire of the earphones, so play it up a little.

Hold the two ends of cut wire up so the audience can clearly see it has been cut in half and place the scissors down. Now after only a moments pause, using your right hand, tuck the two pieces small of wire back into your left hand so they are out of sight. Then holding the actual earphones wire between both hands where the cut was apparently made, rub the wire with your thumbs and fingers of both hands as if magically restoring it! You could say something like, "Don't worry! I'm an electronic wizard! Watch!" Blow on the wire or say your favourite magic words and quickly separate your hands, sliding them well apart. The gimmick remains hidden in your left hand as you show the wires are now back together again and restored!

Now hand the earphones back to the very relieved spectator and retain the gimmick secretly hidden in your left hand, turning your left side of your body away from the spectator/s as you do so and secretly get rid of the gimmick in a side pocket.

Or if using your own earphones, simply wrap the earphones several times around your left hand containing the cut gimmick wire and then just pocket everything!

This trick can also, of course, be performed exactly the same with a length of rope or shoelaces. But earphones, having more costly value and being a personal possession makes the trick all the more interesting and exciting to watch!

The Magic Elbow

The magician causes a coin to completely vanish after rubbing it against his magic elbow! For amazing and deceptive trick, all you require is a coin, an elbow and a shirt/blouse or tee shirt.

Before you perform this trick make sure you have your shirt/blouse or tee shirt tucked into the waistband of your trousers/skirt.

Pick up a coin in your right hand and display it. Now tell your audience that you have a magic elbow and offer to prove it. As you say this raise your left elbow upwards level with your shoulder so your left hand comes to rest naturally by the back of your shirt/blouse collar. You will probably get some funny looks and a few giggles from the audience at this point but proceed to place the coin onto your elbow and start to rub the coin against it. At this point, the audience does not know what you are going to attempt to perform exactly. (Figure 20. Exposed Magician's View)

Now without making it obvious allow the coin to seemingly accidentally drop off of your elbow and onto the floor. What you are doing is setting your audience up and conditioning them into thinking your intention is simply to rub the coin against your elbow. As soon as the coin drops onto the floor act as if it was a mistake and say something like, "Clumsy me! Let me try that again!" and reach down and pick up the coin using your left hand. Then as you are straitening up, without hesitation casually perform the 'French Drop', which you have been taught already and pretend to take the coin into your right hand.

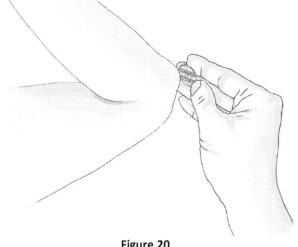

Figure 20

Now in a continuous action resume the same position as before by raising your left elbow, which brings your left hand, secretly hiding the coin to the back of your shirt/blouse collar and while you pretend to rub the coin against your left elbow again, drop the coin down the back of your shirt/blouse disposing of it. (This is why you have to tuck your shirt/blouse in, otherwise, the coin would fall out!)

Continue pretending to rub the coin against your elbow as you casually remove your left hand away from this position. Now slowly lift your right hand showing the coin has completely vanished! What a magic elbow you have indeed!

The Magic Knot

This is a quick and surprising trick you can perform with your school tie, which Eric surprised his rugby team within the changing rooms. You can also perform this trick with a long piece of rope or even a handkerchief by first holding the handkerchief by the diagonally opposite corners and twirling it so it becomes rope-like.

A knot is tied in the centre of a tie and when the magician blows on it the knot dissolves away! To perform this you will need to learn to make a false knot as follows. Hold the tie in your left hand with the narrow end draped about a third of its length over the back of your left hand with the majority of the tie hanging down passing across your palm. Now your palm down right hand grasps the tie about a third of its length up from where wide part of the tie hangs down and moves up to the left hand forming a loop by clipping the tie between your left second and third fingers and thumb, holding it in position (Figure 21. Exposed Magician's View).

The right-hand lets go of the tie, allowing this part to drape over the back of the left hand and then reaches through the loop thus formed from the front and re-grips the tie near the narrow end and in a continuous action pulls it back through the loop and to the right so as to tighten what appears to be a genuine knot but is really a false knot.

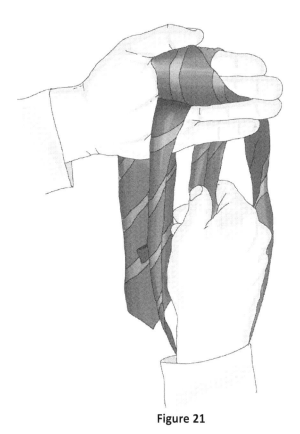

Figure 21

As soon as the knot is formed, move your left hand away so the audience can clearly see the knot. At this point, I like to swing the tie in a circle with my right hand, which helps to convince the spectators it is a real knot. (Figure 22. Magician's View) Then hold the tie by the ends between both hands, stretched out displaying the knot in the centre.

Now to make the knot disappear simply blow on the knot for effect and at the same time pull the tie sharply in opposite directions and the knot will instantly come apart! A real surprise!

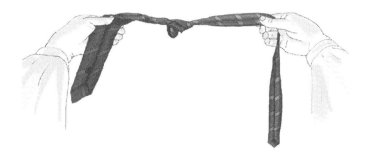

Figure 22

When you are forming the knot it is important that you don't draw too much attention to it, so look at the spectators when you do it. When the knot is formed and you are displaying it, that's when you should look at it! It is important to act like you are genuinely tying a knot and if you believe it so will your spectators!

Here's a fun and very magically trick you can

also perform once you have learnt how to make a false knot. Secretly hide a rubber bouncing ball, a wrapped sweet or even a Yo-Yo for instance in your right hand. It could be any number of things! You can still form the false knot using your right thumb and first finger with your other fingers secretly hiding the object.

Now when you have formed the false knot, hold the up the tie by one end in your left hand and display it hanging down. Your right hand still hiding the object, grips the knot, covering it and pulls sharply downwards and away, immediately throwing the ball on the ground, catching it as it bounces upwards or releases a Yo-Yo, or instead open your right hand to reveal a sweet or a chocolate for a very magical transformation effect!

Think Stop

Every good magician should be able to perform at least a few card tricks and this one although easy to do always impresses! It is always good to be able to perform card tricks with a regular pack as well as a 'Trick Pack' so if someone were to hand you their pack of cards and ask you to show them a trick, you can. This also makes what you perform all the more impressive! In this amazing yet easy to do trick, a freely chosen card is discovered through apparent telepathy!

To perform this trick you only require a regular pack of playing cards and a little acting. The secret relies on a very old principle in magic, which dates back several hundred years called 'The Key Card Principle'. Basically, by placing the 'Key Card' secretly next to the chosen card in the process of cutting the deck you will then be able to easily find the chosen card when the cards are spread face upwards!

Have the pack shuffled by the spectator and as the cards are handed back to you secretly note the value of the bottom card of the deck, which will be your 'Key Card'. If you are unable to get a glimpse of it then casually note what it is as you tap the pack against the table to square the cards. Then spread the cards face down between both your hands for a selection to be made by a spectator sat opposite you at a table. As the card is removed turn your head away as you ask the spectator to remember the card and whilst they are doing this square the pack and place it face down onto the table. Now ask them to place their card face down on top of the pack and to cut the pack and complete the cut by placing the bottom half on top. By doing this they will bring the 'Key Card' directly on top of their chosen card unbeknownst to them. You could 'Overhand Shuffle' the pack if you wish, being careful to keep the middle section where your 'Key Card' and the chosen card are located intact. You could even have a spectator 'Overhand Shuffle' the cards, as the odds of the two cards becoming separated are unlikely.

What really makes this trick powerful is the presentation. Turn the pack face up and spread it along the table so all the card indices can be clearly seen. As you look for your 'Key Card' and the card below it will be the chosen one. Talk to your audience about telepathy and how it is possible for some people to transfer their thoughts to another, to create interest. Then offer to demonstrate and say to the spectator who chose the card, "I will pass my finger along the spread of cards and when my finger passes over your card I want you to please just think 'Stop'" Suiting the actions to the words extend the forefinger of your right hand and slowly move it along the spread from left to right. I sometimes like to grasp the spectator's hand with my other hand to make it even more mysterious. (Figure 23. Magician's View)

Move your hand along the slowly along the spread and purposely go past their card and act like you are finding it difficult to pick up their thoughts. So tell the spectator to concentrate harder and this time to scream the word 'Stop!' in their mind. This is all part of the build-up.

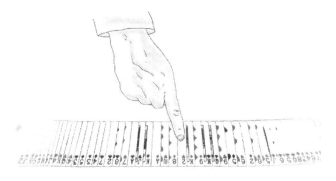

Figure 23

Now say to the audience that you will attempt to have another go and once again move your forefinger slowly along the spread. Here it is good to close your eyes for dramatic effect, as you know the whereabouts of their card, and as you are approaching it, touch the temples of your forehead with your thumb and extended fingers of your other hand, as if to help you concentrate. But really this is to shield your eyes momentarily from view as you secretly open them to spot the exact location of their card. Move your forefinger just a few cards beyond their card and then stop and pause a moment like as if you have just picked up a signal from the spectator.

Then move your hand back the other way over the spread so your finger ends up right above their chosen card and again pause. Now close your eyes again and remove your hand from your forehead so the spectators can see your eyes are closed and will believe they were closed all along. Then dramatically lower your hand so your finger lands on their card and slide the card forwards towards the spectator. Say, "Is that your card?" Acting somewhat unsure yourself and a little exhausted after the demonstration, which will make it all the more believable what the audience have witnessed is genuine telepathy!

Number 18

This is a very clever mathematical trick that will astound your audience based on 'The Nine Principle'. It is a 'Force', which can be used in many different ways. Here is my favourite way of using it. The good news is it is a self-working trick and you don't have to do any arithmetic, the spectator does! All you've got to do is instruct them.

The only set up that is needed is to write down on a slip of paper the value of the 18th card from the top of a pack of cards. Fold the paper into quarters; this will be your prediction. You will also require a pen and a pad or a piece of paper.

Place the pack of cards in full view on the table and hand someone your prediction to look after for safe keeping. Then ask someone to think of any three-digit number containing all different numbers and to write it down, and then to reverse the numbers so they have a new number and to write whichever is the smaller number under the larger number so they can subtract one three-digit number from the other. When they have done the subtraction they will have another new number.

Now lastly, tell them to add these individual numbers together so that they arrive at a random smaller number.

Well, as already mentioned this is a 'Force' and it is not a random number at all as the number will always be the number 18. Here is an example below.

Example

782 (Original thought of number)
- 287 (Reversed)
= 495 (Added together)
= 18   (Total)

Now one of the things that make this force so deceptive in this presentation is that you disguise it in a card trick.

Ask the spectator to announce what the number is and to pick up the pack of cards themselves and to deal the cards one at a time onto the table until they reach the eighteenth card. When the eighteenth card is turned over it will be discovered to match your prediction correctly! A miracle!

Another great way to use this mathematical force is when you are in a restaurant and you predict the name of the dish on the menu eighteenth from the top of the list!

Money, Money, Money

Ever wished that you could produce banknotes out of thin air? Well now you can or at least that's what it will look like when you perform this marvellous trick to your audience.

The magician's hands are shown to be empty and with his sleeves pulled up he rubs his hands together and banknotes keep appearing! It's a good thing that those bullies David and 'Hamburger' didn't see him do this or they would have made the money disappear, in their pockets!

If only you could really produce money out of thin air eh? Well here's a deceptive way to make it at least look like you can. To perform this trick you require several banknotes to make it look effective. You could use fake banknotes if you wish. Stack one banknote squarely on top of the other and fold them in half widthways. Then keep folding the bank notes in half until you form a tight roll shape package.

Now just prior to your performance hide the notes in the crook of your left arm and pull some of the material backwards over the notes so as to hide them and keep your arm slightly bent to keep them in position.

You are now set to make money appear! Face

your audience and with your left hand, casually pull up your right sleeve at the crook of your arm and open your right hand showing it empty. (Figure 24. Exposed Magician's View)

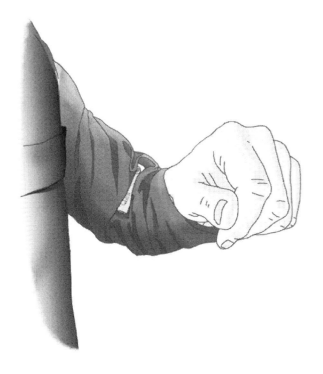

Figure 24

Now in a continuous action, your right-hand moves the material out of the way and positions itself over where the banknotes are hidden and grasps hold of them at the same time you pull your left sleeve upwards to show your left hand empty. Look at the audience the entire time you are doing this and without hesitation bring both the palms of your hands together and rub them vigorously so the banknotes separate from each other, allowing them to drop gradually one or two at a time from your hands as they come into view and fall to the table or ground saying, "Money, money, money!"

The Linking Paper Clips

In the story, Emily showed Eric that she could also do magic and even amazed Eric with this easy to do self-working trick her grandfather taught her. This is a very good trick and you will even amaze yourself when you perform this!

To perform this amazing little trick where two paper clips magically link together, all you require are two paper clips and a bank note, which could be borrowed. The effect far outweighs the method in this one, as the trick is pretty much self-working.

First, fold the banknote widthwise into thirds and secure one clip on the first and second folds, and the other clip on the second and third folds, leaving a little space on the upper corners of the banknote. (Figure 25. Exposed View)

Say to your audience something like, "Have you ever seen the famous trick where the magician magically links large rings together? Well, I don't have any rings but I do have these paper clips so I will demonstrate my mini version of that trick now! Watch closely!"

Now to cause the clips to link together all you have to do is to grip the two upper corners of the bank note between both your hands and then sharply pull your hands apart, where the two paper clips will miraculously link together seemingly in mid-air and drop to the table as you say the magic words your favourite magic words!

Figure 25

The Easiest Four Ace Trick in the World

If you are going to perform card tricks then you've got to be able to perform a trick with the four Aces! This is one of the amazing and skilful looking tricks Eric performed, which stunned the other contestants backstage during the talent competition. Your audience is certainly going to think you're an Ace magician too when you show them this amazing trick!

It is probably the easiest trick in this book but never the less it is also very impressive if it is performed well and will give your audience the impression of you having great skill when actually none is involved!

Before the performance begins secretly remove the four Aces from a pack of cards and hide them squared together under your belt by the small of your back, (Figure 26. Exposed View) and wear a jacket or other item of clothing to cover them. Or just simply hide the four Aces in your back pocket. This trick is ideally performed standing with your audience positioned in front of you.

Now ask a spectator to thoroughly shuffle the cards and once this is down, place the pack behind your back saying, "I will attempt to find an Ace by feel alone, sight unseen!" Now take your time here and act as if you are having some difficulty. Then remove one of the Aces from under your belt and bring it forward saying as you do, "I think I've found one!" Show the audience that you have indeed found an Ace and place it on the table or hand it to someone. Then place your hand once again behind your back as you appear to try and find another Ace, "I've got another!" you announce triumphantly as you bring another Ace into view.

Figure 26

Once you have produced two Aces, hand the deck back to the spectator and ask them to shuffle the cards more thoroughly this time. Then when they have finished shuffling place the cards once again behind your back and say, "But I still have two more Aces to find, which is becoming harder and harder!" Once again build up the suspense. Finally remove the last two Aces together and spread them as you dramatically whip them both into the view of your stunned audience!

It is important to sell this trick to your audience. By that I mean, convince them that what you are doing is a genuinely difficult feat. So I recommend that after you have successfully produced the first Ace, pretend to fail the next time, and actually bring forward and show one of the other cards from the deck to give the impression that it must be a difficult feat, acting a little disappointed and saying something like, "This is a very difficult feat. Let me try again!" and then carry on and produce the other Aces.

You will find that this trick works well for a small or large audience as it is dramatic and visual. To make this trick even more dramatic you could even be blind-folded.

The Lazy Magician

In this amazing card trick, you pass your magical powers onto a spectator who finds his own chosen card! This fun trick is very easy to do and gets the spectator to join in. To accomplish the trick we once again call on our friend 'The Key Card' to help, and simply the misnaming of a card!

Have a pack of cards shuffled and secretly note and remember the value of the bottom card of the deck, which will be your, 'Key Card'. Now say to a spectator that instead of you performing the trick they will. Tell them, "I'm feeling lazy so I will transfer my magic powers over to you so you can perform this trick." Now ask them to spread the cards face down like magicians do and offer you a selection. Take a card yourself and look at it as you only pretend to remember it, without anyone else seeing it.

Now ask them to also choose a card and remember it. Once you have each chosen a card, then ask them to square the pack and place the cards on the table. Now have them return their card to the top of the pack and cut the pack and complete the cut to bury their card somewhere in the centre of the pack. However, in doing so this action has secretly placed the 'Key Card' right next to their chosen card. (Figure 27.)

Next, instruct the spectator to ask you to return your card to the top of the pack and then ask them to cut off only a quarter of the pack and complete the cut, emphasizing the cards have been clearly separated from each other in the pack!

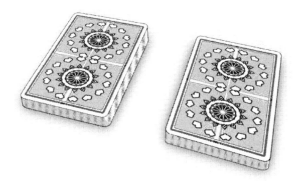

Figure 27

Here you say, "My card was the …" But misname your card, naming your key card instead and then ask them to name their card. Now get them to announce, "I will now cause the … and the … to travel and join each other in the pack!"

Now get them to say their favourite magic words and to make a magical pass over the pack and then ask them to turn the pack over face up and spread the cards across the table to show that both the chosen cards have indeed miraculously joined one another! Lead the applause for them and congratulate them on performing such an amazing trick. The spectator will be amazed them self as to how they did it!

The Pencil Through Bank Note

This is an amazing quick trick using any banknote and any pencil or pen! The good thing about this trick is that no set up is required and you could borrow everything to perform it.

First of all, holding the banknote sideways in your left hand, with your right hand, fold the banknote towards you from the bottom upwards, as if folding it in half but leaving about one centimetre of the end nearest the spectators protruding. Allowing the spectators to clearly see the banknote being folded.

Now as an afterthought suddenly remember to hand out the pencil to be examined and casually allow the banknote to unfold. This is done to precondition the audience into assuming in a moment you will simply just fold the banknote again the same way.

However, while the spectator/s are examining the pencil you refold the note but in a slightly different way as follows. Start to fold the banknote again, but this time as the fold is made, your right second fingertip secretly folds the right side of the note inwards towards the centre forming a channel.

This is all done while the banknote is hidden behind your left hand, which is orientated with the back of your hand towards the audience with the fingers extended towards the right. From the audience view, it should look no different from how you folded the banknote before. (Figure 28. Exposed Magicians View)

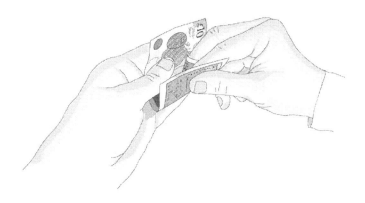

Figure 28

Once you have done this, in a continuous action, casually turn the banknote over sideways from right to left behind your left hand so the secretly folded section remains hidden by your left fingers and display as much of the banknote as possible.

Take the pencil back from the spectator and with the pointed end downwards pretend to pierce a hole right through the centre of the folded banknote but actually you insert the pencil into the secret channel.

For dramatic effect, before you apparently push the pencil through, hold the pencil in place with your left fingers for a moment and then tap or push the pencil seemingly through the banknote and it will look from the front like the pencil is really going through the centre of the banknote and you have damaged it! It's a great illusion! (Figure 29. Exposed Magician's View)

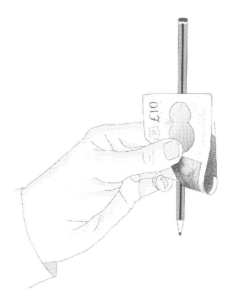

Figure 29

To restore the banknote pull the pencil all the way through and then holding the ends of the banknote, one in each hand, bring it up to your mouth still folded in half. Then, blow on the banknote and then quickly snap it open showing that it is now completely restored! A miracle! Rustle the banknote to remove any telltale creases in it before you hand it back.

You could also present this as a penetration type trick showing that solid can indeed pass through solid!

The Mobile Magician

This trick is appropriately named because it uses a mobile phone and you can perform it anywhere as most of us carry our mobile phone around with us where ever we go! This is the surprisingly delightful trick Eric performed in the story to Emily on their way home from school, where he produced a 3D chocolate for her from just a photo on his phone! But with this set up you will be able to produce a whole manner of different things as well!

You will be able to set up most up to date mobile phones the same way whether you have an 'Apple iPhone' or an Android Phone'. First, you will need to take a photo of the object you wish to produce on a black background. For instance, like a chocolate as in the story using the camera on your phone, making sure the photo appears the same size as the actual 3D object you will produce. Also, take another photo of just the black background and store these two photos next to each other in your photo gallery with the photo of the object to the right of the other.

To perform, first of all secretly hide the object you wish to produce in your left-hand finger-palm position whilst also holding your mobile phone, covering the object from view.

(Figure 30. Exposed Magician's View)

If you wish to produce a chocolate, for instance, say to someone, "Would you like a chocolate?" Then reach into your right trouser or jacket pocket and act as if you are searching for it. But bring your empty hand out saying, "Nothing there!" Now transfer the phone and the chocolate over to your right hand, keeping the object hidden out of sight under the phone, holding it in place with your fingers, and having freed your left hand go in the search of the chocolate in a left trouser pocket.

Figure 30

Acting a little disappointed, bring out your hand showing it empty as well, saying, "Sorry I thought I had one left?" In the process of searching for the chocolate, both hands have been casually shown empty, which is very deceptive. Make sure that you don't look at your hands when you do this! Then act as if you have an idea and casually pass the mobile phone along the object back over to your left hand, all the while being careful to keep it hidden and say, "Ah but being a magician I don't worry about trivial things like that!" Suiting the actions to the words go into your photo gallery on your phone and bring up the photo of the chocolate or whatever it is you are going to produce and display it to the spectators.

Now say, "Look here's a photo I took of a chocolate and if I want a chocolate all I've got to do is to pull it out of the screen!" As you say this, the pad of your right thumb comes onto the far left side of the centre of the screen, fingers palm up underneath the phone, where the chocolate is secretly transferred from your left finger palm position over to your right fingertips and in a continuous movement your right hand moves to the right as your thumb swipes the image over to the right, bringing the next image of the black background into view, where you display the chocolate held between your right thumb and fingertips as if you just pulled it right out of the screen! A real surprise for your audience! (Figure 31. Exposed Magician's Downwards View)

You've got to get the timing right to make it look effective, and when it does; it looks like real magic and will certainly surprise your audience!

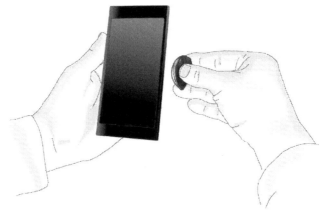

Figure 31

If you don't want to pass the phone and the object to be produced back and forth between your hands, then just keep the phone in your left hand and go straight into the photo gallery and carry on as above from there.

As mentioned already, you can produce a whole manner of different things in this way, like a coin, cash, a playing card or even a small apple. An apple! (Great if you have an 'Apple' phone!)

22nd

I believe this trick to be one of the best self-working mathematical type card tricks in existence. You will even amaze yourself performing this! A chosen card is lost in the pack and two piles are dealt, one face up and the other face down. The spectator confirms that the chosen card is not among the face-up cards and all the face-up cards are discarded. This is repeated until only one card is left. Unbelievably it proves to be the selected card!

To perform this miracle you require a full deck of fifty-two cards without Jokers and all you have to do is have the selected card returned at the twenty-second position from the top of the pack. The best way to do this is as follows. Have the pack first of all shuffled by a spectator, and then as you spread the cards from your left hand over to your right hand to have one selected, secretly count the cards and break the pack open so you have 21 cards in your right hand and the rest in your left hand. It is quicker if you count the cards in groups of three.

When the spectators have memorized the card, have it returned to the top of the left-hand cards and then simply place the cards held in the right hand on top thus positioning the spectator's card second from the top. (Figure 32. Magician's Downwards View)

Figure 32

That's the hardest part of the trick as once you've done that the rest is automatic! You can just sit back relax and enjoy what is about to unfold. If you can perform a full pack false shuffle or give the pack a few false cuts all the better, but it is not necessary.

Tell the spectator's that you will attempt to find the chosen card through a process of elimination. Deal the top card, face up onto the table. The first card must be face up for this to work! Then deal the second card face down to the right of it and continue dealing two piles of cards alternating from left to right dealing face-up cards to the left and face-down cards to the right until the pack is completely exhausted. (Figure 33. Magician's View)

Now ask the spectator if they have seen their card in amongst the face-up cards. They will answer "No," so push the face-up cards aside and pick up the pile of face-down cards and square them in your left hand ready to start the dealing again exactly as before. Face- up cards to the left and face-down cards to the right. Once again ask the spectator if they have seen their cards. Again they will answer "No".

Figure 33

This same procedure is repeated until only one card is left. To everyone's utter amazement when the last face down card is turned over it is seen to be the spectator's chosen card! All throughout the dealing you are stressing the improbability and how the odds are incredibly high against this happening!

The Floating Bread Roll

This is the trick Eric performed in the story to the astonished onlookers in the school dining hall. This trick is ideal to perform in a restaurant or café where there is a basket of bread rolls on the centre of the table. You will also need to use an opaque cloth or paper napkin, or a handkerchief, and to secretly obtain a fork.

Whilst sat down at a dinner table, secretly place the fork on your lap with the handle to your right and lay the napkin on your lap covering the fork. When it's the right moment to perform, grip the uppermost two corners of the napkin, one corner in each hand and using your right hand pick up the fork, gripping it by the end of the handle so that the fork is hidden behind the napkin and angled so that the tines of the fork are pointing towards the centre.

Now lift the napkin up and drape it over the basket of bread rolls and underneath the cover of the napkin stab one of the uppermost bread rolls with the tines of the fork. (Figure 34. Exposed Magician's View)

Then to start with, slowly raise your arms up and bring both your hands closer together so that it looks like one of the rolls is mysteriously floating upwards and away under the napkin.

Figure 34

Just as Eric performed the trick in the story, using the best acting skills you can muster, animate the bread roll by causing it to move up and down and forwards and backwards, and sometimes act as if the bread roll has a mind of its own and wants to get away, floating up so high it pulls you out of your seat! So it appears like you almost lose control of it, and this is the reason you need to use the napkin or it would fly away! Make it appear magical! (Figure 35. Magician's View)

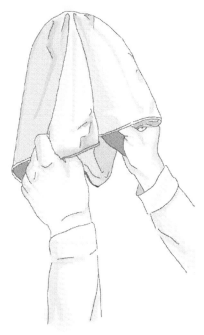

Figure 35

Once you have performed this for only a short while, cause the bread roll to float back down to the bread basket, where your left-hand releases the napkin and is placed palm down on top of the napkin and the bread roll, as if to stop it floating away again. Then using your right hand pull the napkin and fork away towards you, which disengages the fork and allow the fork to drop onto your lap as you flick the napkin completely away to show it is just a napkin.

Instead of using a bread roll you could also use an apple for instance. You will definitely cause a stir and turn a few heads with this fun trick!

The Card in the Balloon

In this amazing and spectacular trick, a balloon is burst and the chosen card suddenly appears as if from inside of it, despite the pack being securely in its case!

To perform this all you require is a round balloon and a pack of regular cards and a pin. As with a lot of card tricks you will need to learn how to control a chosen card to the top of the pack. One of the easiest ways is by using a method you have already been taught, which is to use 'The Key Card Principle'. Basically, remember the bottom card and then have the chosen card returned to the top pack and as already explained have it cut into the centre of the pack placing your 'Key Card' secretly on top of it. You could have the pack 'Overhand Shuffled' if you wish.

Now, in the act of trying to find their chosen card spread through the cards, faces towards you as if searching for it and when you come to your 'Key Card' simply cut all the cards below it to the top and you will bring the chosen card secretly to the top of the pack. Pretend that you are having difficulty in finding their chosen card and say, "I will try to find the card in a more magical way!" As long as you perform it casually it will defy detection!

Now ask one of the spectators to blow up the balloon and tie it, and while they are busy doing that, place the cards back into their case so that their chosen card is nearest to the half-moon cut out in case. Then as you close the flap secretly insert the flap below the chosen card and push the flap all the way inside. (Figure 36. Exposed Magician's View)

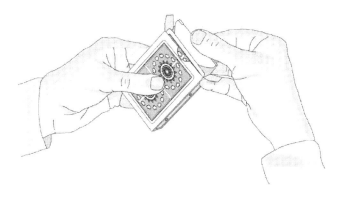

Figure 36

By doing this you have now separated the chosen card from the rest of the pack ready to make a most magical appearance as if it appeared from right inside the balloon.

It is best to stand up when performing this trick. Now holding the case vertically in your right hand, with the chosen card nearest you and your right thumb pad directly pressing against the exposed part of the chosen card, take the balloon back from the spectator in your left hand and pass it to your right and grip the neck of the balloon between your first and second fingers. (Figure 37. Exposed Magician's View)

Figure 37

Your left hand now picks up a pin, which could be conveniently stuck in your lapel and holds it up high to display it. At the same time as this happens slightly push the chosen card upwards about one centimetre so you can grip the card against the neck of the balloon by your thumb and forefinger. The balloon conceals the chosen card being slightly pulled out of the case from the spectator's view.

Now ask the spectator to name their chosen card out loud. Then say your favourite magic words and burst the balloon with the pin. At the same time the balloon pops, allow the case of cards to fall, except for the chosen card, which you continue to grip and in a continuous action swiftly swivel your right hand upwards displaying the chosen card with face of the card towards the audience, as if it just appeared out of the balloon!

If this is your closing trick you could say, "I always like to end my show with a bang!" You are sure to get a big round of applause with this surprising and amazing trick!

Siberian Chain Escape

This is basically the chain escape that Eric learnt and which enabled him to make his escape in the final chapter of the story. Actually, this escape is also effective using a length of rope too.

To learn this escape you will need to acquire a length of chain about three-quarters of a metre long and a padlock and key or piece of rope. Not too wide or thick!

Of course, to demonstrate your amazing ability to escape like 'Harry Houdini', you will need someone's assistance to tie you up. First of all, extend your left arm with your hand palm downwards and wrap the centre of the chain around your wrist so the chain crosses over at the top.

Now give the volunteer the two ends of the chain to hold and immediately lay your right wrist crossways over your left wrist, and then instruct the volunteer to cross over the two ends the chain or rope on top of your right wrist forming a figure of eight and pull tightly and secure the chain in place using the padlock. If using a rope, then simply instruct the volunteer to tightly tie several knots. Get the spectator to check that you are securely tied up before you proceed. (Figure 38. Magician's

View)

If you have instructed the volunteer to tie you up in the correct way it couldn't be easier to escape even though you are seemingly securely tied up and it looks impossible to escape. Now you don't want the spectators to see how you escape so turn your back to them or have your hands covered with something.

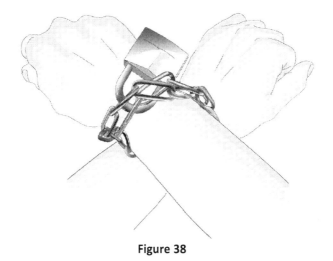

Figure 38

To release yourself from the chains you simply only have to untwist your wrists so your arms and hands line up and then pull your hands out of the larger loop now formed due to untwisting your wrists. (Figure 39. Magician's View)

When you are attempting to escape, drum up as much acting ability as possible, and to help build the suspense, first of all, wriggle about and act as if you are struggling to escape. This is known as showmanship and adds to the drama, so when you do finally escape, it will look impressive!

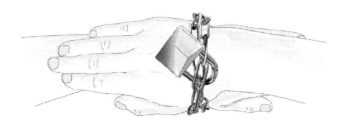

Figure 39

GLOSSARY

Listed in Alphabetical order below are the explanations for magic terms used throughout the book, which you will find useful.

Card Control
A method for secretly controlling the spectator's chosen card either usually to the top or bottom of the pack.

Card Force
A method used to 'Force' a particular playing to be chosen, which the magician has predetermined, unbeknownst to the audience.

Complete Cut
The action of cutting the pack in half and then placing the bottom half of the pack directly on top of the pack. Thus 'Completing the Cut'.

Crimp Card
A playing card which has secretly been slightly crimped or bent in one corner to enable the magician to easily locate and cut at the desired position using the thumb to cut at the 'Crimp Card'.

Bottom or Face of the Pack

The 'Bottom of the Pack' refers to the Bottom or lowermost most playing card of the face-down pack.

Ditch

A method of secretly disposing of an object, for instance, a 'Gimmick' using 'Misdirection' normally disposed of up the sleeve, in your pocket or on your lap.

Escape

An 'Escape' is a feat demonstrated by escaping from a restraint such as chains, like Eric performed in the story, handcuffs or a straitjacket, made famous by 'Harry Houdini'.

Face Down

The face or value of a playing card is orientated facing downwards so the back design is uppermost. Face up The face or value of a playing card orientated facing upwards.

French Drop

A sleight of hand technique for vanishing a coin or other small object where you pretend to remove the coin from one hand to the other but secretly retain the coin hidden in the hand.

Gimmick

A gimmick refers to an object that has been modified or altered so as to facilitate performing a certain trick.

Key Card

A 'Key Card' is a playing card, which is secretly noted by the magician and placed usually directly above or below the spectator's chosen card by means of a complete cut, enabling the magician to locate the chosen card by searching for their 'Key Card'.

Lapping

The term used for a secretly disposing of items onto your lap when sat down at a table.

Mind Reading

The act of seemingly reading a person's mind and then naming what it is they are thinking of.

Misdirection

Misdirection is a technique used by magicians to draw or distract the audiences' attention away from the method used to accomplish the trick.

Overhand Shuffle

This is one of the most common ways to shuffle cards. The pack is held in the right hand by the narrow ends, edgeways over the palm up left hand and the left thumb pulls away small clumps of cards into it until the whole pack is exhausted and the procedure is repeated again. Hence the name 'Over Hand' Shuffle.

Pack of Cards

Also known as a 'Deck of Cards'. Fifty-Two playing cards comprising of Four suits, which are Hearts, Clubs, Diamonds and Spades with thirteen cards in each suite, Ace through to King plus a 'Joker'.

Pre-arranged Pack

A pack of cards, which is secretly set up in a certain order to facilitate the trick.

Prediction

When something is predicted or foretold before it happens. The magician or mentalist normally makes a prediction by writing down the name of something on a slip of paper before it is chosen.

Riffle

The action of flicking the cards quickly by

bending the pack and releasing cards one by one. Usually performed in a 'Riffle Shuffle' or as a way to have a card selected.

Routine
A number of short tricks or 'Effects' strung together in a certain order to make a longer 'Routine'.

Secret Preparation
The 'Secret Preparation' refers to setting up and preparing the tricks you are going to perform in secret prior to your performance, so as not to reveal the 'secrets' or how the tricks are done to your audience.

Self-Working Tricks
Tricks classified as not requiring sleight of hand, often mathematical or use a pre-arranged deck of cards and easy to perform.

Short-Card
A playing card which is shaved very slightly all the way along one of the narrow ends of a playing card or at one corner to enable the magician to easily locate and cut at the desired position by riffling the pack upwards with the thumb to the 'Short Card'.

Shuffle
The pack of cards is mixed or 'Shuffled'.

Sleight of Hand
A term used to describe secret manipulation techniques or 'moves' using your hands to accomplish magic tricks. Steal A method used to secretly remove or 'steal' an object from view using 'Misdirection'.

Switch
A sleight of hand technique used for secretly exchanging one object for another.

Thick Card
Two playing cards which have been glued together to enable the magician to easily locate and cut at the desired position by riffling the pack upwards with the thumb to the 'Thick Card'.

Top of the Pack
The 'Top of the Pack' refers to the top or uppermost playing card of the face-down pack.

SOME WORDS OF WISDOM TO ASPIRING WIZARDS

Well, I hope you have enjoyed reading the story and learning the amazing magic tricks taught in the book. The main thing to do now is to get out socializing; making new friends and entertaining people by performing the amazing magic and advice you have learnt!

Remember to practice and rehearse your magic enough so that you have a polished performance and in no time at all, you will be amazing and entertaining people just like Eric in the story and you will find the more you do it the better you will become and your confidence will grow and grow!

I recommend not trying to learn too many tricks at once! In fact, it is better to learn one trick at a time until you have mastered it before moving on to learn another one.

Also, it is better to learn a fewer number of tricks and to perform them very well rather than to attempt to perform a lot of tricks and not perform them very well! There is a well-known quote by the famous nineteenth-century English magician named David Devant who when approached by a young novice magician boasting he knew three hundred card tricks replied by saying that he knew about eight!

When choosing magic tricks to perform, pick the one's which are not only amazing and impactful but also have good entertainment value. The magic tricks in this book I have chosen for that very reason!

A lot of the methods I teach in this magic book can be used for other magic tricks as well and in some of the tricks, you can also vary which items are used. For instance, instead of vanishing a coin, you could vanish a small ball, or instead of floating a bread roll, you could float an apple using the same method. So be creative and try to come up with your own different magic tricks and ways to perform them!

Sometimes when you are performing magic you will make mistakes and be criticised; it happens to even the best magicians, so don't worry! You mustn't let that put you off because you are still only learning your craft remember. The same applies to anything in life: it is by making mistakes that one learns and improves. So don't be too hard on yourself. It's okay to fail - as long as you keep trying - you're not a failure until you give up! And remember to pat yourself on the back and praise yourself when you do something successfully.

Also, criticism can be positive and helpful, so do listen to people's comments but be shrewd about what advice you decide to take and what advice not to take. Not everybody is right so don't take it too seriously.

Never let anyone put you off from performing magic by telling you that you won't be able to do it, or can't do it! This applies to anything in life. Believe in yourself, be positive and go for it! At least then you can say to yourself that you tried!

As well as performing amazing magic tricks make your performance engaging and entertaining! The real moment of magic is when your spectators unknowingly suspend their disbelief, even for just a moment and become transfixed in wonderment! The most incredible magic happens in the spectators' head, so fill it with wonder! Like all good magicians, this is what you are trying to create when you perform!

And remember, the same as the wise old magician in the story referred to - It's YOU that's the magic and not the tricks! Sometimes it's good to remind yourself of this when you are about to give a performance. So sparkle and make YOUR magic come to life!

The most important thing is to have fun and enjoy what you are performing. If you enjoy yourself then so will your audience. There is an old show business saying, which goes along the lines of, "If the audience likes you as a person then they will like what you do!" This is very true, so sell yourself first and be likeable! By being 'likeable' it will get you much closer to where you want to be in life, whatever it is you want to be!

Here are some golden rules to remember when performing magic. Stick with these and you should do all right!

Always practice and rehearse enough times so that you can give a well-polished performance!

Don't make your magic tricks and routines too

long and drawn out as this would be boring for your audience and they will lose interest. It is better to make your performance of each trick short, simple and direct to have maximum impact!

Choose to perform the type of magic tricks which are amazing, impactful and have entertainment value.
Learn and perform fewer tricks very well rather than lots of tricks not very well!

Never repeat the exact same trick immediately afterwards to the same audience, as they will know what to expect and it won't be a surprise anymore as then they might figure out how you do it!

Never reveal the secrets to your tricks to non-magicians, as the wonderment will be lost and it will spoil it for your audience and what's more, you will get a lot less credit for being a good magician!

Make your performances captivating and entertaining and create a sense of wonder so your audiences will enjoy themselves and be more likely to remember you!

Be yourself, so you come across as relaxed, and remember to smile and use eye contact! Connect with your audience by communicating with them on their level so you find a common ground! This will give the impression of you being both friendly and confident and by taking an interest in them, they in return will take an interest in you! This will put your audience at ease from the start and they will be ready to watch and enjoy your performance!

There is a right time and a place to perform magic! In other words, don't perform to people who clearly don't want to watch magic, or to people who are clearly being awkward. Pick your moment. That way you will get a much better and positive response!

Never admit when a trick has gone wrong! Carry on performing another trick if necessary or make a joke out of it. Remember, the audience doesn't know what to expect.

Never show you are annoyed or get upset when things don't go to plan. Hold your chin up and carry on being positive and likeable! It's better for people to say about you, "They messed that trick up, but wasn't they a nice person!" Rather then, "They messed that trick up and I didn't like that person. I don't want to watch them perform again!"

'Don't hide your light under a bush'! Be a 'Show off', but don't be a 'Cocky Show off'! In other words, perform your magic often and promote yourself, but don't be cocky and arrogant with it! Nobody likes somebody who's cocky!

And most importantly, have FUN!

EPILOGUE

Days, weeks and months went by since Eric triumphantly one 'St. Bartholomew's Got Talent' and Eric came to realize that far more important than winning the competition and receiving the £100.00 cash prize was the popularity he gained and the friendships he made by performing magic! Although, the money did come in handy.

Eric, Emily and Jack, all met up during the start of the Easter Holidays. They were queuing up at the Ramsgate 'Mc Donald's', showing each other the latest tricks they had learnt. By now they had all been bitten by the magic bug and were now keen, budding magicians.

"Wow! That was awesome!" said Eric after witnessing Jack perform a cool card trick.

"Thanks, I learnt it from a really sick book of card tricks!" replied Jack, pleased with himself that he had pulled it off.

"Will you teach me that trick?" said Eric.

"Sure!" replied Jack.

"Yeah, it was really good Jack! I have literally no idea how you did it?" Emily joined in by saying. "I know a good card trick too! Let me borrow your cards a minute …" Jack handed over his cards. "Pick a card," said Emily, as she spread the cards out between her hands, offering Jack the choice of a card.

"… Can I take your order please?" said the slightly miffed 'Mc Donald's' cashier for the second time.

"… Oh sorry!" said the three of them, suddenly realizing that they were now at the front of the queue and were holding up a long queue behind them. "Show us the trick when we sit down Em," said Eric.

The restaurant was very busy and crowded, but the three of them managed to find an empty table and sat down with their food. Emily then performed the card trick she had been eager to perform and both the boys thought it was a really clever trick.

"I've been thinking -" said Eric.

"I thought I could smell wood burning!" joked Jack, interrupting.

"I've been thinking we should form a secret magic club?" repeated Eric, as he casually caused his carton of 'Coke' to levitate away from his hands, trying hard not to spill it. "Then we can share tricks that we've learnt."

"What a good idea!" replied Emily excitedly as she picked up the cards from the cluttered and messy table to avoid getting ketchup on them.

"Sounds good to me, count me in," said Jack, agreeing it would be a good idea.

Eric leaned forwards, "We could use our magic skills to help solve some of the crimes in the area …" quietly announced Eric in earnest.

There had been a sharp rise in local petty crime in recent times and the police were overstretched and struggled to cope with it.

"… Cool! Go on," said Jack, keen to hear more about Eric's idea.

"Okay, here's the plan …" Eric looked quickly left and right and leaned in even closer, but before he could utter another single word he was suddenly interrupted.

"Can I join your club?" A familiar voice from a nearby table was heard to say. It was 'Hamburger'! Sat, all by himself, tucking into his second 'Big Mac' …

LASTLY

I highly recommend taking up magic as a hobby as it is not only very enjoyable but it also can be very rewarding and can open up a lot of doors for you, and create a lot of opportunities! It certainly has for me, which if it wasn't for performing magic I may not have had otherwise?

I have found performing magic to be a great leveller and a means by which to find common ground and communicate and make connections with all types of people from all walks of life and backgrounds. And communication and getting on with people is so important in life, especially a happy life!

Thank you very much for buying my book, and if you would like to purchase any of the marketed magic tricks mentioned in the book you can find them and many more magic tricks and books available to buy through my online magic shop www.zanesmagicshop.com or other well-known magic shops.

Also, if you would like me to write a sequel, and potentially a series of books based on the 'Amazing Fartzini' characters, in which Eric and his friends use their magic skills to help solve crimes and get into all sorts of adventures, then please let me know.

And lastly, be a child! Don't grow up too quickly, as you're only a child once remember. So allow yourself to imagine and dream and have fun! I personally have never grown up!

All the very best in your magical journey of life!

Shane Robinson (A.K.A. Zane)

ACKNOWLEDGMENTS

I would like to thank the numerous magicians who over many years past dreamed up the marvellous magic tricks within these pages!

I would also like to thank Alexander Stone for creating the wonderful illustrations from my imagination, and to especially thank my beloved wife Angela and our son Jake for being so supportive of me in my endeavour to write this book!

ABOUT THE AUTHOR

Shane Robinson was born in Ramsgate, Kent in 1963, whose interest in magic started at the young age of ten. He went on to become a professional magician under the stage name of 'Zane' performing at top venues around the world including cruise liners such as the prestigious and world-famous QE2.

He has also appeared in two critically acclaimed movies 'Funny Bones' and 'Magicians' performing magic.

And, as well as still performing magic he is also the owner of an Internet magic shop called www.zanesmagicshop.com', selling magic tricks suitable for beginners right the way up to professional magicians and is the creator of several magic tricks sold around the world.

He also regularly trades at various public events in the UK selling beginners magic tricks to delighted children and inspiring the next generation of magicians.

He is happily married to Angela and they have a son named Jake.

21819774R00232

Printed in Great Britain
by Amazon